WILLIAM BLIGH was born in Plymouth, England, in 1754. He went to sea when he was sixteen and learned his trade so well that at the age of twenty-two he became sailing-master of the *Resolution* under Captain Cook, from whom he learned the art of navigation. After more than four years at sea he returned home to an England at war. He married Elizabeth Betham, was appointed master of a frigate, and participated in a battle between an English and a Dutch squadron near the Dogger Bank in the North Sea. Before the war ended, he earned the rank of lieutenant. With the coming of peace, Bligh turned to the command of ships in West Indian trade. In 1787, he took charge of the *Bounty* on an expedition to Tahiti to transplant breadfruit plants to the West Indies, where they were to serve as an economical source of food for Negro slaves. The expedition reached Tahiti, collected the breadfruit and set sail for the West Indies. The ship was one month out of Tahiti when the mutiny broke out. Having escaped almost certain death by an amazing voyage in an open boat, Bligh undertook and carried through a second breadfruit expedition. As a captain in the Royal Navy he was later involved in the mutiny at the Nore, and in the battles of Camperdown and Copenhagen—gaining in the latter a special commendation from Nelson. In 1806 he was sent out as Governor of New South Wales and, although again the victim of a rebellion, he was made a Rear-Admiral when he returned to England in 1810. During the last years of his life he lived with his three daughters in Farningham, Kent, where he died in 1817. This edition of William Bligh's account of the mutiny was first published in 1792.

A Voyage to the South Sea
Undertaken by Command of His Majesty
for the Purpose of Conveying the Bread-Fruit Tree
to the West Indies
in His Majesty's Ship the *Bounty*
Commanded by

Lieutenant William Bligh

and an Account of

The Mutiny on Board
H.M.S. *Bounty*

and the Subsequent Voyage of Part of the Crew,
in the Ship's Boat,
From Tofoa, One of the Friendly Islands,
to Timor, a Dutch Settlement in the East Indies

With an Afterword by MILTON RUGOFF

A SIGNET CLASSIC

NEW AMERICAN LIBRARY

A DIVISION OF PENGUIN BOOKS USA INC., NEW YORK
PUBLISHED IN CANADA BY
PENGUIN BOOKS CANADA LIMITED, MARKHAM, ONTARIO

SIGNET CLASSIC TRADEMARK REG. U.S. PAT. OFF. AND FOREIGN COUNTRIES
REGISTERED TRADEMARK—MARCA REGISTRADA
HECHO EN WINNIPEG, CANADA

SIGNET, SIGNET CLASSIC, MENTOR, ONYX, PLUME, MERIDIAN
and NAL BOOKS are published *in the United States* by New American Library,
a division of Penguin Books USA Inc., 1633 Broadway,
New York, New York 10019, and *in Canada* by Penguin Books Canada Limited,
2801 John Street, Markham, Ontario L3R 1B4

7   8   9   10   11   12   13   14   15

PRINTED IN CANADA

Contents

v

CHAPTER VII

CHAPTER VIII

CHAPTER IX

CHAPTER X

CHAPTER XI

CHAPTER XII

CHAPTER XIII

CHAPTER XIV

CHAPTER XV

CHAPTER XVI

CHAPTER XVII

CHAPTER XVIII

CHAPTER XIX

CHAPTER XX

ILLUSTRATIONS

Author's Advertisement

AT the time I published the Narrative of the Mutiny on Board the Bounty, it was my intention that the preceding part of the Voyage should be contained in a separate account. This method I have since been induced to alter. The reason of the Narrative appearing first, was for the purpose of communicating early information concerning an event which had attracted the public notice: and being drawn up in a hasty manner, it required many corrections. Some circumstances likewise were omitted; and the notation of time used in the Narrative, being according to sea reckoning, in which the days begin and end at noon, must have produced a degree of obscurity and confusion to readers accustomed only to the civil mode. And this would have increased, as the remainder of the voyage, on account of the numerous shore occurrences at Otaheite and elsewhere, could not, with clearness and propriety, have been related in any other than the usual manner of reckoning.

Besides remedying these inconveniences, I have thought a fuller account of our passage from Timor to Europe, than that contained in the Narrative, would not be unacceptable. These reasons, with the manifest convenience of comprising the whole Voyage in one continued narrative, in preference to letting it appear in disjointed accounts, will, it is hoped, be allowed a sufficient excuse for having varied from the original intention. Nevertheless, for the accommodation of the purchasers of the Narrative already published, those who desire it, will be supplied with the other parts of the Voyage separate; i.e. the part previous to the mutiny, and the additional account after leaving Timor.

Scale 1 inch = 1040 Statute miles

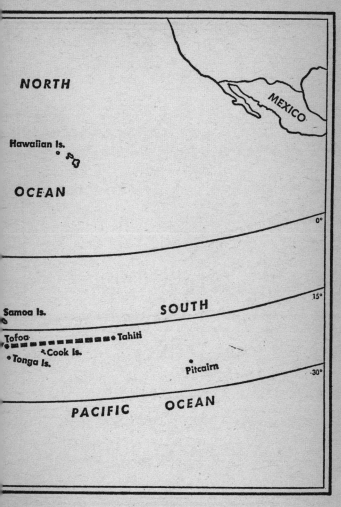

NORTH

MEXICO

Hawaiian Is.

OCEAN

0°

Samoa Is.

SOUTH

15°

Tofoa
Tahiti
Cook Is.
Tonga Is.

Pitcairn

30°

PACIFIC   OCEAN

Route of the *Bounty* from Tahiti to Tofoa thus ●■■■■■■■■●
Route of the *Bounty's* launch from Tofoa to Timor thus ▬▬▬▬▬▬▬

CHAPTER I

Plan of the Expedition—Outfit, and Occurrences to the Time of leaving England—Description of the Bread-Fruit

THE King having been graciously pleased to comply with a request from the merchants and planters interested in his Majesty's West India possessions, that the bread-fruit tree might be introduced into those islands, a vessel, proper for the undertaking, was bought, and taken into dock at Deptford, to be provided with the necessary fixtures and preparations for executing the object of the voyage. These were completed according to a plan of my much honoured friend, Sir Joseph Banks, which, in the event, proved the most advantageous that could have been adopted for the intended purpose.

The ship was named the *Bounty*: I was appointed to command her on the 16th of August 1787. Her burthen was nearly 215 tons; her extreme length on deck, 90 feet 10 inches; extreme breadth, 24 feet 3 inches; and height in the hold under the beams, at the main hatchway, 10 feet 3 inches. In the cockpit were the cabins of the surgeon, gunner, botanist, and clerk, with a steward-room and store-rooms. The between decks was divided in the following manner:—the great cabin was appropriated for the preservation of the plants, and extended as far forward as the after hatchway. It had two large sky-lights, and on each side three scuttles for air, and was fitted with a false floor cut full of holes to contain the garden-pots, in which the plants were to be brought home. The deck was covered with lead, and at the foremost corners of the cabin were fixed pipes to carry off the water that drained from the plants, into tubs placed below to save it for future use. I had a small cabin on one side to sleep in, adjoining to the great cabin, and a place near the middle of the ship to eat in. The bulk-head of this apartment was at the after-part of the main hatchway, and on each side of it were the berths of the mates and midshipmen; between these berths the arms-chest was placed. The cabin of the master,

13

in which was always kept the key of the arms, was opposite to mine. This particular description of the interior parts of the ship is rendered necessary by the event of the expedition.

The ship was masted according to the proportion of the navy; but, on my application, the masts were shortened, as I thought them too much for her, considering the nature of the voyage.

On the 3d of September, the ship came out of dock; but the carpenters and joiners remained on board much longer, as they had a great deal of work to finish.

The next material alteration made in the fitting out, was, lessening the quantity of iron and other ballast.— I gave directions that only 19 tons of iron should be taken on board instead of the customary proportion, which was 45 tons. The stores and provisions I judged would be fully sufficient to answer the purpose of the remainder; for I am of opinion, that many of the misfortunes which attend ships in heavy storms of wind, are occasioned by too much dead weight in their bottoms.

The establishment of men and officers for the ship were as follows:

1	Lieutenant to command
1	Master
1	Boatswain
1	Gunner
1	Carpenter
1	Surgeon
2	Master's Mates
2	Midshipmen
2	Quarter Masters
1	Quarter Master's Mate
1	Boatswain's Mate
1	Gunner's Mate
1	Carpenter's Mate
1	Carpenter's Crew
1	Sailmaker
1	Armourer
1	Corporal
1	Clerk and Steward
23	Able Seamen
44	

Two skilful and careful men were appointed, at Sir Joseph Banks's recommendation, to have the management of the plants intended to be brought home: the one, David Nelson, who had been on similar employment in Captain Cook's last voyage; the other, William Brown, as an assistant to him.—With these two our whole number amounted to forty-six.

It was proposed, that our route to the Society Islands should be round Cape Horn; and the greatest dispatch became necessary, as the season was already far advanced: but the shipwrights not being able to complete their work by the time the ship was ready in other respects, our sailing was unavoidably retarded. However, by the 4th of October the pilot came on board to take us down the river; on the 9th we fell down to Long Reach, where we received our gunner's stores, and guns, four four-pounders and ten swivels.

The ship was stored and victualled for eighteen months. In addition to the customary allowance of provisions, we were supplied with sour krout, portable soup, essence of malt, dried malt, and a proportion of barley and wheat in lieu of oatmeal. I was likewise furnished with a quantity of iron-work and trinkets, to serve in our intercourse with the natives in the South Seas: and from the board of Longitude I received a time-keeper, made by Mr. Kendal.

On the 15th I received orders to proceed to Spithead; but the winds and weather were so unfavourable that we did not arrive there till the 4th of November. On the 24th I received from Lord Hood, who commanded at Spithead, my final orders. The wind, which for several days before had been favourable, was now turned directly against us. On the 28th the ship's company received two months pay in advance, and on the following morning we worked out to St. Helen's, where we were obliged to anchor.

We made different unsuccessful attempts to get down Channel, but contrary winds and bad weather constantly forced us back to St. Helen's, or Spithead, until Sunday the 23rd of December, when we sailed with a fair wind.

During our stay at Spithead, the rate of the time-piece was several times examined by Mr. Bailey's observations at the Portsmouth observatory. On the 19th of December, the last time of its being examined on shore, it was 1' 52", 5 too fast for mean time, and then losing at the rate of

1″, 1 per day; and at this rate I estimate its going when we sailed.

The object of all the former voyages to the South Seas, undertaken by the command of his present majesty, has been the advancement of science, and the increase of knowledge. This voyage may be reckoned the first, the intention of which has been to derive benefit from those distant discoveries. For the more fully comprehending the nature and plan of the expedition, and that the reader may be possessed of every information necessary for entering on the following sheets, I shall here lay before him a copy of the instructions I received from the admiralty, and likewise a short description of the bread-fruit.

> *By the Commissioners for executing the office of Lord High Admiral of Great Britain and Ireland, &c.*

WHEREAS the king, upon a representation from the merchants and planters interested in his majesty's West India possessions, that the introduction of the bread-fruit trees into the islands of those seas, to constitute an article of food, would be of very essential benefit to the inhabitants, hath, in order to promote the interests of so respectable a body of his subjects (especially in an instance which promises general advantage) thought fit that measures should be taken for the procuring some of those trees, and conveying them to the said West India islands: And whereas the vessel under your command hath, in consequence thereof, been stored and victualled for that service, and fitted with proper conveniences and necessaries for the preservation of as many of the said trees as, from her size, can be taken on board her; and you have been directed to receive on board her the two gardeners [David Nelson and William Brown], who from their knowledge of trees and plants, have been hired for the purpose of selecting such as shall appear to be of a proper species and size:

You are, therefore, in pursuance of his majesty's pleasure, signified to us by Lord Sydney, one of his principal secretaries of state, hereby required and directed to put to sea in the vessel you command, the first favourable opportunity of wind and weather, and proceed with her, as expeditiously as possible, round Cape Horn, to the Society Islands, situate in the Southern ocean, in the latitude of about 18° S, and longitude of about 210° E, from Greenwich, where, according to the accounts given by the late Captain Cook, and persons who accompanied him during his voyages, the bread-fruit tree is to be found in the most luxuriant state.

Having arrived at the above-mentioned islands, and taken on board as many trees and plants as may be thought necessary (the better to enable you to do which, you have already been furnished with such articles of merchandise and trinkets as it is supposed will be wanted to satisfy the natives) you are to proceed from thence through Endeavour Straits (which separate New Holland from New Guinea) to Prince's Island, in the Straits of Sunda, or, if it should happen to be more convenient, to pass on the eastern side of Java to some port on the north side of that island, where any bread-fruit trees which may have been injured, or have died, may be replaced by mangosteens, duriens, jacks, nancas, lansas, and other fine fruit trees of that quarter, as well as the rice plant which grows upon dry land; all of which species (or such of them as shall be judged most eligible) you are to purchase on the best terms you can from the inhabitants of that island, with the ducats with which you have also been furnished for that purpose; taking care, however, if the rice plants above-mentioned cannot be procured at Java, to touch at Prince's Island for them, where they are regularly cultivated.

From Prince's Island, or the Island of Java, you are to proceed round the Cape of Good Hope to the West Indies (calling on your way thither at any places which may be thought necessary) and deposit one half of such of the above-mentioned trees and plants as may be then alive at his majesty's botanical garden at St. Vincent, for the benefit of the Windward Islands, and then go on to Jamaica: and, having delivered the remainder to Mr. East, or such person or persons as may be authorized by the governor and council of that island to receive them; refreshed your people, and received on board such provisions and stores as may be necessary for the voyage, make the best of your way back to England; repairing to Spithead, and sending to our secretary an account of your arrival and proceedings.

And whereas you will receive herewith a copy of the instructions which have been given to the above-mentioned gardeners for their guidance, as well in procuring the said trees and plants, and the management of them after they shall be put on board, as for bringing to England a small sample of each species, and such others as may be prepared by the superintendent of the botanical garden at St. Vincent's, and by the said Mr. East, or others, for his majesty's garden at Kew; you are hereby required and directed to afford, and to give directions to your officers and company to afford, the said gardeners every possible aid and assistance, not only in the collecting of the said trees and plants at the places before-mentioned, but for their preservation during their conveyance to the places of their destination.

Given under our hands the 20th November 1787.

> HOWE
> CHAS. BRETT
> RD. HOPKINS
> J. LEVESON GOWER

To Lieut. Wm. Bligh, commanding
his majesty's armed vessel the
Bounty, at Spithead

> By commander of their Lordships,
> P. STEPHENS

In the foregoing orders it is to be observed, that I was particularly directed to proceed round Cape Horn; but, as the season was so far advanced, and we were so long detained by contrary winds, I made application to the Admiralty for discretional orders on that point; to which I received the following answer:

> *By the Commissioners for executing the office of*
> *Lord High Admiral of Great Britain and*
> *Ireland, &c. &c.*

THE season of the year being now so far advanced as to render it probable, that your arrival, with the vessel you command, on the southern coast of America, will be too late for your passing round Cape Horn without much difficulty and hazard; you are, in that case, at liberty (notwithstanding former orders) to proceed in her to Otaheite, round the Cape of Good Hope.

Given under our hands the 18th December 1787.

HOWE

CHAS. BRETT

BAYHAM

*To Lieut. Wm. Bligh, commanding
his majesty's armed vessel Bounty,
Spithead*

By command of their Lordships,

P. STEPHENS

THE BREAD-FRUIT is so well known and described, that to attempt a new account of it would be unnecessary and useless. However, as it may contribute to the convenience of the reader, I have given the following extracts respecting it:

Extract from the account of Dampier's Voyage round the world, performed in 1688

"THE bread-fruit (as we call it) grows on a large tree, as big and high as our largest apple-trees: It hath a spreading head, full of branches and dark leaves. The fruit grows on the boughs like apples; it is as big as a penny-loaf when wheat is at 5s. the bushel; it is of a round shape, and hath a thick tough rind. When the fruit is ripe, it is yellow and soft, and the taste is sweet and pleasant. The natives of Guam use it for bread. They gather it, when full-grown, while it is green and hard; then they bake it in an oven, which scorcheth the rind and makes it black; but they scrape off the outside black crust, and there remains a tender thin crust; and the inside is soft, tender, and white like the crumb of a penny-loaf. There is *neither seed nor stone* in the inside, but all is of a pure substance, like bread. It must be eaten new; for, if it is kept above twenty-four hours, it grows harsh and choaky; but it is very pleasant before it is too stale. This fruit lasts in season *eight months* in the year, during which the natives eat *no other sort of food of bread kind*. I did never see of this fruit any where but here. The natives told us, that there is plenty of this fruit growing on the rest of the Ladrone islands: and I *did never hear of it any where else.*" Vol. I. p. 296.

Extract from the account of Lord Anson's Voyage, published by Mr. Walter

"THERE was, at Tinian, a kind of fruit, peculiar to these (Ladrone) islands, called by the Indians *rhymay,* but by us the *bread-fruit;* for it was constantly eaten by us, during our stay upon the island*, instead of bread; and so *universally preferred,* that no ship's bread was expended in that whole interval. It grew upon a tree which is somewhat lofty, and which towards the top divides into large and spreading branches. The leaves of this tree are of a remarkable deep green, are notched about the edges, and are generally from a foot to eighteen inches in length. The fruit itself is found indifferently on all parts of the branches; it is, in shape, rather elliptical than round; it is covered with a tough rind, and is usually seven or eight inches long; each of them grows singly, and not in clusters. This fruit is fittest to be used when it is full-grown, but still green; in which state, after it is properly prepared by being roasted in the embers, its taste has some distant resemblance to that of an artichoke's bottom, and its texture is not very different, for it is soft and spungy."

Extracts from the account of the first Voyage of Captain Cook. Hawkesworth, Vol. II

"THE bread-fruit grows on a tree that is about the size of a middling oak; its leaves are frequently a foot and a half long, of an oblong shape, deeply sinuated like those of the fig-tree, which they resemble in consistence and colour, and in the exuding of a white milky juice upon being broken. The fruit is about the size and shape of a child's head, and the surface is reticulated not much unlike a truffle: it is covered with a thin skin, and has a core about as big as the handle of a small knife. The eatable part lies between the skin and the core; it is as white as snow, and somewhat of the consistence of new

* About two months; viz. from the latter end of August to the latter end of October, 1742.

bread: it must be roasted before it is eaten, being first divided into three or four parts. Its taste is insipid, with a slight sweetness somewhat resembling that of the crumb of wheaten bread mixed with a Jerusalem artichoke."

P. 80, 81. See also the plate there and at p. 232.

"OF the many vegetables that have been mentioned already as serving them for food, the principal is the bread-fruit, to procure which costs them no trouble or labour but climbing a tree. The tree which produces it does not indeed shoot up spontaneously; but, if a man plants ten of them in his life-time, which he may do in about an hour, he will as completely fulfil his duty to his own and future generations as the native of our less temperate climate can do by ploughing in the cold winter, and reaping in the summer's heat, as often as these seasons return; even if, after he has procured bread for his present household, he should convert a surplus into money, and lay it up for his children.

"It is true, indeed, that the bread-fruit is not always in season; but cocoa-nuts, bananas, plantains, and a great variety of other fruits, supply the deficiency." P. 197.

Extract from the account of Captain Cook's last Voyage

IN THE SOCIETY ISLANDS

"I (Captain Cook) have inquired very carefully into their manner of cultivating the bread-fruit tree at Otaheite; but was always answered, that they never planted it. This, indeed, must be evident to every one who will examine the places where the young trees come up. It will be always observed, that they spring from the roots of the old ones, which run along near the surface of the ground. So that the bread-fruit trees may be reckoned those that would naturally cover the plains, even supposing that the island was not inhabited; in the same manner that the white-barked trees, found at Van Diemen's Land, constitute the forests there. And from this we may observe, that the inhabitant of Otaheite, instead of being obliged to plant his bread, will *rather* be under the necessity of preventing its progress; which, I suppose, is sometimes

PLAN & SECTION
of part of the
BOUNTY ARMED TRANSPORT
showing the manner of
fitting and stowing the Pots
for receiving the
Bread-fruit plants.

done, to give room for trees of another sort, to afford him some variety in his food." Vol. II. p. 145.

IN THE SANDWICH ISLANDS

"THE bread-fruit trees are planted, and flourish with great luxurance, on rising grounds.".—"Where the hills rise almost perpendicularly in a great variety of peaked forms, their steep sides and the deep chasms between them are covered with trees, amongst which those of the bread-fruit were observed particularly to abound." Vol. III. p. 105 and 114, containing Captain King's Narrative.

"THE climate of the Sandwich Islands differs very little from that of the West India Islands, which lie *in the same latitude*. Upon the whole, perhaps, it may be rather more temperate." Captain King, ib. p. 116.

"THE bread-fruit trees thrive in these islands, not in such abundance, but produce double the quantity of fruit they do on the rich plains of Otaheite. The trees are nearly of the same height, but the branches begin to strike out from the trunk much lower, and with greater luxuriance." Capt. King, ib. p. 120.

CHAPTER II

ON Sunday morning the 23d of December 1787, we sailed from Spithead, and, passing through the Needles, directed our course down channel, with a fresh gale of wind at East. In the afternoon, one of the seamen, in furling the main-top-gallant-sail, fell off the yard, and was so fortunate as to save himself by catching hold of the main-top-mast-stay in his fall. At night the wind increased to a strong gale, with a heavy sea. It moderated, however, on the 25th, and allowed us to keep our Christmas with cheerfulness; but the following day it blew a severe storm of wind from the Eastward, which continued till the 29th, in the course of which we suffered greatly. One sea broke away the spare yards and spars out of the starboard main chains. Another heavy sea broke into the ship, and stove all the boats. Several casks of beer, that had been lashed upon deck, were broke loose and washed overboard, and it was not without great difficulty and risk that we were able to secure the boats from being washed away entirely. On the 29th we were in latitude 39° 35′ N and longitude 14° 26′ W when the gale abated, and the weather became fair. Besides other mischief done to us by the storm, a large quantity of our bread was damaged and rendered useless, for the sea had stove in our stern, and filled the cabin with water. From this time to our arrival at Teneriffe we had moderate weather, and winds mostly from the northward.

January 4th. This forenoon we spoke a French ship, bound to the Mauritius. The next day, at nine in the forenoon, we saw the island of Teneriffe, bearing W S W ½ W, about twelve leagues distant. It was covered with a thick haze, except the north-westernmost part, which is a remarkable headland, resembling a horse's head, the ears very distinct. To the eastward of this

head* lie two round rocks, the northern boundary of
Teneriffe. I had a good observation at noon, by which
I make the latitude of the two rocks 28° 44′ N, and their
longitude by our timekeeper 16° 5′ W. To the
southward of these, and near the shore, is a high needle
rock: about four leagues farther to the southward, the
coast inclines towards the West to the road of Santa
Cruz, where we anchored at half past nine on Sunday
morning, in 25 fathoms water, and moored along
shore in the same depth, with the cupola tower of the
church of St. Francis bearing W ½ N, one mile, the East
part of the road E by N, the castle on the South point
S W, and the West part of the Grand Canary S S E.
A Spanish packet, bound to Corunna, an American brig,
and several other vessels, were lying here.

As soon as the ship was anchored, I sent an officer
(Mr. Christian) to wait on the governor, and to acquaint
him I had put in to obtain refreshments, and to repair the
damages we had sustained in bad weather. To this I
had a very polite answer from the governor,† that I
should be supplied with whatever the island afforded.
I had also directed the officer to acquaint him that I
would salute, provided an equal number of guns were to
be returned; but, as I received an extraordinary answer
to this part of my message, purporting, that his excellency
did not return the same number but to persons equal in
rank to himself, this ceremony was omitted.

During this interval I was visited by the port-master
(Capt. Adams) and shortly afterwards several officers
came on board from his excellency, to compliment me
on my arrival. As soon as the ship was moored, I went
on shore, and paid my respects to him.

On Monday morning I began to forward the ship's
business with the utmost dispatch, and gave the necessary directions to Messrs. Collogan and sons, the con-
tractors, for the supplies I wanted. I also got leave of
the governor for Mr. Nelson to range the hills, and
examine the country in search of plants and natural
curiosities.

As there was a great surf on the shore, I bargained for

* S 82° E by the compass.

† Marquis de Brancheforté.

every thing I wanted, to be brought off by the shore boats, and agreed to give 5*s.* per ton for water. Very good wine was bought at £10 per pipe, the contract price; but the superior quality was £15; and some of this was not much inferior to the best London Madeira. —I found this was an unfavourable season for other refreshments: Indian corn, potatoes, pumpkins, and onions, were all very scarce, and double the price of what they are in summer. Beef also was difficult to be procured, and exceedingly poor; the price nearly six pence farthing per pound. The corn was three current dollars per fanega, which is full 5*s.* per bushel; and biscuit at 25*s.* for 100 pounds. Poultry was so scarce that a good fowl cost 3*s.* This is, therefore, not a place for ships to expect refreshments at a reasonable price at this time of the year, wine excepted; but from March to November supplies are plentiful, particularly fruit; of which at this time we could procure none, except a few dried figs and some bad oranges.

During our stay here, the weather was fair, with N E winds and calms, and small drizzling rain in the night. The thermometer from 66° to 69° at noon in the shade. I could make no lunar observations for the longitude, but by the help of the time-keeper I have computed the situation of the town of Santa Cruz to be 28° 28′ N latitude, and 16° 18′ W longitude. I observed the variation by two compasses to be 20° 1′ W: this much exceeded what I could have imagined; for, in 1776, I observed it only 14° 40′ W; a difference of above five degrees in eleven years: and this makes me reflect on the uncertainty of obtaining the exact deviation of the magnetic pole, and of course its annual variation, which never can be accurately ascertained, unless the observations are made always in one spot, and with the same compass.

Teneriffe, though considerably without the tropic, is so nearly within the limits of the trade wind, that navigators generally steer to it from the eastward. The road of Santa Cruz lies on the east side of the island, at the end of a range of craggy hills, barren and very lofty; along which you sail W by S by compass into the road, with a sea unfathomable until near the shore. The anchoring ground may be accounted from 50 fathoms to 20, or even 15. The bank is very steep, and gives but little

time to sound; for which reason it should be done effectually with a heavy lead, or a ship will be too near in before
a stranger is aware of it: he will likewise too soon expect
to find bottom, owning to the great deception of the
adjacent high land. To obviate these difficulties, it is
necessary to observe, that while a town, which lies some
distance to the southward of Santa Cruz, is open with the
castle on the south part of the road, though you may
appear near to the shore, there is no anchorage; but after
it is shut entirely in, you get on the bank. The church
bearing W, or W by S, and the south point of the road
S W ½ S, to S W by W, is a good situation for anchoring:
the depth about twenty-five fathoms. The distance from
the shore will be three quarters of a mile; and the southernmost land that can be seen then will be a half or
quarter point of the compass farther out than the south
point of the road.

The bottom is black soft mud, with some patches of
rocks; for which reason vessels, that lie here any length
of time, buoy their cables. This precaution, besides being
useful in that particular, they think makes them ride
more easy when there is much sea setting into the road,
which, with the wind any way to the southward of E,
or at S W must be very considerable; it is, therefore, usual
to moor with four anchors, though more than two are
scarce ever of use. Mooring is, however, advisable if a
ship is only to remain twenty-four hours, and the tighter
the better, that the cables may keep clear of the ground.

The landing on the beach is generally impracticable
with our own boats, at least without great risk; but there
is a very fine pier, on which people may land without
difficulty if there is not much swell in the road. To this
pier the water is conveyed by pipes for the use of shipping, and for which all merchant-ships pay.

There is a degree of wretchedness and want among the
lower class of people, which is not anywhere so common
as among the Spanish and Portuguese settlements. To
alleviate these evils, the present governor of Teneriffe
has instituted a most charitable society, which he takes the
trouble to superintend; and by considerable contributions,
a large airy dwelling, that contains one hundred and
twenty poor girls, and as many men and boys, has been
built, and endowed with a sufficiency of land round it,

not only for all present purposes, but for enlarging the building for more objects of charity as their funds increase. I had the honour to be shown by his excellency this asylum, (Hospicio they call it) where there appeared in every countenance the utmost cheerfulness and content. The decency and neatness of the dress of the young females, with the order in which they were arranged at their spinning-wheels and looms, in an extensive airy apartment, was admirable. A governess inspected and regulated all their works, which were the manufacturing of ribbons of all colours, coarse linens, and tapes; all which were managed and brought to perfection by themselves, from the silk and flax in their first state; even the dyeing of the colours is performed by them. These girls are received for five years, at the end of which they are at liberty to marry, and have for their portions their wheel and loom, with a sum of money proportioned to the state of the fund, which is assisted by the produce of their labour, and at this time was estimated at two thousand dollars per annum.

The men and boys are not less attended to: they are employed in coarser work, blanketing and all kinds of common woollens: if they become infirm, they spend the remainder of their days here comfortably, and under a watchful inspector, who attends them in the same manner as the governess does the girls. They are all visited every day by the governor, and a clergyman attends them every evening. By this humane institution a number of people are rendered useful and industrious, in a country where the poor, from the indulgence of the climate, are too apt to prefer a life of inactivity, though attended with wretchedness, to obtaining the comforts of life by industry and labour.

The number of inhabitants in the island, I was informed, were estimated at between eighty and one hundred thousand. Their annual export of wine is twenty thousand pipes, and of brandy half that quantity. Vessels are frequently here from St. Eustatia, and from thence a great quantity of Teneriffe wine is carried to the different parts of the West Indies, under the name of Madeira.

Teneriffe is considered of more value than all the other Canaries: the inhabitants, however, in scarce seasons

receive supplies from the Grand Canary; but their vine-
yards here are said to be greatly superior. Their produce
of corn, though exceedingly good, is not sufficient for
their consumption; and, owing to this, the Americans
have an advantageous trade here for their flour and grain,
and take wine in return.

The town of Santa Cruz is about half a mile in extent
each way, built in a regular manner, and the houses in
general large and airy, but the streets are very ill paved.
I am told, that they are subject to few diseases; but if any
epidemic distemper breaks out, it is attended with the
most fatal consequences, particularly the small-pox, the
bad effects of which they now endeavour to counteract
by inoculation. For this reason, they are very circum-
spect in admitting ships to have communication with the
shore without bills of health.

A sloop from London, called the *Chance,* William
Meridith, master, bound to Barbadoes, out nineteen days
from the Downs, came into the road the day before we
sailed. She had suffered much by the bad weather; but,
having brought no bill of health, the governor would
not allow any person to come on shore, unless I could
vouch for them, that no epidemic disease raged in England at the time they sailed, which I was able to do, it
being nearly at the same time that I left the land; and
by that means they had the governor's permission to
receive the supplies they wanted, without being obliged
to perform quarantine.

Having finished our business at Teneriffe, on Thursday the 10th, we sailed with the wind at S E, our ship's
company all in good health and spirits.

I now divided the people into three watches, and gave
the charge of the third watch to Mr. Fletcher Christian,
one of the mates.—I have always considered this as a
desirable regulation, when circumstances will admit of it,
on many accounts; and am persuaded that unbroken rest
not only contributes much towards the health of a ship's
company, but enables them more readily to exert themselves in cases of sudden emergency.

As it was my wish to proceed to Otaheite without
stopping, I ordered every body to be at two thirds allowance of bread: I also directed the water for drinking to

be filtered through dripstones that I had bought at Teneriffe for that purpose.

In the evening we passed the south end of Teneriffe, which is a round lump of land, that, from the lowness of the contiguous land, has at a distance the appearance of a separate island. By our run from the bay of Santa Cruz, I make the latitude of the south end of Teneriffe to be 28° 6′ N.

We ran all night towards the S S W, having the wind at S E. The next morning we could see nothing of the land. I now made the ship's company acquainted with the intent of the voyage; and, having been permitted to hold out this encouragement to them, I gave assurances of the certainty of promotion to every one whose endeavours should merit it.

The winds, for some days after leaving Teneriffe, were mostly from the southward. Fishing-lines and tackle were distributed amongst the people, and some dolphins were caught.

On the 17th the wind came round to the N E, and continued steady in that quarter till the 25th; on which day, at noon, we were in 3° 54′ N. As the cloudiness of the sky gave us reason to expect much rain, we prepared the awnings with hoses for the convenience of saving water, in which we were not disappointed. From this time to our meeting with the S E trade wind we had much wet weather, the air close and sultry, with calms, and light variable winds, generally from the southward.

On the 29th there was so heavy a fall of rain that we caught seven hundred gallons of water.

On the 31st, latitude at noon, 2° 5′ N, found a current setting to the N E, at the rate of 14 miles in the twenty-four hours. The thermometer was at 82° in the shade, and 81° ½ at the surface of the sea, so that the air and the water were within half a degree of the same temperature. At eight o'clock in the evening we observed a violent rippling in the sea, about half a mile to the N W of us, which had very much the appearance of breakers. This I imagine to have been occasioned by a large school (or multitude) of fish, as it was exactly in the track the ship had passed, so that if any real shoal had been there, we must have seen it at the close of the evening, when a careful look-out was always kept. However, if it had

appeared ahead of us, instead of astern, I should certainly have tacked to avoid it. To such appearances I
attribute the accounts of many shoals within the tropics,
which cannot be found any where but in maps. Our
latitude at this time was 2° 8′ N, and longitude 19° 43′
W. The next day we had more of these appearances, from
the number of schools of fish by which the ship was
surrounded.

Saturday the 2nd. This morning, we saw a sail to the
N N W, but at too great a distance to distinguish what
she was.

Monday the 4th. Had very heavy rain; during which
we nearly filled all our empty water casks. So much wet
weather, with the closeness of the air, covered every thing
with mildew. The ship was aired below with fires, and
frequently sprinkled with vinegar; and every little interval
of dry weather was taken advantage of to open all the
hatchways, and clean the ship, and to have all the people's
wet things washed and dried.

With this weather, and light unsteady winds, we advanced but 2½ degrees in twelve days; at the end of
which time we were relieved by the S E trade wind, which
we fell in with on the 6th at noon, in latitude 1° 21′ N,
and longitude 20° 42′ W.

The next afternoon we crossed the equinoctial line, in
longitude 21° 50′ W. The weather became fine, and the
S E trade wind was fresh and steady, with which we kept
a point free from the wind, and got to the southward at a
good rate.

The weather continuing dry, we put some of our bread
in casks, properly prepared for its reception, to preserve
it from vermin: this experiment, we afterwards found,
answered exceedingly well.

On the 16th, at daylight, we saw a sail to the southward. The next day we came up with her, and found her
to be the *British Queen,* Simon Paul, master, from London, bound to the Cape of Good Hope, on the whale-
fishery. She sailed from Falmouth the 5th December,
eighteen days before I left Spithead. By this ship I wrote
to England. At sunset she was almost out of sight astern.

Monday the 18th. In the course of this day's run,
the variation changed from W to E. According to our
observations, the true and magnetic meridians coin-

cided in latitude 20° 0′ S, and longitude 31° 15′ W. At noon we were in latitude 20° 44′ S, and longitude 31° 23′ W. In our advances towards the south, the wind had gradually veered round to the E, and was at this time at E N E. The weather, after crossing the Line, had been fine and clear, but the air so sultry as to occasion great faintness, the quicksilver in the thermometer, in the day-time, standing at between 81° and 83°, and one time at 85°. In our passage through the northern tropic, the air was temperate, the sun having then high south declination and the weather being generally fine till we lost the N E trade wind; but such a thick haze surrounded the horizon, that no object could be seen, except at a very small distance. The haze commonly cleared away at sunset, and gathered again at sunrise. Between the N E and S E trade winds, the calms and rains, if of long continuance, are very liable to produce sickness, unless great attention is paid to keeping the ship clean and wholesome, by giving all the air possible, drying between decks with fires, and drying and airing the people's clothes and bedding. Besides these precautions, we frequently wetted with vinegar; and every evening the pumps were used as ventilators. With these endeavours to secure health, we passed the low latitudes without a single complaint.

The currents we met with were by no means regular, nor have I ever found them so in the middle of the ocean. However, from the channel to the southward, as far as Madeira, there is generally a current setting to the S S E.

On the evening of the 21st, a ship was seen in the N E, but at too great a distance to distinguish of what country. The next day the wind came round to the N and N W, so that we could no longer consider ourselves in the trade wind. Our latitude at noon was 25° 55′ S, longitude 36° 29′ W. Variation of the compass 3° E.

Saturday 23d, towards night the wind died away, and we had some heavy showers of rain, of which we profited, by saving a ton of good water. The next day we caught a shark and five dolphins.

Tuesday 26th, we bent new sails, and made other necessary preparations for encountering the weather that was to be expected in a high latitude. Our latitude at noon was 29° 38′ S, longitude 41° 44′ W. Variation

7° 13′ E. In the afternoon, the wind being westerly, and blowing strong in squalls, some butterflies, and other insects, like what we call horseflies, were blown on board of us. No birds were seen except sheerwaters. Our distance from the coast of Brasil at this time was above 100 leagues.

Sunday 2d, in the forenoon, after seeing that every person was clean, divine service was performed, according to my usual custom on this day. I gave to Mr. Fletcher Christian, whom I had before directed to take charge of the third watch, a written order to act as lieutenant.

Saturday 8th. We were at noon in latitude 36° 50′ S, and longitude 52° 53′ W. The last four days, we several times tried for soundings, without finding bottom, though considerably to the westward of Captain Wallis's track, who had soundings at 54 fathoms depth, in latitude 35° 40′ S, and longitude 49° 54′ W. This day we tried with 240 fathoms of line, but did not find bottom; at the same time, observing a rippling in the water, we tried the current by mooring a keg with 100 fathoms of line, by which it appeared to run to the N N W, at the rate of a mile and a half *per* hour. By the noon observation, however, we were 18 miles to the southward of our reckoning. In the afternoon we saw a turtle floating, and, not having much wind, hoisted a boat out, and sent after it; but it was found to be in a putrid state, with a number of crabs feeding upon it.

The change of temperature began now to be sensibly felt, there being a variation in the thermometer, since yesterday, of 8 degrees. That the people might not suffer by their own negligence, I gave orders for their light tropical clothing to be put by, and made them dress in a manner more suited to a cold climate. I had provided for this before I left England, by giving directions for such clothes to be purchased as were necessary.

Monday 10th. In the forenoon we struck soundings at 83 fathoms depth; our latitude 40° 8′ S, and longitude 55° 40′ W. This I conclude to have been near the edge of the bank; for, the wind being at S S W, we stood towards the S E; and, after running 14 miles in that direction, we could find no bottom with 160 fathoms of line. In the night we stood towards the W S W, with a southerly wind, and got again into soundings. The next day we saw a great number of whales of an immense size, that had two spout-holes on the back of the head.—Upon a complaint made to me by the master, I found it necessary to punish Matthew Quintal, one of the seamen, with two dozen lashes, for insolence and mutinous behaviour. Before this, I had not had occasion to punish any person on board.

On the 12th, we caught a porpoise, by striking it with the grains. Every one eat heartily of it; and it was so well liked, that no part was wasted.

On the 14th, in the afternoon, we saw a land-bird like a lark, and passed part of a dead whale that had been left by some whalers after they had taken the blubber off. Saw, likewise, two strange sail. The next day, at noon, our latitude was 43° 6′ S, and longitude 58° 42′ W. Had soundings at 75 fathoms; the bottom a fine greenish sand. Saw two hawks.

On the 16th another ship was seen to the W N W, standing to the northward. Latitude, at noon, 43° 34′ S. We continued running to the southward, keeping in soundings.

On the 19th, at noon, by my account, we were within 20 leagues of Port Desire; but the wind blowing fresh from the N W with thick foggy weather, I did not attempt to make the land. We passed a good deal of rock-weed, and saw many whales, and albatrosses and other sea-birds.

On the 20th, at noon, our latitude was 50° 24′ S, and longitude 65° 50′ W. In the afternoon, the wind, which had for some time past been northerly, suddenly shifted to the W S W, and blew hard, We steered to the S S E; and on the 23rd, at two o'clock in the morning, we discovered the coast of Terra del Fuego bearing S E. At nine in the forenoon we were off Cape St. Diego, the eastern part of Terra del Fuego. Observed the variation here to be 21° 23′ E. The wind being unfavourable, I thought it more advisable to go round to the eastward of Staten Land, than to attempt passing through Straits le Maire. The two opposite coasts of the Straits exhibited very different appearances. The land of Terra del Fuego hereabouts, though the interior parts are mountainous, yet near the coast is of moderate height, and, at the distance we were from it, had not an unpromising appearance. The coast of Staten Land, near the Straits, is mountainous and craggy, and remarkable for its high peaked hills. Straits le Maire is a fair opening, which cannot well be mistaken; but if any doubt could remain, the different appearances of the opposite shores would sufficiently make the Straits known.

I did not sail within less than 6 leagues of the coast, that we might have the wind more regular, and avoid being exposed to the heavy squalls that came off from the land. At noon Cape St. Anthony bore S, and the westernmost of New Year's Isles S E ¼ S, 5 or 6 leagues. Latitude observed 54° 28′ S, longitude 64° 4′ W.

The sight of New Year's Harbour almost tempted me to put in; but the lateness of the season, and the people being in good health, determined me to lay aside all thoughts of refreshment, until we should reach Otaheite. At two o'clock in the afternoon, the easternmost of New Year's Isles, where Captain Cook observed the latitude to be 55° 40′ S, bore from us S four leagues. We saw the entrance isles of New Year's Harbour; at the back of which the land is very craggy and mountainous. This must be a very convenient port to touch at, as the access to it is safe and easy. The harbour lies S S E, by compass, from the N E part of the easternmost of the New Year's Islands.

About two leagues to the westward of Cape St. John, I observed the separation of the mountains that Captain Cook had taken notice of, which has the appearance of Staten Land, being there divided into two islands.

At sunset, Cape St. John bore S S E 5 or 6 leagues. The land hereabouts is of less height, and not so rugged as near New Year's Harbour. The night coming on, I could get no good view of the coast near the Cape; and at daylight, next morning, we were at too great a distance.

Monday 24th. We had stood to the southward all night, with the wind at W S W and S W. At eight in the morning, Cape St. John bore N W, 10 leagues distant. Soon after we lost sight of the land.

From the result of my lunar observations, assisted by the time-keeper, I make the longitude of the west side of Straits le Maire to be 64° 48′ W; the easternmost of the New Year's Isles 63° 52′ W; and the longitude of Cape St. John 63° 19′ W.

In our run from the latitude of 12° S to 48° S, the ship was set 2° 30′ to the eastward by currents; and from the latitude of 48° S to Staten Land, the currents set us to the westward 2° 43′; which I imagine to have been occasioned by an indraught into the Straits of Magellan.

From the time we lost sight of the land, to the end of the month, we were struggling with bad weather and contrary winds: but on the morning of the 31st the wind came to the N N E, and made us entertain great hopes that we should be able to accomplish our passage round the Cape without much difficulty. At noon we were in latitude 60° 1′ S, and in 71° 45′ W longitude, which is 8° 26′ W of the meridian of Cape St. John. This flattering appearance was not of long continuance: in the night the wind became variable, and next day settled again in the W and N W, with very bad weather.

On the 2nd, in the morning, the wind, which had blown fresh all night from the N W, came round to the S W, and increased to a heavy gale. At six in the morning the storm exceeded what I had ever met with before; and the sea, from the frequent shifting of the wind, running in contrary directions, broke exceeding high. Our ship, however, lay to very well, under a main and fore-stay sail. The gale continued, with severe squalls of hail and sleet, the remainder of this, and all the next day.—On the 4th, the wind was less violent, but far from moderate. With so much bad weather, I found it necessary to keep a constant fire, night and day; and one of the watch always attended to dry the people's wet clothes: and this, I have no doubt, contributed as much to their health as to their comfort.

Our companions in this inhospitable region were albatrosses, and two beautiful kinds of birds, the small blue petterel, and pintada. A great many of these were frequently about the wake of the ship, which induced the people to float a line with hooks baited, to endeavour to catch them; and their attempts were successful. The method they used, was to fasten the bait a foot or two before the hook, and, by giving the line a sudden jerk when the bird was at the bait, it was hooked in the feet or body.

On the 6th the weather was moderate, and continued

so till the 9th, with the wind veering between the N W
and S W; of which we were able to take advantage.

On the 7th, observed the variation 27° 9′ E; our
latitude 60° 24′ S; and longitude 75° 54′ W. On the
9th, at noon, we were in latitude 59° 31′ S, and our
longitude 76° 58′ W, which is farther to the W than
we had yet been. The weather was now unfavourable
again, blowing strong from the westward, with a high sea.

On the 10th, we saw some fish, which appeared
spotted, and about the size of bonetos: these were the
only fish we had seen in this high latitude.

The stormy weather continued with a great sea. The
ship now began to complain, and required to be pumped
every hour; which was no more than we had reason to
expect from such a continuance of gales of wind and high
seas. The decks also became so leaky, that I was obliged
to allot the great cabin, of which I made little use, except
in fine weather, to those people who had wet berths, to
hang their hammocks in; and by this means the between
decks was less crowded.

Every morning all the hammocks were taken down
from where they hung, and when the weather was too bad
to keep them upon deck, they were put in the cabin; so
that the between decks were cleaned daily, and aired with
fires, if the hatchways could not be opened. With all this
bad weather, we had the additional mortification to find,
at the end of every day, that we were losing ground; for
notwithstanding our utmost exertions, and keeping on the
most advantageous tacks (which, if the weather had
been at all moderate, would have sufficiently answered
our purpose) yet the greater part of the time, we were
doing little better than drifting before the wind.

Birds as usual were about the ship, and some of them
caught; and, for the first time since we left Staten Land,
we saw some whales. This morning, owing to the violent
motion of the ship, the cook fell and broke one of his ribs,
and another man, by a fall, dislocated his shoulder. The
gunner, who had the charge of a watch, was laid up with
the rheumatism: and this was the first sick list that appeared on board the ship. The time of full moon, which
was approaching, made me entertain hopes that after
that period we should experience some change of wind or
weather in our favour; but the event did not at all

answer our expectations. The latitude, at noon this day, was 58° 9′ S, and longitude 76° 1′ W.

As we caught a good many birds, but which were all lean, and tasted fishy, we tried an experiment upon them, which succeeded admirably. By keeping them cooped up, and cramming them with ground corn, they improved wonderfully in a short time; so that the pintada birds became as fine as ducks, and the albatrosses were as fat, and not inferior in taste to fine geese. Some of the latter birds were caught that measured 7 feet between the extremities of the wings, when spread. This unexpected supply came very opportunely; for none of our live stock remained except hogs, the sheep and poultry not being hardy enough to stand the severity of the weather.

This morning, the wind died away, and we had a calm for a few hours, which gave us hopes that the next would be a more favourable wind. A hog was killed for the ship's company, which gave them an excellent meal. Towards noon, to our great disappointment, the wind sprung up again from the westward, and in the afternoon blew strong, with snow and hail storms.

This was the second day after the full moon; but, as I have remarked before, it had no influence on the weather. At noon our latitude was 58° 31′ S, and longitude 70° 7′ W, which is near seven degrees to the eastward of our situation on the morning of the 9th instant, when we had advanced the farthest in our power to the westward, being then in 76° 58′ W, three degrees to the west of Cape Deseada, the west part of the Straits of Magellan; and at this time we were 3° 52′ to the east of it, and hourly losing ground.

It was with much concern I saw how hopeless, and even unjustifiable it was, to persist any longer in attempting a passage this way to the Society Islands. We had been thirty days in this tempestuous ocean. At one time we had advanced so far to the westward as to have a fair prospect of making our passage round; but from that period hard gales of westerly wind had continued without intermission, a few hours excepted, which, to borrow an expression in Lord Anson's voyage, were "like the elements drawing breath to return upon us with redoubled violence." The season was now too far advanced for us to expect more favourable winds or weather, and we had sufficiently experienced the impossibility of beating round against the wind, or of advancing at all without the help of a fair wind, for which there was little reason to hope. Another consideration, which had great weight with me, was, that if I persisted in my attempt this way, and should, after all, fail to get round, it would occasion such a loss of time, that our arrival at Otaheite, soon enough to return in the proper season by the East Indies, would be rendered precarious. On the other hand, the prevalence of the westerly winds in high southern latitudes, left me no reason to doubt of making a quick passage to the Cape of Good Hope, and thence to the eastward round New Holland. Having maturely considered all circumstances, I determined to bear away for the Cape of Good Hope; and at five o'clock on the evening of the 22d, the wind then blowing strong at W, I ordered the helm to be put a weather, to the great joy of every person on board. Our sick list at this time had increased to eight, mostly with rheumatic complaints: in other respects the people were in good health, though exceedingly jaded.

The passage round Cape Horn, into the South Seas, during the summer months, has seldom been attended with difficulty, and is to be preferred, in the moderate seasons, to the more distant route to the eastward round the Cape of Good Hope and New Holland. If we had been one month earlier, or perhaps less, I doubt not but we should have effected our passage.

The soundings that are met with off the coast of America, from the latitude of 36° S to the southward, are very convenient to enable ships to judge of their distance from the land, as thick fogs are very frequent near that coast. If the winds are favourable, to go through Straits le Maire must considerably shorten the passage around Cape Horn, as all the distance saved is so much gained to the westward. I am informed, that several harbours have been lately discovered by the South Sea whalers, on the north side of Staten Island, that afford safe anchorage, with supplies of wood and water.

While we were off Cape Horn, I did not observe that our situation was at all affected by currents.

CHAPTER III

*Passage towards the Cape of Good Hope, and search after
Tristan da Cunha—Arrival at False Bay—Occurrences
there—Reports concerning the Grosvenor's People—Departure from the Cape*

THE westerly winds and stormy weather continuing,
gave me no reason to repent of my determination.
On the 25th, at noon, we were in latitude 54° 16′ S,
and longitude 57° 4′ W. The nearest of the Falkland
Islands, by my reckoning, then bore N 13° W; distance
23 leagues. Our stock of water being sufficient to serve us
to the Cape of Good Hope, I did not think it worth while
to stop at these islands, as the refreshment we might
obtain there would scarce repay us for the expence of
time: we therefore continued our course towards the N E
and E N E.

On the 9th of May, at eight o'clock in the evening, we
were near the situation of Tristan da Cunha, our latitude
being 37° 7′ S, and longitude 15° 26′ W. All the afternoon the weather had been clear enough for land of a
moderate height to be seen at least 7 leagues; I therefore
concluded that we had not yet passed the meridian of the
island; for the most western position given to it from any
authority, is 15° 0′ W.

As I wished to make this island, we kept our wind on
different tacks during the night, that we might be nearly
in the same place at daylight in the morning, as on the
preceding evening: in the morning, no land being in
sight, we continued to steer to the eastward.

We ran on all day, having clear weather, but without
seeing anything to indicate our being near land. At noon
our latitude observed was 37° 27′ S, which being more
to the southward than we had reason to expect, I altered
the course to the northward, and steered N E all the afternoon. At six o'clock in the evening, we were in latitude
37° 0′ S, and longitude 12° 42′ W, having a clear horizon, but not the least sign of being in the neighbourhood

of land. With the night came thick rainy weather, and we were now to the eastward of the situation ascribed to Tristan da Cunha; I therefore determined to give over the search, and to resume our course towards the Cape of Good Hope.

The island of Tristan da Cunha, by Robertson's Elements, is laid down in 37° 12' S latitude, and 13° 23' W longitude. In Captain Cook's general map, prefixed to his last voyage, it is placed in the same latitude, but in 15° W longitude. From our track, and the clearness of the weather, I am convinced, if the latitude ascribed to it as above is correct, that it is not to be found between the meridians of 16° 30' W, and 12° 30' W. On the 13th I had a number of lunar observations for the longitude, the mean of which agreed exactly with the time-keeper.*

In this passage the weather was generally so cloudy, that I had few opportunities to make observations of any kind, except for the noon latitudes. I could not determine when we crossed the line of no variation. The two nearest observations to it were, the first in 39° 51' S latitude, and 26° 11' W longitude, where the variation of the compass was found to be 3° 17' E; and the other in latitude 35° 30' S, and longitude 5° 21' W, where I observed the variation 11° 35' W; between these we had no intermediate observation for the variation.

Thursday 22nd, at two in the afternoon, we saw the Table Mountain of the Cape of Good Hope. As it is reckoned unsafe riding in Table Bay at this time of the year, I steered for False Bay. The next evening we anchored in the outer part, and on the forenoon of the 24th got the ship secured in Simon's Bay, which is in the inner part of False Bay. When moored, Noah's ark bore S 35° E three-quarters of a mile, and the hospital S 72° W. We found lying here, one outward bound Dutch Indiaman, five other Dutch ships, and a French ship.

After saluting the fort, which was returned by an equal

* In Mr. Dalrymple's Collection of Plans, which I had not with me, the northernmost of the *Islands of Tristan d'Acunha* is placed in latitude 37° 22' S, and longitude 13° 17' W. I think it probable we missed them by being too much to the northward.

number of guns, I went on shore, and dispatches were sent away to Cape Town, to acquaint the governor of our arrival. A Dutch ship at this time lying in Table Bay, bound for Europe, I sent letters by her to the Admiralty. It is very unusual for ships to be in Table Bay so late in the year, on account of the strong N W winds. April is the time limited.

I gave the necessary directions for getting our wants supplied. The ship required to be caulked in every part, for she was become so leaky, that we had been obliged to pump every hour in our passage from Cape Horn. This we immediately set about, as well as repairing our sails and rigging. The severe weather we had met with, and the leakiness of the ship, made it necessary to examine into the state of all the stores and provisions. Of the latter, a good deal was found damaged, particularly the bread.—The time-keeper I took on shore to ascertain its rate, and other instruments, to make the necessary astronomical observations.—Fresh meat, with soft bread, and plenty of vegetables, were issued daily to the ship's company, the whole time we remained here. A few days after our arrival, I went over to Cape Town, and waited on his excellency M. Vander Graaf, the governor, who obligingly arranged matters so much to our advantage, that we scarcely felt the inconvenience of being at a distance from the Cape Town, whence we received all our supplies.

The Cape Town is considerably increased within the last eight years. Its respectability, with regard to strength, has kept pace with its other enlargements, and rendered it very secure against any attempt which is not made with considerable force. Great attention is paid to military order and discipline; and monthly signals are established to communicate with their shipping as they arrive near the coast, that they may not run unawares into the hands of an enemy. I found everything much dearer than when I was here in 1780. Sheep cost four Spanish dollars each, and were so small, that it answered better to purchase the mutton, for the ship's daily use, at four pence per pound.

During our stay here, I took care to procure seeds and plants that would be valuable at Otaheite, and the differ-

ent places we might touch at in our way thither. In this
I was greatly assisted by Colonel Gordon, the commander
of the troops. In company with this gentleman, the loss
of the *Grosvenor* East Indiaman was mentioned: on this
subject, Colonel Gordon expressed great concern, that,
from anything he had said, hopes were still entertained
to flatter the affectionate wishes of the surviving friends
of those unfortunate people. He said that, in his travels
into the Caffre country, he had met with a native who
described to him, that there was a white woman among
his countrymen, who had a child, and that she frequently
embraced the child, and cried most violently. This was
all he (the colonel) could understand; and, being then
on his return home, with his health much impaired by
fatigue, the only thing that he could do, was to make a
friend of the native, by presents, and promises of reward,
on condition that he would take a letter to this woman,
and bring him back an answer. Accordingly he wrote
letters in English, French and Dutch, desiring that some
sign or mark might be returned, either by writing with
a burnt stick, or by any means she should be able to
devise, to satisfy him that she was there; and that on receiving such token from her, every effort should be made
to ensure her safety and escape. But the Caffre, although
apparently delighted with the commission which he had
undertaken, never returned, nor has the colonel ever
heard anything more of him, though he had been instructed in methods of conveying information through the
Hottentot country.

To this account, that I may not again have occasion to
introduce so melancholy a subject, I shall add the little
information I received respecting it, when I revisited the
Cape, in my return towards Europe.—A reputable farmer
of the name of Holhousen, who lives at Swellendam, eight
days' journey from the Cape, had information from some
Caffre Hottentots, that at a crawl, or village, in their
country, there were white men and women. On this
intelligence, Mr. Holhousen asked permission of the
governor to make an expedition, with some of the farmers, into the country, requiring a thousand rix-dollars to
bear his expenses. The governor referred him to Mr.
Wocke, the Landros of Graverennet, a new colony, in his

way. But from the place where Mr. Holhousen lives, to the Landros, Mr. Wocke's residence, is a month's journey, which he did not choose to undertake at an uncertainty, as Mr. Wocke might have disapproved of the enterprise. It was in October last that Mr. Holhousen offered to go on this service. He was one of the party who went along the sea-coast in search of these unfortunate people, when a few of them first made their appearance at the Cape. I am, however, informed, that the Dutch farmers are fond of making expeditions into the country, that they may have opportunities of taking away cattle; and this, I apprehend, to be one of the chief reasons why undertakings of this kind are not encouraged.

On the 13th of June, the *Dublin* East Indiaman arrived from England; on board of which ship, was a party of the 77th regiment under the command of Colonel Balfour.

The result of my lunar observations gave for the longitude of Simon's Bay, 18° 48′ 34″ E; the latitude 34° 11′ 34″ S. The time-keeper likewise made the longitude 18° 47′ E. The longitude, as established by former observations, is 18° 33′ E. The variation of the compass on shore was 24° 4′ W; but, on board of the ship, it was only 22° 28′ W.—The time of high water was three-quarters past two on the full and change, and it then flowed six feet.

With respect to the Cape Promontory, it lies about three miles E of the meridian of Simon's Town. All the tables of latitude and longitude place the Cape in 34° 29′ S latitude; but from many observations off it, with good instruments, I make it to lie in 34° 23′ S, which agrees with its situation as laid down in Major Rennel's map. The part which I call the Cape, is the southernmost point of the land between Table Bay and False Bay; but the Dutch consider the westernmost part of the coast to be the Cape.

On the 29th, being ready for sea, I took the time-keeper and instruments on board. The error of the time-keeper was 3′ 33″, 2 too slow for the mean time at Greenwich, and its rate of going 3″ per day, losing. The thermometer, during our stay here, was from 51 to 66 degrees.

We had been thirty-eight days at this place, and my people had received all the advantage that could be derived from the refreshments of every kind that are here to be met with. We sailed at four o'clock this afternoon, and saluted the platform with thirteen guns as we ran out of the bay, which were returned.

CHAPTER IV

Passage towards Van Diemen's Land—Make the Island of St. Paul—Arrival in Adventure Bay—Natives seen—Sail from Van Diemen's Land

WE lost sight of the land the day after leaving False Bay, and steered towards the E S E, having variable winds the first week, with much thunder, lightning, and rain. The remainder of this passage, the winds were mostly between the S and W, blowing strong. There were almost every day great numbers of pintada, albatrosses, blue petterels, and other oceanic birds, about us; but it was observed, that if the wind came from the northward, only for a few hours, the birds generally left us, and their presence again was the forerunner of a southerly wind.

The variation of the compass was 30° 34′ W, which was the greatest variation we found in this track. Our latitude 36° 28′ S, and longitude 39° 0′ E.

The latitude, at noon, was 40° 30′ S, and longitude 60° 7′ E. We were at this time scudding under the fore-sail and close-reefed main-top-sail, the wind blowing strong from the W. An hour after noon the gale increased, and blew with so much violence, that the ship was almost driven forecastle under, before we could get the sails clewed up. As soon as the sails were taken in, we brought the ship to the wind, lowered the lower yards, and got the top-gallant-masts upon deck, which eased the ship very much. We remained lying to till eight the next morning, when we bore away under a reefed fore-sail. In the afternoon the sea ran so high, that it became very unsafe to stand on: we therefore brought to the wind again, and remained lying to all night, without accident, excepting that the man at the steerage was thrown over the wheel, and much bruised. Towards noon, the violence of the storm abated, and we again bore away under the reefed fore-sail. Our latitude, at noon, 38° 49′ S: in the afternoon saw some whales.

We continued running to the eastward in this parallel, it being my intention to make the island St. Paul. On Monday the 28th, at six in the morning, we saw the island, bearing E by N, 12 leagues distant: between ten and eleven o'clock, we ran along the south side, at about a league distant from the shore. There was a verdure that covered the higher parts of the land; but I believe it was nothing more than moss, which is commonly found on the tops of most rocky islands in these latitudes. We saw several whales near the shore. The extent of this island is five miles from E to W; and about two or three from N to S. As we passed the east end, we saw a remarkable high sugar-loaf rock, abreast of which, I have been informed, is good anchorage in 23 fathoms, the east point bearing S W by S, by true compass. I had this information from the captain of a Dutch packet, in which I returned to Europe. He likewise said there was good fresh water on the island, and a hot spring, which boiled fish in as great perfection as on a fire. By his account, the latitude, which he observed in the road, is 38° 39′ S; and from the anchoring place, the island of Amsterdam was in sight to the northward. We had fair weather all the forenoon, but just at noon, a squall came on, which was unfavourable for our observation. I had, however, two sets of double altitudes, and a good altitude exactly at noon, according to the time-keeper. The result of these give for the latitude of the centre of St. Paul, 38° 47′ S. The longitude I make 77° 39′ E. The variation of the compass, taking the mean of what it was observed to be the day before we saw the island, and the day after, is 19° 30′ W.

At noon, we were 3 leagues past the island. We kept on towards the E S E, and for several days continued to see rock-weed, which is remarked to be generally the case after ships pass St. Paul's; but to the westward of it, very seldom any is seen.

In latitude 44° 16′ S, longitude 122° 7′ E, I observed the variation of the compass to be 6° 23′ W. I had no opportunity to observe it again till in the latitude of 43° 56′ S, longitude 133° 16′ E, when it was 1° 38′ E; so that we had passed the line of no variation. In 1780, on board the *Resolution,* latitude 44° 23′ S, longitude 131° 28′ E, the variation was observed 6° 0′ W, which is a

remarkable difference. We had much bad weather, with
snow and hail, and in our approach to Van Diemen's
Land, nothing was seen to indicate the nearness of the
coast, except a seal, when we were within the distance of
20 leagues.

At two o'clock this afternoon, we saw the rock named
the Mewstone, that lies near the S W cape of Van
Diemen's Land, bearing N E about 6 leagues. The wind
blew strong from the N W. As soon as we had passed
the Mewstone, we were sheltered from a very heavy sea
which ran from the westward. At eight o'clock at night
we were abreast of the south cape, when the wind became
light and variable. Saw several fires inland.

The Mewstone is a high bold rock, that lies 5 leagues
to the S E of the S W cape, and is the part that all ships
bound this way should endeavour to make. Its latitude
is 43° 46' or 47'. Several islands lie to the northward,
between that and the main, among which, bearing N by W
from the Mewstone, is a high rock much resembling it;
and N N E from the Mewstone, on the mainland, is a
remarkable high mountain, which in this direction, appears notched like a cock's comb; but as viewed from the
eastward, seems round.

All the 20th, we were endeavouring to get into Adventure Bay, but were prevented by variable winds. The
next morning, at five o'clock, we anchored in the outer
part, and at sunrise weighed again; at noon, we anchored
well in the bay, and moored the ship, Penguin Island
bearing N 57° ½ E, about two miles distant; Cape
Frederick Henry N 23° E; and the mouth of the Lagoon
S 16° E.

In our passage from the Cape of Good Hope, the winds
were mostly from the westward, with very boisterous
weather: but one great advantage that this season of the
year has over the summer months is, in being free from
fogs. I have already remarked, that the approach of
strong southerly winds is announced by many kinds of
birds of the albatross or petterel tribe, and the abatement
of the gale, or a shift of wind to the northward, by their
keeping away. The thermometer also very quickly shows
when a change of these winds may be expected, by vary-
ing sometimes six and seven degrees in its height. I have
reason to believe, that after we passed the island St. Paul,

there was a weatherly current; the ship being every day to
the westward of the reckoning, which in the whole, from
St. Paul to Van Diemen's Land, made a difference of four
degrees between the longitude by the reckoning and the
true longitude.

The ship being moored, I went in a boat to look out
for the most convenient place to wood and water at,
which I found to be at the west end of the beach: for the
surf, though considerable, was less there than at any other
part of the bay. The water was in a gully about 60 yards
from the beach; it was perfectly good, but being only a
collection from the rains, the place is always dry in the
summer months; for we found no water in it when I was
here with Captain Cook in January, 1777.—We had very
little success in hauling the seine; about twenty small
flounders, and flat-headed fish, called foxes, were all that
were taken.

I found no signs of the natives having lately frequented
this bay, or of any European vessels having been here
since the *Resolution* and *Discovery* in 1777. From some
of the old trunks of trees, then cut down, I saw shoots
about 25 feet high, and 14 inches in circumference.

In the evening, I returned on board. The next morning, the 22d, at daylight, a party was sent on shore for
wooding and watering, under the command of Mr.
Christian and the gunner; and I directed that one man
should be constantly employed in washing the people's
clothes. There was so much surf that the wood was
obliged to be rafted off in bundles to the boat. Mr. Nelson
informed me that, in his walks to-day, he saw a tree,
in a very healthy state, which he measured, and found to
be 33½ feet in girt; its height was proportioned to its
bulk.

Saturday the 32d, the surf was rather greater than
yesterday, which very much interrupted our wooding and
watering. Nelson to-day picked up a male opossum that
had been recently killed, or had died, for we could not
perceive any wound, unless it had received a blow on the
back, where there was a bare place about the size of a
shilling. It measured 14 inches from the ears to the beginning of the tail, which was exactly the same length.

Most of the forest trees were at this time shedding their
bark. There are three kinds, which are distinguished from

each other by their leaves, though the wood appears to be the same. Many of them are full 150 feet high; but most of those that we cut down were decayed at the heart. There are, besides the forest trees, several other kinds that are firm good wood, and may be cut for most purposes, except masts; neither are the forest trees good for masts, on account of their weight, and the difficulty of finding them thoroughly sound. Mr. Nelson asserted that they shed their bark every year, and that they increase more from the seed than by suckers.

I found the tide made a difference of full 2 feet in the height of the water in the lake, at the back of the beach. At high water, it was very brackish, but at low tide, it was perfectly fresh to the taste, and soap showed no sign of its being the least impregnated. We had better success in fishing on board the ship, than by hauling the seine on shore; for, with hooks and lines, a number of fine rock cod were caught.—I saw to-day several eagles, some beautiful blue-plumaged herons, and a great variety of paroquets. A few oyster-catchers and gulls were generally about the beach, and in the lake a few wild ducks.

Being in want of plank, I directed a saw-pit to be dug, and employed some of the people to saw trees into plank. The greater part of this week the winds were moderate, with unsettled weather. On Friday it blew strong from the S W, with rain, thunder, and lightning. We continued to catch fish in sufficient quantities for everybody, and had better success with the seine.—We were fortunate, also, in angling in the lake, where we caught some very fine tench. Some of the people felt a sickness from eating mussels, that were gathered from the rocks; but I believe it was occasioned by eating too many. We found some spider-crabs, most of them not good, being the female sort, and out of season. The males were tolerably good, and were known by the smallness of their two fore claws, or feeders. We saw the trunk of a dead tree, on which had been cut "A.D. 1773." The figures were very distinct; even the slips made with the knife were discernible. This must have been done by some of Captain Furneaux's people, in March, 1773, fifteen years before. The marks of the knife remaining so unaltered, I imagine the tree must have been dead when it was cut; but it serves to show the durability of the wood, for it was perfectly sound at this time. I shot two gannets: these birds were of the same size as those in England; their colour is a beautiful white, with the wings and tail tipped with jet black, and the top and back of the head of a very fine yellow. Their feet were black, with four claws, on each of which was a yellow line the whole length of the foot. The bill was four inches long, without nostrils, and very taper and sharp-pointed.

The east side of the bay being not so thick of wood as the other parts, and the soil being good, I fixed on it, at Nelson's recommendation, as the most proper situation for planting some of the fruit-trees which I had brought from the Cape of Good Hope. A circumstance much against anything succeeding here, is, that in the dry season, the fires made by the natives are apt to communicate to the dried grass and underwood, and to spread in such a manner as to endanger everything that cannot bear a severe scorching. We, however, chose what we thought the safest situations, and planted three fine young apple-trees, nine vines, six plantain-trees, a number of orange and lemon-seed, cherry-stones, plum, peach, and apricot-stones, pumpkins, also two sorts of Indian corn, and apple and pear kernels. The ground is well adapted for the trees, being of a rich loamy nature. The spot where we made our plantation was clear of underwood; and we marked the trees that stood nearest to the different things which were planted. Nelson followed the circuit of the bay, planting in such places as appeared most eligible. I have great hopes that some of these articles will succeed. The particular situations I had described in my survey of this place, but I was unfortunately prevented from bringing it home. Near the watering place, likewise, we planted on a flat, which appeared a favourable situation, some onions, cabbage-roots, and potatoes.

For some days past, a number of whales were seen in the bay. They were of the same kind as those we had generally met with before, having two blow-holes on the back of the head.

On the night of the 1st September, we observed, for the first time, signs of the natives being in the neighbourhood. Fires were seen on the low land, near Cape Frederick Henry, and at day-light we saw the natives with our glasses. As I expected they would come round to us, I remained all the forenoon near the wooding and watering parties, making observations, the morning being very favourable for that purpose. I was, however, disappointed in my conjecture, for the natives did not appear, and there was too great a surf for a boat to land on the part where we had seen them.

The natives not coming near us, I determined to go after them, and we set out, in a boat, towards Cape Frederick Henry, where we arrived about eleven o'clock. I found landing impracticable, and therefore came to a grapnel, in hopes of their coming to us, for we had passed several fires. After waiting near an hour, I was surprised to see Nelson's assistant come out of the wood: he had wandered thus far in search of plants, and told me that he had met with some of the natives. Soon after we heard their voices like the cackling of geese, and twenty persons came out of the wood, twelve of whom went round to some rocks, where the boat could get nearer to the shore than we then were. Those who remained behind were women.

We approached within 20 yards of them, but there was no possibility of landing, and I could only throw to the shore, tied up in paper, the presents which I intended for them. I showed the different articles as I tied them up, but they would not untie the paper till I made an appearance of leaving them. They then opened the parcels, and, as they took the articles out, placed them on their heads. On seeing this, I returned towards them, when they instantly put every thing out of their hands, and would not appear to take notice of any thing that we had given them. After throwing a few more beads and nails on shore, I made signs for them to go to the ship, and they, likewise, made signs for me to land; but as this could not be effected, I left them, in hopes of a nearer interview at the watering place.

When they first came in sight, they made a prodigious clattering in their speech, and held their arms over their heads. They spoke so quick, that I could not catch one single word they uttered. We recollected one man, whom we had formerly seen among the party of the natives that came to us in 1777, and who is particularized in the account of Captain Cook's last voyage, for his humour and deformity. Some of them had a small stick, two or three feet long, in their hands, but no other weapon.

Their colour, as Captain Cook remarks, is a dull black: their skin is scarified about their shoulders and breast. They were of a middle stature, or rather below it. One of them was distinguished by his body being coloured with red oker, but all the others were painted black, with a kind of soot, which was laid on so thick over their faces and shoulders, that it is difficult to say what they were like.

They ran very nimbly over the rocks, had a very quick sight, and caught the small beads and nails, which I threw to them, with great dexterity. They talked to us sitting on their heels, with their knees close into their armpits, and were perfectly naked.

In my return towards the ship, I landed at the point of the harbour near Penguin Island, and from the hills, saw the water on the other side of the low isthmus of Cape Frederick Henry, which forms the bay of that name. It is very extensive, and in, or near, the middle of the bay, there is a low island. From this spot, it has the appearance of being a very good and convenient harbour.

The account which I had from Brown, the botanist's assistant, was, that in his search for plants, he had met an old man, a young woman, and two or three children. The old man at first appeared alarmed, but became familiar on being presented with a knife. He nevertheless sent away the young woman, who went very reluctantly. He saw some miserable wigwams, in which were nothing but a few kangaroo skins spread on the ground, and a basket made of rushes.

Among the wood that we cut here, we found many scorpions and centipedes, with numerous black ants that were an inch long. We saw no mosquitoes, though in the summer months they are very troublesome.

What is called the New Zealand tea plant grew here in great abundance; so that it was not only gathered and dried to use as tea, but made excellent brooms. It bears a small pointed leaf, of a pleasant smell, and its seed is contained in a berry, about the size of a pea, notched into five equal parts on the top. The soil, on the west and south sides of the bay, is black mould, with a mixture of fine white sand, and is very rich. The trees are lofty and large, and the underwood grows so close together, that in many places it is impassable. The east side of the bay is a rich loamy soil; but, near the tops of the hills, is very much encumbered with stones and rocks: the underwood thinly placed and small. The trees on the S, S E, and S W sides of the hills grow to a larger size than those that are exposed to the opposite points; for the sides of the trees, open or exposed to the north winds, are naked, with few branches; while the other sides are in a flourishing state. From this I do not infer, that the equatorial are more hurtful than the polar winds; but that the trees, by their situation, were more sheltered from the one than from the other.

A calm prevented our sailing to-day. The friendly interview which we had had with the natives made me expect that they would have paid us a visit; but we saw nothing more of them, except fires in the night, upon the low land to the northward.

The result of the observations which I made here, reduced to Penguin Island, place it in 43° 21′ 11″ S latitude, and in longitude 147° 33′ 29″ E, which scarcely differs from the observations made in 1777. The variation of the compass, observed on shore, was 8° 38′ E; and on board the ship 8° 29′ E. It was high water, at the change of the moon, at 49 minutes past six in the morning. The rise was 2 feet 8 inches. Southerly winds, if of any continuance, make a considerable difference in the height of the tides.

This forenoon, having a pleasant breeze at N W, we weighed anchor, and sailed out of Adventure Bay. At noon the southernmost part of Maria's Isles bore N 52° E, about 5 leagues distant; Penguin Island S 86° W; and Cape Frederick Henry N 65° W. In this position we had soundings at 57 fathoms, a sandy bottom. Latitude observed 43° 22′ S.

The southern part of Maria's Islands lie in latitude 43° 16′ S. The country is not in general woody, but in some of the interior parts, there appeared great abundance. Among these islands, I have no doubt of there being many convenient places for shipping. On the east side, in latitude 42° 42′ S, and longitude 148° 24′ E, in July, 1789, Captain Cox, of the *Mercury,* found a convenient and secure harbour from all winds, which he named

Oyster Bay. Here he found wood, water, and fish, in great abundance. It has two outlets, and lies north, a little easterly, distant 34 miles from the south-easternmost island, or point, seen from Adventure Bay.

Adventure Bay is a convenient and safe place for any number of ships to take in wood and water, during the summer months: but in the winter, when the southerly winds are strong, the surf, on all parts of the shore, makes the landing exceedingly troublesome. The bay of Frederick Henry may, perhaps, be found preferable, as it appears to be equally easy of access. The soundings in Adventure Bay are very regular: near the west shore are some patches of weed, but no shoal or danger, the depth on them being from 5 to 9 fathoms.

CHAPTER V

*Rocky Islands discovered—See the Island Maitea, and arrive
at Otaheite—Ship crowded by the Natives*

BEING clear of the land, we steered towards the E S E,
it being my intention to pass to the southward of New
Zealand, as I expected in that route to meet with constant
westerly winds; in which, however, I was disappointed,
for they proved variable, and frequently from the eastward blowing strong, with thick misty weather. The thermometer varied from 41 to 46 degrees.

On the 14th at noon, we were in 49° 24′ S latitude,
and in 168° 3′ E longitude, which is on the same meridian with the south end of New Zealand. We altered our
course, steering to the northward of E, and frequently
saw rock-weed, which I supposed to have drifted from
New Zealand. The sea now became rougher, from our
being exposed to a long swell, which came from the N E.

On the 19th, at daylight, we discovered a cluster of
small rocky islands, bearing E by N 4 leagues distant
from us. We had seen no birds, or anything to indicate
the nearness of land, except patches of rock-weed, for
which the vicinity of New Zealand sufficiently accounted.
The wind being at N E prevented our near approach to
these isles; so that we were not less than 3 leagues distant
in passing to the southward of them. The weather was too
thick to see distinctly: their extent was only 3½ miles
from east to west, and about half a league from north to
south: their number, including the smaller ones, was
thirteen. I could not observe any verdure on any of them:
there were white spots like patches of snow; but, as Captain Cook, in describing the land of New Zealand, near
Cape South, says, in many places there are patches like
white marble, it is probable that what we saw might be
of the same kind as what he had observed. The westernmost of these islands is the largest; they are of sufficient
height to be seen at the distance of 7 leagues from a ship's
deck. When the easternmost bore north, I tried for sound-

ings, being then 10 miles distant from the nearest of them,
and found bottom at 75 fathoms, a fine white sand: and
again at noon, having run 6 leagues more to the E S E,
we had soundings at 104 fathoms, a fine brimstone-
coloured sand. The latitude of these islands is 47° 44' S;
their longitude 179° 7' E, which is about 145 leagues to
the east of the Traps, near the south end of New Zealand.
Variation of the compass here 17° E. While in sight of
the islands, we saw some penguins, and a white kind of
gull with a forked tail. Captain Cook's track, in 1773,
was near this spot, but he did not see the islands: he saw
seals and penguins hereabouts, but considered New Zealand to be the nearest land. I have named them after the
ship, the Bounty Isles.

This day we saw a seal, some rock-weed, and a great
many albatrosses. I tried for soundings, but found no
bottom at 230 fathoms depth. Our latitude 47° 32' S,
longitude 182° 36' E.

Were in 40° 27' S latitude, and 214° 4' E longitude.
It being calm, and a number of small blubbers about the
ship, I took up some in a bucket, but I saw no difference
between them and the common blubbers in the West
Indies. We frequently, in the night time, observed the sea
to be covered with luminous spots, caused by prodigious
quantities of small blubbers, that, from the strings which
extend from them, emit a light like the blaze of a candle,
while the body continues perfectly dark.

The 3d in the morning, we saw a seal. Captain Cook
has remarked seeing seaweed, when nearly in the same
place. Our latitude 40° 21' S, longitude 215° E. Variation of the compass 7° 45' E. Being now well to the eastward of the Society Islands, I steered more to the
northward.

We continued to have the southern oceanic birds accompany us, and a few whales. The people caught albatrosses, and fattened them in the same manner which they
had done when off Cape Horn. Some of these measured
near 8 feet between the tips of the wings, when spread.

On Thursday the 9th, we had the misfortune to lose
one of our seamen, James Valentine, who died in the
night, of an asthmatic complaint. This poor man had been
one of the most robust people on board, until our arrival
at Adventure Bay, where he first complained of some

slight indisposition, for which he was bled, and got better. Some time afterwards, the arm in which he had been bled, became painful and inflamed: the inflammation increased, with a hollow cough, and extreme difficulty of breathing, to his death.

The 13th, in the afternoon, we saw two land birds, like what are called sand-larks. Our latitude at this time was 28° 3′ S, and longitude 223° 26′ E. The next morning we saw a tropic bird, and some fish. The winds were light and variable, with calms, from this time to the 19th, when a breeze sprung up from the N E, which gradually came round to the eastward, and proved to be the trade wind. Our latitude on the 19th, at noon, was 24° 13′ S, longitude 222° 17′ E. Variation of the compass 5° 19′ E.

On the 25th, at half past seven in the morning, we saw the Island Maitea, called Osnaburg by Captain Wallis, who first discovered it. At noon it bore S W by W ¼ W, 6 miles distant. Our latitude 17° 50′ S, longitude 212° 24′ E. Variation 5° E. As Captain Wallis and Captain Cook had both passed near the south side, I ran along the north side, which is remarkably steep. The island is high and round, and not more than 3 miles in its greatest extent. The south side, where the declivity from the hill is more gradual, is the chief place of residence of the natives; but the north side, from the very summit down to the sea, is so steep, that it can afford no support to the inhabitants. We steered pretty close in to the northward of the east end, where we saw but few habitations: a very neat house on a small eminence, delightfully situated in a grove of cocoa-nut trees, particularly attracted our notice. About twenty of the natives followed us along shore, waving and showing large pieces of cloth; but the surf on the shore was too high to think of having any communication with them. I observed a great number of cocoa-nut trees, but did not see one plantain-tree. There were other trees, but of what kind we could not distinguish: near the east end are two remarkable rocks and a reef runs off to the eastward about half a league.

The latitude of Maitea is 17° 53′ S; and by our time-keeper, its longitude is 1° 24′ E from Point Venus. Variation of the compass 5° 36′ E.

We continued our course to the westward, and at six in the evening we saw Otaheite, bearing W ¾ S; the island Maitea, then in sight, bearing E ½ S, 8 leagues distant. As there was great probability that we should remain a considerable time in Otaheite, it could not be expected that the intercourse of my people with the natives should be of a very reserved nature: I therefore ordered that every person should be examined by the surgeon, and had the satisfaction to learn, from his report, that they were all perfectly free from any venereal complaint.

On the 26th, at four o'clock in the morning, having run 25 leagues from Maitea, we brought to till daylight, when we saw Point Venus bearing S W by W, distant about 4 leagues. As we drew near, a great number of canoes came off to us. Their first inquiries were, if we were *Tyos*, which signifies friends; and whether we came from *Pretanie* (their pronunciation of Britain), or from Lima: they were no sooner satisfied in this, than they crowded on board in vast numbers, notwithstanding our endeavours to prevent it, as we were working the ship in; and in less than ten minutes, the deck was so full that I could scarce find my own people. At nine in the forenoon, we were obliged to anchor in the outer part of Matavai Bay, in 13 fathoms, being prevented by light variable winds from placing the ship in a proper berth. In this station the west part of One-tree Hill bore S by E ½ E 1 mile distant.

This passage of fifty-two days from Van Diemen's Land may be rated as moderate sailing. We passed New Zealand with the spring equinox, and the winds, though strong, were at no time violent. To the southward of 40° 0′ S they were variable; between the latitudes of 40 and 33° S, the wind kept in the N W quarter; afterwards, till we got into the trade, the winds were variable, mostly from the eastward, but light, and inclinable to calms. The ship was 3° 22′ in longitude to the eastward of the dead reckoning, which the time-keeper almost invariably proved to be owing to a current giving us more easting than the log. Our track was as distant from any course of former ships as I could conveniently make it; and though we made no new discoveries, except the small cluster of islands near New Zealand, yet in other parts of the track, as has been noticed, we met with signs of being in the neighbourhood of land.

It may not be unworthy of remark, that the whole

distance which the ship had run by the log, in direct and contrary courses, from leaving England to our anchoring at Otaheite, was 27,086 miles, which, on an average, is at the rate of 108 miles each twenty-four hours.

CHAPTER VI

*Account of an English ship lately sailed from Otaheite—
Death of Omai—Captain Cook's picture sent on board—
Otoo visits the ship—His visit returned—Natives well dis-
posed towards us—Account of the cattle left by Captain
Cook—Bread-fruit plants promised—Visit to the Earee
Rahie—Presents made to the Arreoys*

THE ship being anchored, our number of visitors continued to increase; but as yet we saw no person that
we could recollect to have been of much consequence.
Some inferior chiefs made me presents of a few hogs, and
I made them presents in return. We were supplied with
cocoa-nuts in great abundance, but bread-fruit was scarce.

Many inquiries were made after Captain Cook, Sir
Joseph Banks, and many of their former friends. They
said a ship had been here, from which they had learnt
that Captain Cook was dead; but the circumstances of his
death they did not appear to be acquainted with; and I
had given particular directions to my officers and ship's
company, that they should not be mentioned. The ship
spoken of, they informed me, stayed at Otaheite one
month, and had been gone four months, by some of their
accounts; according to others, only three months. The
captain they called Tonah. I understood likewise from
them, that Lieutenant Watts was in the ship; who, having
been here in the *Resolution* with Captain Cook, was well
known to them.—One of my first inquiries, as will naturally be imagined, was after our friend Omai; and it was
a sensible mortification and disappointment to me to hear
that not only Omai, but both the New Zealand boys who
had been left with him, were dead. Every one agreed in
their information that they died a natural death. Otoo,
who was the chief of Matavai when Captain Cook was
here the last time, was absent at another part of the
island; they told me messengers were sent to inform him
of our arrival, and that he was expected to return soon.
There appeared among the natives in general great goodwill towards us, and they seemed to be much rejoiced at

our arrival. This whole day we experienced no instance of dishonesty. We were so much crowded, that I could not undertake to remove to a more proper station, without danger of disobliging our visitors, by desiring them to leave the ship: this business was, therefore, deferred till the next morning.

Early in the morning, before the natives began to flock off to us, we weighed anchor, to work farther into the bay, and moored at about a quarter of a mile distance from the shore; Point Venus bearing N 16° E; the west part of One-tree Hill S W by S; and the point of the reef N 37° W; the ship lying in 7 fathoms water.

Several chiefs now came on board, and expressed great pleasure at seeing me. Among these were Otow, the father of Otoo, and Oreepyah, his brother; also another chief of Matavai, called Poeeno; and to these men I made presents. Two messengers likewise arrived from Otoo, to acquaint me of his being on his way to the ship; each of whom brought me, as a present from Otoo, a small pig, and a young plantain-tree, as a token of friendship. The ship was now plentifully supplied with provisions; every person having as much as he could consume.

As soon as the ship was secured, I went on shore with the chief Poeeno, and accompanied by a multitude of the natives. He conducted me to the place where we had fixed our tents in 1777, and desired that I would now appropriate the spot to the same use. We then went across the beach, and through a walk delightfully shaded with bread-fruit trees, to his own house. Here we found two women at work staining a piece of cloth red. These I found were his wife and her sister. They desired me to sit down on a mat, which was spread for the purpose, and with great kindness offered me refreshments. I received the congratulations of several strangers, who came to us and behaved with great decorum and attention. The people, however, thronged about the house, in such numbers, that I was much incommoded by the heat, which being observed, they immediately drew back. Among the crowd I saw a man who had lost his arm just above the elbow; the stump was well covered, and the cure seemed as perfect as could be expected from the greatest professional skill.

I made inquiries about the cattle that had been left

here by Captain Cook, but the accounts I received were
very unfavourable, and so various, that, for the present,
I shall forbear speaking of them. After staying about an
hour, I got up to take leave, when the women, in a very
obliging manner, came to me with a mat, and a piece of
their finest cloth, which they put on me after the Otaheite
fashion. When I was thus dressed, they each of them took
one of my hands, and accompanied me to the water-side,
and at parting promised that they would soon return my
visit.

In this walk, I had the satisfaction to see that the island
had received some benefit from our former visits. Two
shaddocks were brought to me, a fruit which they had
not, till we introduced it. And among the articles which
they brought off to the ship, and offered for sale, were
capsicums, pumpkins, and two young goats.

On my return to the ship, I found that a small disturbance had been occasioned by one of the natives making
an attempt to steal a tin pot; which, on being known to
Oreepyah, he flew into a violent rage, and it was with
some difficulty that the thief escaped with his life. He
drove all his countrymen out of the ship; and when he
saw me, he desired, if at any time I found a thief, that I
would order him to be tied up and punished with a severe
flogging.

This forenoon, a man came on board with Captain
Cook's picture, which had been drawn by Mr. Webber,
in 1777, and left with Otoo. It was brought to me to be
repaired. The frame was broken, but the picture no way
damaged, except a little in the back ground. They called it
Toote (which has always been their manner of pro-
nouncing Captain Cook's name) *Earee no Otaheite,* chief
of Otaheite. They said Toote had desired Otoo, whenever
any English ship came, to show the picture, and it would
be acknowledged as a token of friendship. The youngest
brother of Otoo, named Whydooah, visited me this afternoon: he appeared stupefied with drinking Ava. At sunset
all our male visitors left the ship.

The next morning early, I received a message from
Otoo, to inform me of his arrival, and requesting that I
would send a boat for him; which I immediately did, with
an officer (Mr. Christian) to conduct him on board. He
came with numerous attendants, and expressed much

satisfaction at our meeting. After introducing his wife to me, we joined noses, the customary manner of saluting, and, to perpetuate our friendship, he desired we should exchange names. I was surprised to find, that, instead of Otoo, the name by which he formerly went, he was now called Tinah. The name of Otoo, with the title of *Earee Rahie,* I was informed had devolved to his eldest son, who was yet a minor, as is the custom of the country. The name of Tinah's wife was Iddeah: with her was a woman dressed with a large quantity of cloth, in the form of a hoop, which was taken off and presented to me, with a large hog, and some bread-fruit. I then took my visitors into the cabin, and after a short time produced my presents in return. The present I made to Tinah (by which name I shall hereafter call him) consisted of hatchets, small adzes, files, gimblets, saws, looking-glasses, red feathers, and two shirts. To Iddeah I gave ear-rings, necklaces, and beads; but she expressed a desire also for iron, and therefore I made the same assortment for her as I had for her husband. Much conversation took place among them on the value of the different articles, and they appeared extremely satisfied; so that they determined to spend the day with me, and requested I would show them all over the ship, and particularly the cabin where I slept. This, though I was not fond of doing, I indulged them in; and the consequence was, as I had apprehended, that they took a fancy to so many things, that they got from me nearly as much more as I had before given them. Afterwards, Tinah desired me to fire some of the great guns: this I likewise complied with, and, as the shot fell into the sea at a great distance, all the natives expressed their surprise by loud shouts and acclamations.

I had a large company at dinner; for, besides Tinah and his wife, there was Otow, the father of Tinah, Oreepyah, and Whydooah, two of his brothers, Poeeno, and several other chiefs. Tinah is a very large man, much above the common stature, being not less than 6 feet 4 inches in height, and proportionably stout: his age about thirty-five. His wife (Iddeah) I judged to be about twenty-four years of age: she is likewise much above the common size of the women at Otaheite, and has a very animated and intelligent countenance. Whydooah, the younger brother of Tinah, was highly spoken of as a warrior, but had the character of being the greatest drunkard in the country; and indeed, to judge from the withered appearance of his skin, he must have used the pernicious drink called Ava, to great excess. Tinah was fed by one of his attendants, who sat by him for that purpose, this being a particular custom among some of the superior chiefs; and I must do him the justice to say, he kept his attendant constantly employed: there was indeed little reason to complain of want of appetite in any of my guests. As the women are not allowed to eat in presence of the men, Iddeah dined with some of her companions, about an hour afterwards, in private, except that her husband Tinah favoured them with his company, and seemed to have entirely forgotten that he had already dined.

Provisions were brought off to the ship in the greatest plenty; and, to prevent as much as possible any thing which might occasion disputes, I desired Mr. Peckover, the gunner, to undertake the management of our traffic with the natives. Some of the hogs brought to-day weighed 200 lb. and we purchased several for salting. Goats were likewise brought off for sale, and I bought a she-goat and kid for less than would have purchased a small hog.—Our friends here expressed much disappointment, that there was no portrait-painter on board; Tinah in particular, who wished to have had pictures of his father and family.

An intimacy between the natives, and our people, was already so general, that there was scarce a man in the ship who had not his *tyo* or friend. Tinah continued with me the whole afternoon, in the course of which he ate four times of roast pork, besides his dinner. When he left the ship, he requested I would keep for him all the presents I had given to him, as he had not, at Matavai, a place sufficiently safe to secure them from being stolen; I therefore showed him a locker in my cabin for his use, and gave him a key to it. This is perhaps not so much a proof of his want of power, as of the estimation in which they hold European commodities, and which makes more than the common means of security requisite to prevent theft.

I had sent Nelson and his assistant to look for plants, and it was no small pleasure to me to find, by their report, that, according to appearances, the object of my mission would probably be accomplished with ease. I had given directions to every one on board not to make known to the islanders the purpose of our coming, lest it might enhance the value of the bread-fruit plants, or occasion other difficulties. Perhaps so much caution was not necessary, but at all events I wished to reserve to myself the time and manner of communication. Nelson met with two fine shaddock-trees, which he had planted in 1777: they were full of fruit, but not ripe.

In the morning I returned Tinah's visit, for I found he expected it. He was in a small shed about a quarter of a mile to the eastward of Matavai point, with his wife and three children, not their own, but who they said were relations. In my walk I had picked up a numerous attendance, for every one I met followed me; so that I had collected such a crowd, that the heat was scarce bearable, every one endeavouring to get a look to satisfy their curiosity: they however carefully avoided pressing against me, and welcomed me with cheerful countenances, and great good-nature.

I made Tinah understand, that my visit was particularly to him, and gave him a second present, equal to the first, which he received with great pleasure; and to the people of consequence, that were about him, I also presented some article or other. There were great numbers of children; and, as I took notice of the little ones that were in arms and gave them beads, both small and great, but with much drollery and good-humour, endeavoured to benefit by the occasion. Boys of ten and twelve years old were caught up in arms and brought to me, which created much laughter; so that in a short time I got rid of all I had brought on shore.

In my return I called on Poeeno, and an elderly chief, a relation of his, called Moannah, the principal men of this district, and with whom I judged it my interest to be on good terms. I gave them several valuable articles; and, as the situation here was eligible for a garden, I planted melon, cucumber, and sallad-seeds. I told them many other things should be sown for their use; and they appeared much pleased when they understood I intended to plant such things as would grow to be trees and produce fruit. I saw large patches of tobacco growing without culture, and many pumpkin vines.—The bread-fruit trees and cocoa-nut trees at this time were full of fruit.

I went on board to dinner, and Moannah accompanied me. In the afternoon I returned to Poeeno's, with some additional seeds to improve the little garden I had begun to make in the forenoon. While I was giving directions, I received a message from Tinah, inviting me to come to him at his brother Oreepyah's house, which was near the beach. At this place I found a great number of people collected, who, on my appearance, immediately made way for me to sit down by Tinah. The crowd being ordered to draw back, a piece of cloth, about two yards wide and forty-one yards in length, was spread on the ground; and another piece of cloth was brought by Oreepyah, which he put over my shoulders, and round my waist, in the manner the chiefs are clothed. Two large hogs, weighing each above 200 pounds, and a quantity of baked bread-fruit and cocoa-nuts, were laid before me, as a present, and I was desired to walk from one end of the cloth spread on the ground to the other, in the course of which, *Tyo* and *Ehoah** were repeated with loud acclamations. This ceremony being ended, Tinah desired I would send the things on board, which completely loaded the boat; we, therefore, waited till he came back, and then I took them on board with me; for I knew they expected some return.—The present which I made on this occasion, was equal to any that I had made before; but I discovered that Tinah was not the sole proprietor of what he had given to me, for the present I gave was divided among those who, I guessed, had contributed to support his dignity; among whom were Moannah, Poeenah, and Oreepyah; Tinah, however, kept the greatest part of what I had given, and every one seemed satisfied with the proportion he allotted them.

The Otaheite breed of hogs seems to be supplanted by the European. Originally they were of the China sort, short, and very thick-necked; but the superior size of the European have made them encourage our breed.

At break of day, Tinah and his wife came again to the ship, and, as their attendants were numerous, I provided a breakfast for them of broiled and roasted pork, which they preferred to tea. Our arrival being known all over the island, we had this day a great number of strangers on

* *Tyo* and *Ehoah* are words of the same signification; i.e., *friend*.

board, who came from the most remote parts, and in the forenoon some hooks and thimbles were cut out from the blocks. This induced me to order all the natives out of the ship, except the chiefs and their attendants. In executing these orders, a daring fellow attacked the sentinel, but escaped among the crowd. Every one knew the consequence of offending the sentinel, and were exceedingly alarmed at the appearance of anger I thought necessary to assume.

Among those who visited us to-day, were two chiefs of great consequence, Marremarre and his son Poohaitaiah Otee, Earees of the districts of Itteeah and Attahooroo. Otee was fed at dinner in the same manner as Tinah. It was evident that the attention which I showed to these chiefs seemed to give uneasiness to Tinah. At sunset my visitors took leave, and were carried on shore by one of the ship's boats, which has always been regarded as a mark of distinction, and, on that account, preferred by them to going in their own canoes. At their request, a race was rowed between our five-oared cutter and one of their double canoes with four paddles. Great exertions were used on both sides, but the cutter first reached the shore. In their return to the ship, Oreepyah stopped them, till a large piece of cloth, that he had sent for, was brought; which he tied to the boat-hook, and desired should be carried off as a trophy of their victory.

The next morning, at sunrise, Moannah came on board with a message from Tinah, to acquaint me that he was *mattow* (afraid to see me) till he had recovered some things that had been stolen from the ship, and which he had sent after. I knew there was something wrong, as no canoes came off to us, and, on looking about, we found the buoy of the best bower anchor had been taken away, I imagine, for the sake of some iron hoops that were on it. That this might not create any coolness, I sent a boat to Tinah, to invite him and his friends to come on board; which they immediately did, and were no longer under any apprehensions. I had made an appointment with Oreepyah, for him to go with me to Oparre this morning; but the accident just mentioned caused him to break his engagement, he having gone, I was informed, in search of what had been stolen.

Oparre is the district next to the westward of Matavai.

One of my reasons for going to Oparre, was to see if
Nelson would be able to procure plants there; but I gave
the credit of my visit to young Otoo, the son of Tinah,
who was the *Earee Rahie,* and lived with the rest of
Tinah's children at Oparre. I prepared a magnificent
present for this youth, who was represented to me as the
person of the greatest consequence, or rather of the highest rank, in the island. At noon I left the ship, accompanied by Tinah, his wife Iddeah, and Poeeno. Moannah
was to have been of the party, but he insisted on remaining in the ship, to prevent his countrymen from attempting
to steal anything.

After half an hour's sailing, we arrived at Oparre.
During this time, Tinah gave me a more circumstantial
account of the cattle and sheep, that had been left with
him: he related, that after five years from the time of
Captain Cook's departure (counting 63 moons) the people of the Island Eimeo joined with those of Attahooroo,
a district of Otaheite, and made a descent on Oparre: that
after some resistance, by which many men were killed,
Tinah and his people fled to the mountains, leaving all
their property to the mercy of the victorious party, who
destroyed almost everything which they found not convenient to take away with them. Some of the cattle were
killed and eaten, but the greater part were taken to
Eimeo. The cows, he said, had produced eight calves, and
the ewes ten young ones. The ducks, among which they
classed the geese, had greatly increased; but the turkeys
and peacocks, whatever was the cause, had not bred. It
seemed to give Tinah great pleasure to observe how much
I was concerned for the destruction of so many useful
animals; but the cause of his satisfaction, I found, did not
proceed from any expectation that I should replace them,
but from the belief that I would take vengeance on the
people who had deprived him of them; for with respect
to the loss of the cattle, he appeared so unconcerned and
indifferent, that I was very angry with him. There is, however, sufficient excuse for his resentment against the
people of Eimeo; for the large extensive houses which we
had seen in this part of Otaheite, in the year 1777, were
all destroyed, and at present they had no other habitations
than light sheds, which might be taken by the four corners,
and removed by four men; and of the many large canoes

which they then had, not more than three remained.
Tinah, understanding from my conversation, that I intended visiting some of the other islands in this neighbourhood, very earnestly desired I would not think of leaving
Matavai. "Here," said he, "you shall be supplied plentifully with everything you want. All here are your friends,
and friends of King George: if you go to the other islands,
you will have everything stolen from you." I replied, that,
on account of their good will, and from a desire to serve
him and his country, King George had sent out those
valuable presents to him; "and will not you, Tinah, send
something to King George in return?"—"Yes," he said,
"I will send him any thing I have"; and then began to
enumerate the different articles in his power, among which
he mentioned the bread-fruit. This was the exact point to
which I wished to bring the conversation; and, seizing an
opportunity, which had every appearance of being un-
designed and accidental, I told him the bread-fruit trees
were what King George would like; upon which he promised me a great many should be put on board, and seemed
much delighted to find it so easily in his power to send
anything that would be well received by King George.

On landing at Oparre, an immense crowd of natives, as
usual, immediately thronged about us. I inquired for
Oreepyah, whom I expected to have met me here, but he
was not yet returned from his search after the thieves; we
therefore went under a shed of his to wait for him, and in
about a quarter of an hour he joined us, bringing with
him an iron scraper, and one of the hoops of the buoy. I
thanked him for the trouble which he had taken, and
assured him that I was perfectly satisfied; for he still
seemed apprehensive of my displeasure.

We took leave for a short time of Oreepyah, and I proceeded with Tinah to make my visit to the young Otoo,
the *Earee Rahie*. When we had walked about five minutes, Tinah stopped, and informed me that no person
could be permitted to see his son, who was covered above
the shoulders. He then took off his upper garments, and
requested I would do the same. I replied, that I had no
objection to go as I would to my own king, who was the
greatest in all the world; and, pulling off my hat, he threw
a piece of cloth round my shoulders, and we went on.
About a quarter of a mile farther towards the hills,

through a delightful shade of bread-fruit trees, we stopped at the side of a small serpentine river: here I was in view of a house on the other side, at about fifty yards distance. From this house the young king was brought out on a man's shoulders, clothed in a piece of fine white cloth, and I was desired by Tinah to salute him by the name of *Too Earee Rahie*. The present which I had prepared was divided into three parts, and two other children made their appearance in the same manner. The first present I gave to a messenger who attended for that purpose; and I was instructed by Tinah to say, that it was for the *Earee Rahie;* that I was his friend; that I hated thieves; and that I came from Britannia. The second present was sent in the same manner, with a similar message, to one of the other children; and likewise the third.

As I could not see the *Earee Rahie* distinctly, I desired to be permitted to go over the river to him; but this, it seems, could not be complied with: therefore, after seeing the presents delivered, I returned with Tinah towards Oreepyah's house. I was informed that Tinah had four children by his wife Iddeah. Otoo, or Too, the *Earee Rahie,* appeared to be about six years old: the second is a girl, named Terrenah Oroah: the third, a boy, Terree-tappanooai; and a fourth, an infant girl, whom I did not see, named Tahamydooah.

When we came to the place where we had first stopped, Tinah took the cloth from my shoulders, and desired me to put my hat on; I expressed a desire to see more of the place, and he took me back by a different way. On passing a trunk of a tree, rudely carved, I was desired again to pull my hat off, and all uncovered their shoulders. This I discovered to be nothing more than the boundary of the king's land; on which, whoever set their feet, uncovered themselves out of respect.

We stopped at a house belonging to Tinah, where I was treated with a concert of one drum and three flutes, with singing by four men. I made some presents to the performers, and we removed to Oreepyah's house, where, after paying my compliments to him, which I found was expected, Tinah made me a present of a large hog, and some cocoa-nuts. He then introduced an uncle of his, called Mowworoah, a very old man, much tattooed, and almost blind. To this chief I made a present; and soon after I embarked, with Tinah, Oreepyah, their wives, and Poeeno. A vast number of people were collected on the beach to see us depart; and as soon as the boat had put off, Tinah desired me to fire my pocket pistol, the *poopooe ete ete,* as he called it: the report seemed to electrify the whole crowd; but finding no harm done, they gave great shouts of approbation.

Nelson, who accompanied me in this expedition, had but little opportunity to search after plants, the natives having crowded so much about him: he saw enough, however, to assure him that they were to be procured here as plentifully as at Matavai.

In our passage to the ship, which we rowed in one hour, nothing but *Britannie* was enquired after, and of the number of ships and guns. When I told them we had ships of 100 guns, they could not believe it, till I drew one on paper; they then asked me if it was not as big as Tarrah, which is a high projecting head-land, halfway between Matavai and Oparre, called by us One-tree Hill. Tinah much wished that one of these large ships should be sent to Otaheite, and that myself should come in her, and bring him a number of things that he wanted; among which he particularly desired beds and high-backed elbow chairs might not be forgotten: a request perfectly according with the indolent character of Tinah.

As we had occasion to fix a tent on Point Venus, this morning we moved the ship nearer to it, and moored again in 6 fathoms, the point bearing N N E.

Tinah and several other chiefs dined on board with me. After dinner I went on shore with Tinah, and made a visit to his father, Otow. I likewise went to the garden which I had made near Poeeno's house, and found everything had been taken care of. After this, I was invited to an entertainment called *Heiva,* which Tinah had ordered, and which consisted of singing and dancing by three men and a young girl. When this performance was finished I returned to the ship.

At daylight, I sent Mr. Christian with a party to erect our tent, and soon after followed myself with Tinah, Moannah, and Poeeno. With their consent I fixed a boundary, within which the natives were not to enter without leave, and the chiefs cautioned them against it. The principal use of the tents on shore was for a lodge-

ment for the plants; and I had now, instead of appearing
to receive a favour, brought the chiefs to believe that I
was doing them a kindness in carrying the plants, as a
present from them to the *Earee Rahie no Britanee.* The
party at the tent consisted of nine persons, including Nelson and his assistant.

Tinah dined with me on board, and was to-day my only
visitor: nevertheless, the ceremony of being fed he so
scrupulously observed, that, even after all the attendants
were sent away, and we were left by ourselves, I was
obliged to lift the wine to his mouth. The wives of the
Earees are sometimes subject to this restriction after the
birth of a child, but are released after a certain time, on
performing a ceremony called *Oammo.*

After dinner, Tinah invited me to accompany him with
a present of provisions to a party of the *Arreoys,* a society
described in the accounts of the former voyages: in this
ceremony, he made me the principal person. Our way to
the place where the offering was to be made, was by the
side of a river, along the banks of which I had always
walked before this time; but on the present occasion a
canoe was provided for me, and dragged by eight men.
On arriving at the landing-place, I saw a large quantity
of bread-fruit, with some hogs ready dressed, and a quantity of cloth. At about forty yards distant sat a man, who,
I was informed, was a principal *Arreoy.* A lane being
made by the crowd, he was addressed by one of Tinah's
people, standing on the canoe, in a speech composed of
short sentences, which lasted about a quarter of an hour.
During this, a piece of cloth was produced, one end of
which I was desired to hold, and five men, one with a
sucking pig, and the others having each a basket of bread-
fruit, prepared to follow me. In this order we advanced to
the *Arreoy,* and laid the whole down before him. I then
spoke several sentences dictated to me by Tinah, the
meaning of which I did not understand; and, my pronunciation not being very exact, caused a great deal of mirth.
This speech being finished, I was shown another *Arreoy,*
who had come from Ulietea, and to him likewise I was
required to deliver an oration. Tinah understanding from
me, that I had children in my own country, he desired
me to make one more offering on their account. There
still remained three baskets of bread-fruit, a small pig,

and another piece of cloth: with these, assisted as before, I made the offering in favour of my children to the man whom I had first addressed. He made no reply to all my fine speeches, but sat with great gravity, and received everything as a matter of right, and not of courtesy.

All that I could make out of this strange ceremony was, that the *Arreoys* are highly respected, and that the society is chiefly composed of men distinguished by their valour or some other merit, and that great trust and confidence is reposed in them; but I could not comprehend what this had to do with my children, or why it should be imagined that an offering made on their account to a society of men, who destroy all their children, should be propitious. I learnt from Tinah, in talking about his children, that his first-born child was killed as soon as it came into the world, he being then an *Arreoy;* but before his second child was born, he quitted the society. The *Arreoys* are allowed great latitude in their amours, except in times of danger. Then, as they are almost all fighting men *(tata toa)* they are restricted, that they may not weaken or enervate themselves.

These ceremonies being ended, I returned to the ship.

Such of the natives, as I conversed with about the institution of so extraordinary a society as the *Arreoy,* asserted that it was necessary, to prevent an over population. *Worrow worrow no te mydidde, worrow worrow te tata.* We have too many children, and too many men, was their constant excuse. Yet it does not appear, that they are apprehensive of too great an increase of the lower class of people, none of them being ever admitted into the *Arreoy* society. The most remarkable instance, related to me, of the barbarity of this institution, was of Teppahoo, the *Earee* of the district of Tettaha, and his wife, Tetteehowdeeah, who is sister to Otow, and considered as a person of the first consequence. I was told that they have had eight children, every one of which was destroyed as soon as born. That any human beings were ever so devoid of natural affection, as not to wish to preserve alive one of so many children, is not credible. It is more reasonable to conclude, that the death of these infants was not an act of choice in the parents; but that they were sacrificed in compliance with some barbarous superstition, with which we are unacquainted. What strengthens this conjecture is, that they have adopted a nephew as their heir, of whom they are excessively fond.

In countries so limited as the islands in the South Seas, the natives of which, before they were discovered by European navigators, probably had not an idea of the existence of other lands, it is not unnatural that an increasing population should occasion apprehensions of universal distress. Orders of celibacy, which have proved so prejudicial in other countries, might perhaps in this have been beneficial; so far at least as to have answered their purpose by means not criminal. The number of inhabitants at Otaheite have been estimated at above 100,000. The island, however, is not cultivated to the greatest advantage: yet, were they continually to improve in husbandry, their improvement could not, for a length of time, keep pace with an unlimited population.

An idea here presents itself, which, however fanciful it may appear at first sight, seems to merit some attention: —While we see among these islands so great a waste of the human species, that numbers are born only to die; and, at the same time, a large continent so near to them as New Holland, in which there is so great a waste of land uncultivated, and almost destitute of inhabitants; it naturally occurs, how greatly the two countries might be made to benefit each other; and gives occasion to regret that the islanders are not instructed in the means of emigrating to New Holland, which seems as if designed by nature to serve as an asylum for the superflux of inhabitants in the islands. Such a plan of emigration, if rendered practicable to them, might not only be the means of abolishing the horrid custom of destroying children, as it would remove the plea of necessity, but might lead to other important purposes. A great continent would be converted from a desert to a populous country; a number of our fellow-creatures would be saved; the inhabitants of the islands would become more civilized; and it is not improbable, but that our colonies in New Holland would derive so much benefit as to more than repay any trouble or expense, that might be incurred in endeavouring to promote so humane a plan.

The latter, however, is a remote consideration, for the intertropical parts of New Holland are those most suited to the habits and manner of living of the islanders; and likewise the soil and climate are the best adapted to their modes of agriculture. Man placed by his Creator in the warm climates, perhaps, would never emigrate into the colder, unless under the tyrannous influence of necessity; and ages might elapse before the new inhabitants would spread to our settlers, though they are but barely within the limits of frost, that great cause of nine-tenths of the necessities of Europeans. Nevertheless, besides forwarding the purposes of humanity and general convenience, in bringing a people without land to a land without people, the benefit of a mutual intercourse with a neighbouring and friendly colony would in itself be no inconsiderable advantage.

Among people so free from ostentation as the Otaheiteans, and whose manners are so simple and natural, the strictness with which the punctilios of rank are observed is surprising. I know not if any action, however meritorious, can elevate a man above the class in which he was born, unless he were to acquire sufficient power to confer dignity on himself. If any woman of the inferior classes has a child by an *Earee,* it is not suffered to live. Perhaps the offspring of Teppahoo and Tetteehowdeeah were destined to satisfy some cruel adjustment of rank and precedency.

CHAPTER VII

THE trade for provisions I directed to be carried on at the tent by Mr. Peckover, the gunner. Moannah likewise resided there, as a guard over his countrymen; but though it appeared to be the wish of all the chiefs, that we should remain unmolested, it was not possible entirely to prevent them from pilfering.

My table at dinner was generally crowded. Tinah, Oreepyah, Poeeno, and Moannah, were my regular guests, and I was seldom without some chiefs from other districts. Almost every individual of any consequence has several names, which makes it frequently perplexing, when the same person is spoken of, to know who is meant. Every chief has perhaps a dozen or more names in the course of thirty years; so that the person who has been spoken of by one visitor, will not perhaps be known to another, unless other circumstances lead to a discovery. The father of Tinah, at this time called Otow, was known in 1769 by the name of Whappai.

I showed Tinah the preparations I was making to take on board the bread-fruit plants, which pleased him exceedingly, but he did not forget to remind me, that when the next ship came out he hoped King George would send him large axes, files, saws, cloth of all kinds, hats, chairs, and bedsteads, with arms, ammunition, and in short every thing he could think of mentioning.

This afternoon, the gudgeon of the rudder belonging to the large cutter was drawn out and stolen, without being perceived by the man that was stationed to take care of her. Several petty thefts having been committed by the natives, mostly owing to the negligence of our own people; and as these kind of accidents generally created alarm, and had a tendency to interrupt the good terms on which we were with the chiefs, I thought it would have a good effect to punish the boat-keeper in their presence, many of them happening to be then on board; and accordingly I ordered him a dozen lashes. Tinah, with several of the chiefs, attended the punishment, and interceded very earnestly to get it mitigated: the women showed great sympathy, and that degree of feeling which characterises the amiable part of their sex.

The natives brought off to-day two different kinds of roots that grow like yams: one they call Ettee, which is a sweet root, common also to the Friendly Islands, and may be eaten as a sweetmeat: the other they call Appay, a root like the Tyah or Eddie in the West Indies. A fruit called Ayyah, which is the jambo of Batavia, was likewise brought off to us: they are as large as middle-sized apples, very juicy and refreshing, and may be eaten in large quantities. Also some Avees, which are the real Otaheite apple; but they were not yet in season. These are a delicious high-flavoured fruit, and before they are ripe, answer the culinary purposes of our apples.

A chief called Tootaha, who came from the island Ulietea, was introduced to me to-day, by Tinah, as one of his particular friends. I was told that he was a priest, and a person of great knowledge. I desired Tinah to take what he thought proper as a present for him; and I must do Tinah the justice to say, he was more sparing than I should have been. I likewise received a visit to-day from Oedidee, the man who had been at sea with Captain Cook in 1773 and 1774, as related in the account of that voyage. He still retained some of the English words which he had learnt in that expedition.

The weather variable, with lightning, and frequent showers of rain. Wind E N E.

This was the first day of our beginning to take up plants: we had much pleasure in collecting them, for the natives offered their assistance, and perfectly understood the method of taking them up and pruning them.

The crowd of natives was not so great as hitherto it had been; the curiosity of strangers was satisfied; and, as the weather began to be unsettled and rainy, they had almost all returned to their homes; so that only the people of Matavai and Oparre remained with us, except a few chiefs from other islands: our supplies however were abundant; and what I considered as no small addition to

our comforts, we ceased to be incommoded, when on
shore, by the natives following us, and could take our
walks almost unnoticed. In any house that we wished to
enter, we always experienced a kind reception, and without officiousness. The Otaheiteans have the most perfect
easiness of manners, equally free from forwardness and
formality. When they offer refreshments, if they are not
accepted, they do not think of offering them the second
time; for they have not the least idea of that ceremonious
kind of refusal which expects a second invitation. In like
manner, at taking leave, we were never troubled with
solicitations to prolong our visit, but went without ceremony, except making use of a farewell expression at parting. Another advantage, seldom found in warm countries,
was, in this part of Otaheite being free from mosquitoes,
though, at particular times of the year, the inhabitants
are pestered with great numbers of flies.

Moannah continued our constant friend at the tent,
and, with Tinah and all his friends, dined with me every
day.

The ship's barber had brought with him from London,
a painted head, such as the hair-dressers have in their
shops, to show the different fashions of dressing hair;
and it being made with regular features, and well coloured, I desired him to dress it, which he did with much
neatness, and with a stick, and a quantity of cloth, he
formed a body. It was then reported to the natives that
we had an English woman on board, and the quarterdeck
was cleared of the crowd, that she might make her appearance. Being handed up the ladder, and carried to the
after-part of the deck, there was a general shout of
Huaheine no Brittanne myty. Huaheine signifies woman,
and myty, good. Many of them thought it was living,
and asked if it was my wife. One old woman ran with
presents of cloth and bread-fruit, and laid them at her
feet; at last they found out the cheat; but continued all
delighted with it, except the old lady, who felt herself
mortified, and took back her presents, for which she was
laughed at exceedingly. Tinah and all the chiefs enjoyed
the joke, and, after making many enquiries about the
British women, they strictly enjoined me, when I came
again, to bring a ship full of them.

Some very fine sugar-cane was brought to me; each

of the pieces was six inches round. I had before told Tinah that our sugar was made of it, and he was very desirous to discover the means; for they were so fond of our loaf sugar, that a present to any chief would have been incomplete without a piece of it. Another article in great estimation, and likewise expected to make part of a present, was scissors, which they made use of to keep their beards in order.

By this time Nelson had, with assistance from the ship, completed a large garden near the tents; in which were sown seeds of different kinds, that we had collected at the Cape of Good Hope. I likewise distributed fruit-stones and almonds for planting, among the chiefs, who, I hope, will endeavour to make them succeed: and, as they are very fond of sweet-smelling flowers, with which the women delight to ornament themselves, I gave them some rose-seed.

We had very variable weather, much rain, and some westerly winds; so that a considerable swell ran into the bay, and a number of spotted white and black porpusses made their appearance.

I had the mortification to see that our garden-ground had been much trod over; and, what was worse, the chiefs appeared but little concerned at it. To this kind of carelessness and indifference I attribute the miscarriage of many of the plants left here by Captain Cook. I had now in a flourishing state, two orange plants, some vines, a fig-tree, and two pine-apple plants, which I gave to Poeeno, whose residence is a place favourable for their growth.

We got on successfully with our plants, having a hundred potted at the tent, and in a fair way of doing well. The cabin also was completed, and ready to receive them on board.

I have before remarked, that my friend Tinah was rather of a selfish disposition, and this afternoon he showed a stronger instance of it than I was witness to at any time before or after. His brother Oreepyah sent on board to me, a present of a large hog, and a quantity of bread-fruit: but these kind of presents are much more expensive than purchasing at the market. Soon after Oreepyah himself came on board. Tinah was with me at the time, and whispered me to tell Oreepyah not to

bring any more hogs or fruit, and to take those back
which he had sent. This advice, as may be supposed, did
not produce the effect intended. Oreepyah appears to
be a man of great spirit, and is highly respected by his
countrymen. Among other visitors to-day, was one of
the men who had been to Lima in 1776.

Our plants had now increased to 252: as they were all
kept on shore at the tent, I augmented the guard there,
though, from the general conduct of the natives, there did
not appear the least occasion for so much caution.

While I was at dinner, Tinah desired I would permit a
man to come down into the cabin, whom he called his
Taowah, or priest; for I was obliged to keep a sentinel at
the hatchway to prevent being incommoded at my meals
with too much company; a restriction which pleased the
chiefs, who always asked leave for any particular person
to be admitted of whom they wished me to take notice.
The company of the priest brought on a religious conversation. He said, their great God was called Oro; and
that they had many others of less consequence. He asked
me if I had a God?—if he had a son? and who was his
wife? I told them he had a son, but no wife. Who was
his father and mother? was the next question. I said, he
never had father or mother; at this they laughed exceedingly. You have a God then who never had a father
or mother, and has a child without a wife! Many other
questions were asked, which my little knowledge of the
language did not enable me to answer.

The weather was now fine again, and a great number
of people were come from other parts of the island. Tinah
informed me that there was to be a *heiva* and a wrestling-
match on shore, and that the performers waited for our
attendance; we therefore set off, with several of our
friends, and, about a quarter of a mile from the tents,
we found a great concourse of people formed into a ring.
As soon as we were seated, a dancing *heiva* began, which
was performed by two girls and four men: this lasted half
an hour, and consisted of wanton gestures and motions,
such as have been described in the account of former
voyages. When the dance ended, Tinah ordered a long
piece of cloth to be brought; his wife Iddeah, and myself,
were desired to hold the two first corners, and, the remaining part being supported by many others, we carried

it to the performers, and gave it them. Several other chiefs made a like present or payment. The performers were strollers, that travelled about the country as in Europe.

After this, the wrestling began, and the place soon became a scene of riot and confusion. A party of the *Arreoys* also began to exercise a privilege, which it seems they are allowed, of taking from the women such of their clothes as they thought worth it; so that some of them were left little better than naked. One young woman, who was attacked, opposed them with all her strength, and held fast her cloth, though they almost dragged her along the ground. Observing that I took notice of her, she held out her hand, and begged my assistance; and at my request she escaped being pillaged.

Soon after, a ring was again made, but the wrestlers were so numerous within it, that it was impossible to restore order. In the challenges, they lay one hand upon their breast, and on the bending of the arm at the elbow, with the other hand, they strike a very smart blow, which, as the hand is kept hollow, creates a sound that may be heard at a considerable distance; and this they do so frequently, and with such force, that the flesh becomes exceedingly bruised, and, the skin breaking, bleeds considerably. At this time, the sound from so many resembled that of a number of people in a wood felling trees. This is the general challenge; but when any two combatants agree to a trial, they present their hands forward, joining them only by the extremities of the fingers. They begin by watching to take an advantage; at length they close, seize each other by the hair, and are most commonly parted before either receives a fall. Only one couple performed any thing like the part of good wrestlers; and, as they were an equal match, this conflict lasted longer than any of the others; but they also were parted.

Iddeah was the general umpire, and she managed with so much address as to prevent any quarrelling, and there was no murmuring at her decisions. As her person was large, she was very conspicuous in the circle. Tinah took no part in the management. Upon the whole, this performance gave me a better opinion of their strength than of their skill or dexterity.

For some time past, Tinah had talked of going to the island of Tethuroa, which lies 8 or 10 leagues north from Otaheite, to fetch his mother; but I found I had only half understood him; for this morning he enquired when we were to sail there in the ship: however, he seemed to feel no great disappointment at my not complying with his wish. Tethuroa, he informed me, is the property of his family. He likewise spoke to me about an island called Roo-opow, the situation of which he described to be to the eastward of Otaheite four or five days sail, and that there were large animals upon it with eight legs. The truth of this account he very strenuously insisted upon, and wished me to go thither with him. I was at a loss to know whether or not Tinah himself gave credit to this whimsical and fabulous account; for though they have credulity sufficient to believe any thing, however improbable, they are at the same time so much addicted to that species of wit which we call humbug, that it is frequently difficult to discover whether they are in jest or earnest. Their ideas of geography are very simple: they believe the world to be a fixed plane of great extent; and that the sun, moon, and stars, are all in motion around it. I have been frequently asked by them, if I have not been as far as the sun and moon; for they think we are such great travellers, that scarce any undertaking is beyond our ability.

Another island, called Tappuhoi, situated likewise to the eastward, was described to me by Tinah, the inhabitants of which were said to be all warriors, and that the people of Otaheite did not dare to go there. He told me, that very lately a canoe from Tappuhoi was at the island Maitea; that as soon as they landed they began to fight with the people of Maitea, who killed them all, except a young lad, and a woman, who have since been at Otaheite. I saw the boy, but could get no information from him. It is most probable, that this unfortunate visit of the canoe from Tappuhoi was not designed, but occasioned by adverse winds, which forced them so far from their own island; and that the people of Maitea began the attack, taking advantage of their superior numbers, on account of some former quarrel.

Thursday 13th. I had a large company to dine with me to-day. Some of my constant visitors had observed, that we always drank his Majesty's health, as soon as the cloth was removed; but they were by this time become so fond of wine, that they would frequently remind me of the health in the middle of dinner, by calling out: King George Earee no Brittannee; and would banter me if the glass was not filled to the brim. Nothing could exceed the mirth and jollity of these people, when they met on board.

I was assured Oediddee, and several others, that the vines planted at the island Huaheine by Captain Cook, had succeeded and bore fruit; and that some of the other plants, both at Huaheine, and at Oaitepeha, a district on the S E part of Otaheite, had been preserved, and were in a thriving state. I was likewise informed, that there was a bull and a cow alive at Otaheite, but on different parts of the island; the former at a place called Itteah, the latter at the district of Tettaha. All the rest were taken away or destroyed by the people of Eimeo. As Tettaha was at no great distance, I determined to go thither myself, the first opportunity, and make enquiries, in hopes that the breed might still be preserved.

I had much discourse with my guests about Omai: they confirmed to me, that he died about thirty months after Captain Cook left the islands. Soon after Captain Cook's departure from Huaheine, there were some disputes between the people of that island and those of Ulietea, in which also the natives of Bolabola took a part. Omai, who was become of consequence from the possessing three or four muskets, and some ammunition, was consulted on the occasion. Such was his opinion and assurances of success, that a war was determined on, and took place immediately.—Victory soon followed, through the means of those few arms, and many of the Ulietea and Bolabola men were killed. In this contest their flints proved bad, or probably the locks of the muskets had got out of order: this they remedied by a lighted stick, one man presenting the musket, and another with the burnt stick setting fire to the priming; without which contrivance, their arms would have proved useless. This expedition, it seems, consumed all their ammunition. Peace was soon after established, but I did not understand that Omai had increased his possessions or his rank. Nevertheless, I have reason to conclude, that he was in some degree of favour

with his countrymen, from the general good character
which they give of him. It appears, that he always remembered England with kindness; for his accounts to
his countrymen had been such as to give them, not only
a great idea of our power and consequence, but of our
friendship and goodwill towards him.

Tyvarooah, the eldest of the New Zealand boys that
were left with him, died a short time after Omai: about
Coah, the youngest, I had always doubtful accounts till I
came to Huaheine, where I learnt that he likewise was
dead.

AFTER dinner, I went on shore, and while I was at the tents, from having exposed myself too much in the sun, I was taken ill, and continued in much pain for near an hour. This was soon known among the natives, and I was exceedingly surprised to see Tinah, and all the principal people, both men and women, collecting round me, and offering their assistance. For this short illness, I was made ample amends, by the pleasure I received from the attention and appearance of affection in these kind people.

Friday 14th.—This morning I had numberless enquiries after my health. The weather being fine, I invited Tinah, Oreepyah, and Poeeno, to accompany me to Tettaha, in order to enquire after the cow; and soon after sun-rise we set off in the launch. Tettaha is nearly four leagues from Point Venus. On our arrival, Tinah sent a man to give notice of our visit. The chief of the district, whose name was Teppahoo, did not appear, but sent a messenger to demand, if I came only to see the cow, or to take it away with me. In answer to this, I sent assurances, that I only desired to see it; and the chiefs who were with me spoke to the same effect. I was then desired to proceed in the boat farther along shore to the westward. In our way Tinah made me stop among some fishing canoes to purchase fish for him, which he ate raw, with salt water for sauce. When we arrived at the landing place, a great number of people had collected, and soon after Teppahoo arrived. Oreepyah and I went with him about a quarter of a mile, when I was shown one of the most beautiful heifers I ever saw. I asked if they had any more, but they all said there was no other than a bull at Itteah, as before-mentioned. I could not refrain from expressing my displeasure at the destruction, and the foolish separation of these fine animals. I had shared with Captain Cook in the trouble of this business, and had been equally anxious for the success.

The district of Tettaha is not so luxuriant and fruitful as the country about Matavai. As I saw nothing of consequence to detain me, I made a present to Teppahoo, and, after inviting him to visit me on board the ship, which he promised to do, I took leave. Tinah had remained all this time in the boat. I observed that no respect was shown to him at this place, nor was he able to procure a cocoa-nut, or a bread-fruit, otherwise than by purchasing it. The heifer being here, is a proof of this district not having been friendly to the people of Matavai and Oparre.

In our way back, having to row against the wind, we stopped to refresh at Oparre, and it was eight o'clock by the time we arrived at the ship. I kept my fellow travellers on board to supper, and they did not fail to remind me of the king's health.

Our collection of bread-fruit plants at the tents continued increasing. This morning I sent twelve on board, in pots, to discover where they would thrive the best, the air being more temperate on board the ship than on shore. While I was absent from the ship, Teppahoo had been on board, and left a hog as a present for me.

After dinner to-day, Tinah, who was my constant visitor, left the table sooner than usual. When he was gone, Oreepyah, his brother, and Oediddee, told me a piece of scandal, which had been before hinted to me, but which till now I had not heard of with certainty: this was, that Iddeah, Tinah's wife, kept a gallant, who was a *towtow*, or servant, and the very person who always fed Tinah at dinner: and this was so far from being without Tinah's knowledge or consent, that they said it was by his desire. They added many other circumstances, and, as I appeared to doubt, they took several opportunities, in the course of the day, of mentioning it to other people, who all declared it was true.

Tuesday 18th. This afternoon, I saw Teppahoo, and invited him on board: before we parted, I bargained with him for the heifer, which he promised to bring in five days. My intention was, that if I got the heifer, I would endeavour to purchase the bull at Itteah: but if that could not be done, then I could send the heifer as a present to the possessor of the bull, which might equally well answer my purpose.

It has been mentioned, that Tinah had a place in my cabin to keep those things which I gave him, as being more secure on board than on shore. I had remarked lately, that his hoard seemed to diminish the more I endeavoured to increase it: at length I discovered that Iddeah kept another hoard in the master's cabin, which she regularly enriched from her husband's, whenever I made him a present, apprehending that I should cease giving, when I saw Tinah's locker full. At his request, I set the carpenters to work to make him a chest large enough for himself and wife to sleep on. Captain Cook had formerly given him such a chest, but it had been taken from him by the Eimeo people.

This forenoon, I received a message from Teppahoo, to acquaint me the heifer was brought to Matavai. I immediately went on shore, and found that he had been as good as his word. The purchase money was paid, which consisted of a shirt, hatchet, a spike nail, a knife, a pair of scissors, a gimlet, and file; to which was added, a small quantity of loaf-sugar. Teppahoo appeared well pleased with his bargain; and I sent the heifer to Poeeno's residence, near which was plenty of grass.

In the afternoon, I was invited to a *heiva*, the most extraordinary part of which was an oration, with some ceremonies in compliment to us. Twelve men were divided into four ranks, with two women in the front: behind them all stood a priest, who made a speech which lasted ten minutes, and which was listened to with some attention. During this, the picture of Captain Cook, which had been brought for that purpose, was placed by my side. When the priest left off speaking, a piece of white cloth was wrapt round the picture, and another piece round me. The priest then spoke again for a short time, and an old man placed a piece of plaited cocoa-nut leaf at my feet; the same was done to Tinah, and one piece was put under the picture. After this the dancing began, which was in the same style that we had already seen.

The head of the ship was the figure of a woman, and not ill carved. As we were painting the ship's upper works, I directed this figure to be painted in colours, with which the islanders were much pleased. Not only the men, but the women, desired me to bring English women when I came again. To-day Oedid-dee, thinking I was not convinced of the truth of what he had told me about Iddeah, mentioned the affair to the lady herself in my hearing, at which she laughed, but said he did ill to tell me of it. However, it was evident she was not much offended; for they were both very much diverted in discoursing upon the subject.

I find it is not at all uncommon for brothers to have connection with the wives of each other, particularly elder brothers with the wives of their younger brothers, which is generally allowed, and no offence taken: but if any person, not belonging to the family, endeavours at the same intimacy, it is resented as an injury. Inclination seems to be the only binding law of marriage at Otaheite.

As I purposed to get instruments on shore at Point Venus, to make observations, I desired Tinah to order a house to be brought there for me; which was done, and fixed in half an hour, being only a light shed supported by posts.

To-day I bought a turtle, that was caught on the reefs. As Tinah was going to leave me for a few days, I had it dressed for his dinner. He told me that his mother, Oberree-roah, was arrived from the island Tethuroa, and begged that I would send for her in the morning, and take care of her till he returned; which I willingly promised.

Tuesday the 25th. This morning, I sent a boat to Oparre, which returned in the afternoon with Oberree-roah, and two women, her servants. As she was old and corpulent, it was with difficulty that we helped her up the ship's side. As soon as she was in the ship, she sat down on the gangway, and, clasping my knees in her arms, expressed her pleasure at seeing me by a flood of tears. Her servants then produced three pieces of cloth, which, with a large hog, some bread-fruit, plantains, and cocoanuts, she had brought as a present. As she was fatigued by her journey, she wished to remain on board all night; and I directed accommodations to be prepared, which was done with little trouble, as nothing more was necessary than a mat, and some cloth spread on the deck. She had with her a favourite cat, bred from one that had been given her by Captain Cook. She told me all the misfortunes that had befallen her son and friends, since

Captain Cook left Otaheite. All the accounts agree in
some of the cattle being now alive at the island Eimeo:
in the number they differ; but that there are eight, is the
least account. In the morning Oberree-roah being desirous
to go on shore, I made her a present of several things,
which she did not care to take with her then, but requested that I would keep them safe for her. Only
Moannah and Poeeno dined with me to-day. They told
me that Tinah and his brother Oreepyah were not on good
terms together; and it was imagined that they would fight as
soon as the ship was gone. I had observed a coolness between them, and had at times endeavoured to make them
more cordial, but with very little effect. Their quarrel had
arisen from a disagreement between their wives.

In the afternoon, a canoe from Ulietea arrived, in
which was an *Earee,* or chief, of that island, who is a
nephew to Oberree-roah. He brought a sheep with him:
the poor animal was infected with the mange, and in
very poor condition. The climate had not, as far as I
could judge, altered the quality of the wool, with which
he was well covered, except a part about the shoulders.
I imagine this animal to be the English ewe left by
Captain Cook. The owner assured me that there were ten
sheep at Huaheine; the truth of which I much doubted.
I was surprised, and rather mortified, to find that he set
so little value on this, as to let me have it, at the first
word, for a small adze. I sent it to be kept at Poeeno's,
with the heifer.

Friday the 28th. Tinah and his wife returned to
Matavai, and, from appearances which I have no reason
to mistrust, were sincerely glad to see me again after their
short absence. They brought, as usual, a present of a
hog and fruit. This morning there was an eclipse of the
sun, but the weather was so cloudy, that I had only an
opportunity of observing the end of the eclipse, which
was at $19^h 43' 53''$.

I sent a man to shear the ewe, by which a remedy
could more easily be applied to cure the disease with
which it was infected. The garden made near the tents
was not in a prosperous condition: most of the melons
and cucumbers were destroyed by insects; and the soil,
being sandy, was not favourable to the other seeds. I

therefore chose another spot of ground, farther from the sea-side, and had an assortment of seeds sown.

December the 1st. In the night, the rudder of one of the boats was stolen from the tents. On landing in the morning, neither Tinah nor any of his family came near me, being, I was informed, afraid of my displeasure. As the loss was not great, I immediately sent to assure them that I had no anger, except against the person who committed the theft. In consequence of this message, Tinah and some of the other chiefs came to the tents, and promised that they would exert themselves to discover the thief, and get the rudder restored. This was the first theft, of any consequence, that had been committed since the tents were on shore; and my suspicions fell chiefly on the people who were here from some of the other islands. Tinah had just begun to build a house for himself, and I promised that our carpenters should assist him. Whydooah, the youngest brother of Tinah, had lately been one of my constant visitors, and seemed to have left off his former custom of getting drunk with the Ava. He was esteemed one of their best warriors; and I was told that in the quarrel with the people of Eimeo, he killed Maheine the chief of that island.

The weather for some time past had been very unsettled. This afternoon, the wind blew fresh from the N W, which occasioned the sea to break very high across the Dolphin bank; and in the night such a heavy broken sea came into the bay, that we were obliged to batten all the hatchways down, and to keep every body upon deck all night, though the rain came down in torrents. The ship rolled in a most violent manner. In the morning, the wind increasing, and there being no possibility of putting to sea, we struck yards and topmasts, and trusted to our anchors. The river swelled so much with the rain, that the point of land on which the tents stood became an island; and, to preserve the bread-fruit plants from being endangered, the people were obliged to cut a passage for the river through a part of the beach, at a distance from the tents. The sea broke very high on the beach; nevertheless, a canoe put off, and, to my surprise, Tinah, his wife, and Moannah, made their way good through the surf, and came on board to see me. There was no other person in the canoe, for the weather did not admit of useless passengers: each of them had a paddle, which they managed with great activity and skill. These kind people embraced me with many tears, and expressed their apprehensions for the safety of the ship. Towards noon, however, the sea abated considerably, but the wind continued to blow strong from the N W. At sunset, Iddeah went on shore, but Tinah would remain with me the whole night.

Sunday the 7th. The wind continued between the N and N W, but had so much moderated, that I no longer considered our situation to be alarming. At noon Iddeah returned to the ship, with a large hog, and a supply of bread-fruit, and cocoa-nuts; and soon after, she and Tinah left the ship, having exacted a promise from me, that if the weather was moderate, I would go on shore in the morning, and visit their parents and sister, who, they told me, had been much alarmed on our account. I received a visit likewise from Poeeno and his wife. This woman had always shown great regard for us; and now, on our meeting, before I could be aware of it, she began beating her head violently with a shark's tooth, so that her face was covered with blood in an instant. I put a stop to this as soon as I could, and, with the drying up of the blood, her agitation subsided. This ceremony is frequently performed, upon occasions either of joy or grief. Her husband said, that, if any accident happened to the ship, I should live with him, and that they would cut down trees, and build me another ship.

From this sample of the weather, and the information of the natives, I was convinced it would not be safe to continue in Matavai Bay much longer; and I determined to get everything ready for sailing as speedily as I could.

The night proved moderate; and in the morning, I went on shore, where I was received by Oberree-roah, and several other friends, with great affection.

The plants received no injury from the bad weather, having been carefully covered from the spray of the sea: some were in a dormant state, and others were striking out young shoots. Nelson thought that it was better to refrain a few days from taking them on board; I therefore consented to defer it. He was of opinion that the plants could be propagated from the roots only, and I directed some boxes to be filled, as we could stow them where no others could be placed.

This afternoon, in hauling the launch on shore to be repaired, many of the natives assisting, one of them, a fine boy about ten years old, was thrown down, and a roller which was placed under the boat went over him. The surgeon being ill, I sent off for his assistant. Fortunately no limb was broken, nor did he receive any material injury. The surgeon had been a long time ill, the effect of intemperance and indolence. He had latterly scarce ever stirred out of his cabin, but was not apprehended to be in a dangerous state; nevertheless, this evening he appeared to be so much worse than usual, that it was thought necessary to remove him to some place where he could have more air; but to no effect, for he died in an hour afterwards. This unfortunate man drank very hard, and was so averse to exercise, that he never would be prevailed on to take half a dozen turns upon deck at a time, in the whole course of the voyage.

As I wished to bury the surgeon on shore, I mentioned it to Tinah; who said there would be no objection, but that it would be necessary to ask his father's consent first; which he undertook to do, and immediately left me for that purpose. By this circumstance it appears, that though the eldest son of an Earee succeeds to the title and honours of the father as soon as he is born, yet a considerable portion of authority remains with the father, even after the son is of age. When Tinah returned, I went with him to the spot intended for the burial place, taking with us two men to dig the grave; but on our arrival, I found the natives had already begun it. Tinah asked me, if they were doing right? "There," says he, "the sun rises, and there it sets." The idea that the grave should be E and W, I imagine they learnt from the Spaniards, as the captain of one of their ships was buried at Oeitepeha in 1774. Certain it is, they had not the information from any body belonging to our ship; for I believe we should not have thought of it. The grave, however, was marked out very exactly. At four in the afternoon, the body was interred: the chiefs, and many of the natives, came to see the ceremony, and showed great attention during the service. Some of the chiefs were very inquisitive about what was to be done with the surgeon's cabin, on account of apparitions. They said, when a man died in Otaheite, and was carried to the Tupapow, that as soon as night came, he was surrounded by spirits, and if any person went there by himself, they would devour him: therefore they said that not less than two people together should go into the surgeon's cabin for some time. I did not endeavour to dissuade them from this belief, otherwise than by laughing, and letting them know that we had no such apprehensions.

In the afternoon, the effects of the deceased were disposed of, and I appointed Mr. Thomas Denman Ledward, the surgeon's mate, to do duty as surgeon.

I went in a boat to examine the harbours about Oparre, and found two formed by the reefs. The westernmost is the most convenient for sailing in or out, but is not well sheltered from a N W wind or sea. This harbour is called by the natives Taowne: it is about a league and a half distant from Point Venus, and may be known by a remarkable mountain, called by the natives Wawry, which bears S S E from the entrance.

The easternmost harbour is called Toahroah. It is small, but as secure as a reef harbour can well be. It is about three miles distant from Point Venus. The chief objection to this harbour is the difficulty of getting out with the common trade wind, the entrance being on the east side, not more than 100 yards wide, and the depth without, inconvenient for warping. On the south side of the entrance is a Morai: the reef side is to be kept on board, and a look-out to be kept from aloft, whence the shoal water is better discerned than from the deck.

This forenoon, we performed divine service. Many of the principal natives attended, and behaved with great decency. Some of the women at one time betrayed an inclination to laugh at our general responses; but, on my looking at them, they appeared much ashamed. After the service, I was asked if no offering was to be made for the Eatua to eat.

The weather had been fair all the last week, and at this time appeared quite settled; so that I was under no apprehensions of danger from continuing a little longer in Matavai Bay.

CHAPTER IX

WEDNESDAY the 17th. This morning I took a walk into the country, accompanied by Nelson and my old friend Moannah. The breadth of the border of low land, before we arrived at the foot of the hills, was near three miles. This part of our journey was through a delightful country, well covered with bread-fruit and cocoa-nut trees, and strewed with houses, in which were swarms of children. We then proceeded along a valley, still among houses, with plantations of yams, tarro, the cloth-plant, and their favorite root the Ava: there were bread-fruit trees on the sides of the hills, which were dwarfs in comparison of those on the low land. Our walk was very much interrupted by a river, the course of which was so serpentine, that we had to cross it several times, being carried over on men's shoulders.

On arriving at a Morai, I saw a number of the natives collected, and was informed that the priests were performing their devotions. Sixteen men were sitting on their heels; in the front was a pole covered with a plaited cocoa-nut branch, and before each of the men there was a number of small pieces of the same leaf plaited, which they call *Hahyree,* and each had likewise a piece round his wrist. One, who appeared to be the chief priest, prayed aloud, and was answered by all the rest together: after a few short sentences and responses, they rose, and each carried an hahyree, which they placed at the foot of the pole, and returned to prayer: this was repeated till all the hahyree were delivered, and then the ceremony ended. I must not forget to mention, that they had placed, near the pole, an offering of plantains and bread-fruit, which they left for the Eatua. They very kindly asked us to partake of a roasted hog, that had been prepared for them whilst they were praying; but as I wished to make the most of the morning, before the sun was too high, I declined their offer, and Moannah bespoke refreshments to be ready for us when we returned.

We continued our walk up the valley, which became very narrow, and had advanced a considerable way beyond all the houses and plantations, when we were suddenly stopped by a cascade, that fell into the river from a height of above 200 feet: the fall at this time was not great, but in the heavy rains must be considerable. The natives look upon this as the most wonderful sight in the island. The fall of water is the least curious part; the cliff, over which it comes, is perpendicular, forming an appearance as if supported by square pillars of stone, and with a regularity that is surprising. Underneath is a pool 8 or 9 feet deep, into which the water falls; and in this place all the natives make a point of bathing once in their lives, probably from some religious idea.

The hills here approach each other within a few yards, and are well covered with wood. As the road appeared difficult, I did not care to proceed towards the mountain. I cannot with certainty say how far this curious precipice is from the bay, but think, in the road by which we went, it cannot be less than 7 miles. It is called Peeah Roah.

In our return, we found a young pig prepared for us, and we made a hearty meal. We dined in the house of an old acquaintance of Nelson's; for whom he had, in 1777, planted the two shaddock plants, formerly mentioned, which he had brought from the Friendly Islands. These we had the satisfaction to see were grown to fine trees, and full of fruit.

In their plantations they do not take much pains, except with the Ava and the cloth-plant, both of which they are careful to keep clear of weeds. Many of the plantations of the cloth-plant were fenced with stone, and surrounded with a ditch. The yams and plantains are mostly on the higher grounds. As soon as we had finished our dinner, we returned towards the ship. I was much delighted, in this walk, with the number of children that I saw in every part of the country: they are very handsome and sprightly,

and full of antic tricks. They have many diversions that are
common with the boys in England; such as flying kites,
cats cradle, swinging, dancing or jumping in a rope,
walking upon stilts, and wrestling.

Friday the 19th. The wind to-day blew fresh, but
continued regular from the E and E S E. We had likewise
much rain, and a long swell set into the bay. I had not
yet determined, whether, on leaving Matavai Bay, I
would go to the island Eimeo, or to the harbour of Toahroah near Oparre: this uncertainty made Tinah, and the
rest of my friends, very anxious; and they appeared much
distressed on my desiring them, this afternoon, to send on
board all the things which they wished to have repaired
by the forge, without delay, that what they wanted might
be done before the ship left Matavai, which I told them
would be in a few days. They very earnestly entreated I
would stay one month longer. I represented this as impossible, and asked Tinah if he would not go with me
to Eimeo; but he said, that, notwithstanding my protection, he was certain the Eimeo people would watch for an
opportunity to kill him. He remained on board with me
all night, but his wife went on shore, and returned early in
the morning, bringing with her some axes, and other
things, that were in need of repair.

When I went on shore, I found Otow, Oberree-roah,
Moannah, and several others, in great tribulation at the
thoughts that we were so soon to leave them. All the
people of Matavai, I saw, were much concerned at my
intention of going to Eimeo, and took every opportunity
to prejudice me against the people of that island; to which
I paid very little attention, as their motive was obvious.
Their expressions of friendship and affection for me, however, I could not disregard, as I had no doubt of their
being genuine and unaffected; and I felt my unwilling-
ness to leave these kind people so much increased, that
the next day, I sent the master in the launch to re-
examine the depth of water between this bay and Toahroah harbour. He returned in the evening, and acquainted
me, that he found a good bottom, with not less than 16
fathoms depth all the way. The harbour of Toahroah
appearing every way safe, I determined to get the ship
there as speedily as possible, and I immediately made my
intention public, which occasioned great rejoicing.

This day, we took the plants on board, being 774 pots, all in a healthy state; for whenever any plant had an unfavourable appearance, it was replaced by another. The number of those rejected was 302, of which not one in ten but was found to be growing at the root.

The natives reckon eight kinds of the bread-fruit tree, each of which they distinguish by a different name. 1. *Patteah.* 2. *Erorro.* 3. *Awanna.* 4. *Mi-re.* 5. *Oree.* 6. *Powerro.* 7. *Appeere.* 8. *Rowdeeah.* In the first, fourth, and eighth class, the leaf differs from the rest; the fourth is more sinuated; the eighth has a large broad leaf, not at all sinuated. The difference of the fruit is principally in the first and eighth class. In the first, the fruit is rather larger and more of an oblong form: in the eighth, it is round and not above half the size of the others. I inquired if plants could be produced from the seed, and was told they could not, but that they must be taken from the root. The plants are best collected after wet weather, at which time the earth balls round the roots, and they are not liable to suffer by being moved.

The most common method of dividing time at Otaheite is by moons; but they likewise make a division of the year into six parts, each of which is distinguished by the name of the kind of bread-fruit then in season. In this division they keep a small interval called *Tawa,* in which they do not use the bread-fruit. This is about the end of February, when the fruit is not in perfection; but there is no part of the year in which the trees are entirely bare.

Thursday the 25th. At daylight we unmoored, and I sent the tents in the launch to Oparre, with directions that after landing them, the launch should meet the ship in the entrance of Toahroah harbour, to show the safest part of the channel. At half past ten, we got the ship under sail, and ran down under top-sails: when we were near the launch, it fell calm, and the ship shot past her. We immediately let the anchor go, but, to our great surprise, we found the ship was aground forwards. She had run on so easy, that we had not perceived it at the time. This accident occasioned us much trouble, as we were obliged to send anchors out astern to get the ship afloat: in doing this, one of the cables swept a rock, and was not got clear again without much difficulty. When the ship was moored, Point Venus bore N 46° E. The east point

of the harbour N 65° E ¼ of a mile. Our distance from
shore half a cable's length; depth of water 8½ fathoms.

The next morning, on my landing, I was welcomed by
all the principal people; I may say by the whole crowd,
and congratulated on the safety of the ship. Tinah
showed me a house near the water-side, abreast the ship,
which he desired I would make use of, and which was
large enough for all our purposes. He and his brother
Oreepyah then desired I would stay and receive a formal
address and present, which they called Otee. To this I
assented, and a stool was brought for me to sit on. They
then left me with Moannah, and in a short time I saw
Tinah returning with about twenty men, who all made a
stop at some distance, and a priest said a short prayer to
the Eatua, to which the rest made reply. A man was
then sent to me three several times, at each time bringing
me a small pig, and the stem of a plantain leaf. The first
they told me was for the God of Brittannee, the next for
King George, and the last for myself. Moannah then got
up, and, without being dictated to, made an oration for
me; the purport of which I understood to be, that I received their offering with thanks; that we were good
people and friends; and therefore he exhorted them to
commit no thefts: he told them to bring their pigs, cocoa-
nuts, and bread-fruit, and they would receive good things
in return; that we took nothing without their consent;
and finally, that every man was to quit the place (the
house we occupied) at night; for if they made any visit
in the dark, they would be killed. With this speech the
ceremony ended.

I found this a delightful situation, and in every respect
convenient. The ship was perfectly sheltered by the
reefs in smooth water, and close to a fine beach without
the least surf. A small river, with very good water, runs
into the sea about the middle of the harbour. I gave
directions for the plants to be landed, and the same party
to be with them as at Matavai. Tinah fixed his dwelling
close to our station.

Some of the natives took advantage of the butcher's
negligence, and stole his cleaver. I complained of this
to the chiefs who were on board, and they promised that
they would endeavour to recover it; but an article so

valuable as this was to the natives, I had no great expectation of seeing restored.

The ship continued to be supplied by the natives as usual. Cocoa-nuts were in such plenty, that I believe not a pint of water was drunk on board the ship in the twenty-four hours. Bread-fruit began to be scarce, though we purchased, without difficulty, a sufficient quantity for our consumption: there was, however, another harvest approaching, which they expected would be fit for use in five or six weeks. The better kind of plantains also were become scarce; but a kind which they call Vayhee were in great plenty. This fruit does not hang on the trees like the other kinds, but grows upon an upright stalk of considerable strength and substance. Though this plantain is inferior in quality to most of the others, it affords great subsistence to the natives. We received, almost every day, presents of fish, chiefly dolphin and albacore, and a few small rock fish. Their fishing is mostly in the night, when they make strong lights on the reefs, which attract the fish to them. Sometimes, in fine weather, the canoes are out in such numbers, that the whole sea appears illuminated. In the canoes they fish with hook and line, and on the reefs they strike the fish with a spear. Some likewise carry out small nets, which are managed by two men. In the day-time their fishing canoes go without the reefs, sometimes to a considerable distance, where they fish with rods and lines, and catch bonetas, and other fish. Whenever there is a show of fish, a fleet of canoes immediately proceeds to sea. Their hooks being bright, are used without bait, in the manner of our artificial flies. Their rods are made of bamboo; but when there are any very large fish, they make use of an outrigger over the fore part of the canoe, about twenty-five feet in length, which has two prongs at the extremity, to each of which is fastened a hook and line; and when a fish takes the hook, it is raised by ropes managed by two men in the stern of the canoe.

Contrary to my expectation, Tinah, this afternoon, brought on board the cleaver that had been stolen. The thief had taken it to Attahooroo, and Tinah told me, which I could easily believe, that it was given up with great reluctance. The next morning I offered Tinah a present of axes, and other things; but, as he suspected this was meant by way of return for getting the cleaver restored, he would not be prevailed with to accept a single article.

I had constantly the company of Tinah, his wife, and some of his relations; but the royal children, though so near us, never came in sight of the ship. The river separated them from the place occupied by our people on shore; and, for fear of giving alarm or offence, I gave strict orders that no one should attempt to go near their place of residence.

Monday the 5th. At the relief of the watch, at four o'clock this morning, the small cutter was missing. I was immediately informed of it, and mustered the ship's company; when it appeared, that three men were absent, Charles Churchill, the ship's corporal, and two of the seamen, William Musprat, and John Millward; the latter of whom had been sentinel from twelve to two in the morning. They had taken with them eight stand of arms and ammunition; but what their plan was, or which way they had gone, no one on board seemed to have the least knowledge. I went on shore to the chiefs, and soon received information, that the boat was at Matavai; and that the deserters had departed in a sailing canoe for the island Tethuroa. On this intelligence, I sent the master to Matavai to search for the small cutter, and one of the chiefs went with him; but before they had got half way, they met the boat with five of the natives, who were bringing her back to the ship. This service, rendered me by the people of Matavai, pleased me much, and I rewarded the men accordingly.

I told Tinah, and the other chiefs, that I expected they would get the deserters brought back; for that I was determined not to leave Otaheite without them. They assured me, that they would do everything in their power to have them taken; and it was agreed that Oreepyah and Moannah should depart the next morning for Tethuroa. Oreepyah inquired if they had pocket pistols, "for," said he, "though we may surprise and seize them before they can make use of their muskets; yet if they have pistols, they may do mischief, even while they are held." I quieted these apprehensions, by assuring them, that the deserters had no pistols with them.

At daylight, Oreepyah and Moannah set off in two

canoes for Tethuroa, but the weather became so boisterous, that they were obliged to return in the forenoon, and
I was happy to see them get safe in, as the sea ran very
high without the harbour. From the first of this month,
the weather and winds had been much unsettled, with a
great deal of rain. Our former station at Matavai appeared not at all safe, the sea at times breaking high over
the Dolphin bank, and making a great swell in the bay.
Oreepyah and Moannah both promised me, that they
would sail again as soon as the weather should be fine.

The wind continued to blow strong at sea, though in
the harbour we had, at times, but light breezes. Poeeno,
from Matavai, came to see me to-day: he said, he was
apprehensive that I was displeased with him, on account
of our deserters having been carried to Tethuroa, by a
canoe from Matavai. This, he declared, had been done
before he heard of it; and that the only service in his
power, he had not neglected to do for me, which was the
sending our boat back. As this was really an act of
friendship, I received him with great cordiality; and he
assured me, that there could not be no doubt, from the
directions Tinah had given, of the deserters being brought
to the ship, as soon as the weather would admit canoes
to go after them.

One of the officers, this morning, on shore, inadvert-
ently plucked a branch from a tree called Tutuee, that
bears the oil nut, which was growing at a Morai. On
entering with it into the house occupied by our people,
all the natives, both men and women, immediately went
away. When I went on shore, I found this branch tied
to one of the posts of the house, although the effect it
had on the natives was known. I was much displeased at
this piece of wantonness, and ordered the branch to
be taken away; but the natives, notwithstanding, would
not come near the place. They said the house was *taboo,*
which I understand to signify interdicted, and that none
of them might approach it till the *taboo* was taken off,
which could only be done by Tinah. To take anything
away from a Morai is regarded as a kind of sacrilege,
and, they believe, gives great offence to the Eatua. At
my request, Tinah took off the *taboo,* but not before the
afternoon. This was performed by an offering of a
plantain leaf at the Morai, and a prayer made to the.

Eatua. After this ceremony, the house was resorted to by the natives, as usual.

I had not yet given up the hope of obtaining the bull from Itteah, though I had hitherto received no satisfactory answer to the messages which Tinah had sent at my desire: I therefore spoke to Poeeno, who undertook to negotiate this business, and I commissioned him to make very liberal offers. He left me after dinner, to return to Matavai. In the evening, a messenger arrived from him, to acquaint me, that, in his absence, the sheep which I had trusted to his care, had been killed by a dog; and that he had sent the culprit, hoping that I would kill him for the offence he had committed. This poor sheep had been so much diseased, that I could not help suspecting he died without the dog's assistance, and that the story of the dog was invented to prevent my attributing it to want of care. This doubt did not appear in my answer; as for the dog, I told the messenger to do with him what he pleased.

Tuesday the 13th. This morning, the weather being more moderate than it had been for some days past, Oreepyah sailed with two canoes for Tethuroa. Some business prevented Moannah from accompanying him, but he followed the next day with two other canoes. The wood that we had got at Matavai being expended, I applied to Tinah, who sent three trees down to the waterside before night, which when cut up made a good launch load.

I saw two instances of jealousy to-day, one of which had nearly produced fatal consequences. A man was detected with a married woman, by the husband, who stabbed him in the belly with a knife: fortunately the intestines escaped, and the wound did not prove dangerous. The other instance was, a girl, who had constantly lived with my coxswain, beating another girl, that she discovered to have been too intimate with him.

In walking to-day with Tinah near a Tupapow, I was surprised by a sudden outcry of grief. As I expressed a desire to see the distressed person, Tinah took me to the place, where we found a number of women, one of whom was the mother of a young female child that lay dead. On seeing us their mourning not only immediately ceased, but to my astonishment, they all burst into an immoderate fit of laughter, and, while we remained, appeared much diverted with our visit. I told Tinah the woman had no sorrow for her child, otherwise her grief would not have so easily subsided; on which he jocosely told her to cry again: they did not, however, resume their mourning in our presence. This strange behaviour would incline us to think them hard-hearted and unfeeling, did we not know that they are fond parents, and, in general, very affectionate: it is therefore to be ascribed to their extreme levity of disposition; and it is probable, that death does not appear to them with so many terrors, as it does to people of a more serious cast.

Sunday the 18th. I received a message from Poeeno, to acquaint me that he had been successful in his negotiation for the bull, which he had driven part of the way by land, but could not get farther on account of the rivers, and therefore desired a boat should be sent for him. I accordingly ordered the launch to be got ready, and at two o'clock the next morning, Mr. Fryer, the master, set off in her.

In the afternoon, the launch returned with the bull, and my friend Poeeno. For the night I directed that the bull should remain at Oparre, and the next day he was taken to the cow at Matavai.

Wednesday the 21st. To-day, Poeeno brought to me the person from whom he had the bull, to receive the stipulated payment, which was one of every article of traffic that I had in my possession. This man, whose name was Oweevee, they told me, was inspired by a divine spirit; and that in all matters of consequence he was consulted, for that he conversed with the Eatua. It was, they said, the Eatua that ordered him to demand the bull from Tinah, which not to have complied with, would have been the height of impiety. I endeavoured to convince them of the roguery of this man, thinking I had a fair argument to prove it by his selling that which the Eatua had ordered him to keep; but here I was easily defeated, for it seems the Eatua told him to sell me the beast. This being the case, I said, I would not give the animals to any person; that they were now mine, and that I would leave them under the protection of Poeeno and Tinah, who I hoped would take care of them for me till I returned. They both entered into my views, and promised the animals should be attended to, and told me, that while they were considered as my property, no one would attempt to take them away.

Thursday the 22nd. This afternoon, I received a message from Teppahoo, to inform me that our deserters had passed this harbour, and were at Tettaha, about five miles distant. I ordered the cutter to be got ready, and a little before sunset left the ship, taking Oediddee with me. By his advice I landed at some distance from the place where the deserters were; but thinking it necessary to have the boat within call, and Oediddee assuring me that there was safe landing farther on, I directed the boat to proceed along shore, whilst Oediddee and I walked along the beach. The night was very dark and windy, and the shore being rocky, I soon lost sight of the boat. A few of the natives had joined us in our walk; and, from their manner, I had reason to suspect them of a design to close upon us, with an intention, no doubt, to plunder: I was provided with pocket-pistols, and on producing one, they left us. Oediddee was so much alarmed that I could scarce prevail on him to proceed. When we arrived at Teppahoo's house, we were very kindly received by him and his wife. The cutter was arrived, but, there being a very high surf, she could not come within a hundred yards of the shore.

The deserters, I was informed, were in a house close to us, and I imagined there would be no great difficulty in securing them, with the assistance of the natives. They had, however, heard of my arrival; and when I was near the house, they came out, without their arms, and delivered themselves up. I sent directions off to the boat for one of my people to come on shore, and for the boat to return to the place where I had landed. My next business was to secure the arms, which I delivered to Teppahoo to take charge of for the night. One musket and two bayonets were missing, which they said were lost, by the canoe in which they came from Tethuroa having overset. I then took leave of Teppahoo, who presented us with a plentiful supply of provisions, and we proceeded with the deserters towards the boat; but as the wind had increased, and it rained hard, I determined to remain on shore till the morning; and having found shelter for the people, we passed the remainder of the night without accident. At daylight, I sent for the arms, and we returned to the ship.

I learnt from the deserters, that at Tethuroa they had seen Oreepyah and Moannah, who had made an attempt to secure them. They said it was their intention to have returned to the ship; and it is probable that they were so much harassed by the natives watching for an opportunity to surprise them, that they might wish to have the merit of returning of their own accord, to avoid the disgrace of being seized and brought back. At the time they delivered themselves up to me, it was not in their power to have made resistance, their ammunition having been spoiled by the wet.

In consequence of my having been kept all night from the ship by the tempestuous weather, the time-keeper went down at 10^h $5''$ $36'$. Its rate, previous to this, was $1''$, 7 losing in 24 hours, and its error from the mean time at Greenwich was $7'$ $29''$, 2 too slow. I set it going again by a common watch, corrected by observations, and endeavoured to make the error the same as if it had not stopped; but being over cautious, made me tedious in setting it in motion, and increased the error from mean time at Greenwich. The rate of going I did not find to have altered.

At dinner, Tinah congratulated me on having recovered my men, but expressed some concern that they had not been brought by Oreepyah and Moannah; lest I should imagine they had not done everything in their power. To this I replied, that I was perfectly satisfied of their good intentions to serve me, and that I considered myself under great obligations to them for the trouble they had been at on my account. I learnt afterwards that they had actually seized and bound the deserters, but had been prevailed upon, by fair promises of their returning peaceably to the ship, to let them loose: the deserters, however, finding an opportunity to get possession of their arms again, set the natives at defiance.

This afternoon, I punished one of the seamen, Isaac Martin, with nineteen lashes, for striking an Indian. This was a transgression of so serious a nature, and such a direct violation of my orders, that I would on no account be prevailed on to forgive it, though great intercession was made by some of the chiefs.

Oreepyah and Moannah were not yet returned from Tethuroa. This place is resorted to by the principal people of this part of Otaheite, at particular seasons, when fish are in great plenty there. It was described to me to be a group of small keys, surrounded by a reef: their produce is chiefly cocoa-nuts and plantains. During the season, bread-fruit and other provisions are daily carried over from Otaheite. Not less than a hundred sail of canoes were at Tethuroa when our deserters were there.

Teppahoo and his wife were become my constant visitors: he had for some time past been ill, and had made Oparre his place of residence, for the benefit of our surgeon's advice and assistance. At this time he complained of a hoarseness and sore-throat. Mr. Ledward, on examining him, discovered there had been two holes in the roof of his mouth, which, though healed, had the appearance of having been large: the adjacent parts appeared sound, yet the surgeon was of opinion that they were cancerous, and would in the end occasion his death.

This morning, I ordered all the chests to be taken on shore, and the inside of the ship to be washed with boiling water, to kill the cockroaches. We were constantly obliged to be at great pains to keep the ship clear of vermin, on account of the plants.—By the help of traps and good cats, we were freed from rats and mice. When I was at Otaheite with Captain Cook, there were great numbers of rats about all the houses, and so tame, that they flocked round the people at their meals for the offals, which were commonly thrown to them; but, at this time, we scarcely ever saw a rat, which must be attributed to the industry of a breed of cats left here by European ships.

After breakfast, I walked with Tinah to Matavai, to see the cattle and the gardens. Tinah had already taken so large a dose of the Ava, that he was perfectly stupefied. Iddeah, however, was with us, and she is one of the most intelligent persons I met with at Otaheite. We went first to Poeeno's house, and saw the bull and cow together in a very fine pasture. I was informed that the cow had taken the bull; so that, if no untoward accident happens, there is a fair chance of the breed being established. In the garden, near Poeeno's house, many things had failed. The Indian corn was in a fine state, and I have no doubt but they will cultivate it all over the country. A fig-tree was in a very thriving way, as were two vines, a pineapple plant, and some slips of a shaddock-tree. From this place, we walked to the garden at Point Venus; but I had the mortification to find almost everything there destroyed by the hogs. Some underground pease and Indian corn had escaped, and likewise the caliloo green and ocra of Jamaica.

We returned to the ship; and after dinner I was not a little surprised to hear Tinah seriously propose that he and his wife should go with me to England. He said he would only take two servants; that he much wished to see King George, who, he was sure, would be glad to see him. Tinah and many of his countrymen were become extremely eager to get a knowledge of other countries, and were continually inquiring about the situations of the islands which we told them of in these seas. To quiet his importunity, I was obliged to promise, that I would ask the king's permission to carry them to England, if I came again; that then I should be in a larger ship, and could have accommodations properly fitted up. I was sorry to find, that Tinah was apprehensive he should be attacked by his enemies, as soon as our ship left Otaheite, and that if they joined, they would be too powerful for him. The illness of Teppahoo, with whom he was on good terms, gave him much uneasiness; Teppahoo's wife being a sister of Otow's and aunt to Tinah. They have no children, as has been before related; and if Teppahoo were to die, he would be succeeded, as Earee of the district of Tettaha, by his brother, who is an enemy of Tinah. I have on every occasion endeavoured to make the principal people believe that we should return again to Otaheite, and that we should revenge any injury done in our absence to the people of Matavai and Oparre.

The wife of Oediddee is likewise an aunt to Tinah, and sister to Otow. His native place is Ulietea, where he has some property; but which, I imagine, is not of such consequence to him as the countenance of the chiefs with whom he is connected at Otaheite.

CHAPTER X

I WAS present, this afternoon, at a wrestling match,
where a young man, by an unlucky fall, put his arm out
of joint at the elbow: three stout men immediately took
hold of him, and two of them fixing their feet against his
ribs, replaced it. I had sent for our surgeon, but before he
arrived, all was well, except a small swelling of the mus-
cles, in consequence of the strain. I enquired what they
would have done if the bone had been broken; and, to
show me their practice, they got a number of sticks and
placed round a man's arm, which they bound with cord.
That they have considerable skill in surgery is not to be
doubted. I have before mentioned an instance of an
amputated arm being perfectly healed, and which had
every appearance of having been treated with great
propriety.

The part of the beach nearest the ship was become the
general place of resort towards the close of the day. An
hour before sunset, the inhabitants began to collect, and
here they amused themselves with exercising the lance,
dancing, and various kinds of merriment, till nearly dark,
when they retired to their homes. Of this cheerful scene,
we were spectators and partakers, every fine evening.

Friday the 6th. An occurrence happened to-day that
gave me great concern, not only on account of the danger
with which the ship had been threatened, but as it tended
greatly to diminish the confidence and good understanding which had hitherto been constantly preserved between
us and the natives. The wind had blown fresh in the
night, and at daylight we discovered that the cable, by
which the ship rode, had been cut near the water's edge,
in such a manner, that only one strand remained whole.
While we were securing the ship, Tinah came on board.
I could not but believe he was perfectly innocent of the

transaction; nevertheless, I spoke to him in a very peremptory manner, and insisted upon his discovering and bringing to me the offender. I was wholly at a loss how to account for this malicious act. My suspicions fell chiefly, I may say wholly, on the strangers that came to us from other parts of the island; for we had on every occasion received such unreserved and unaffected marks of good will from the people of Matavai and Oparre, that in my own mind I entirely acquitted them. The anger which I expressed, however, created so much alarm, that old Otow and his wife (the father and mother of Tinah) immediately quitted Oparre, and retired to the mountains in the midst of heavy rain, as did Teppahoo and his family. Tinah and Iddeah remained, and expostulated with me on the unreasonableness of my anger against them. He said, that he would exert his utmost endeavours to discover the guilty person; but it might possibly not be in his power to get him delivered up, which would be the case, if he was either of Tiarraboo, Attahooroo, or of the island Eimeo. That the attempt might have been made as much out of enmity to the people of Matavai and Oparre as to me; every one knowing the regard I had for them, and that I had declared I would protect them against their enemies. All this I was inclined to believe; but I did not think proper to appear perfectly satisfied, lest Tinah, who was naturally very indolent, should be remiss in his endeavours to detect the offender. To guard as much as possible against future attempts of this kind, I directed a stage to be built on the forecastle, so that the cables should be more directly under the eye of the sentinel; and I likewise gave orders that one of the midshipmen should keep watch forward.

In the afternoon, Oreepyah returned from Tethuroa. He told me, that Moannah and himself had narrowly escaped being lost in the bad weather, and that Moannah had been obliged to take shelter at Eimeo. Several canoes had been lost lately in their passage to or from Tethuroa. The oversetting of their canoes is not the only risk they have to encounter, but is productive of another danger more dreadful; for at such times many become a prey to the sharks, which are very numerous in these seas. I was informed likewise, that they were sometimes attacked by a fish, which, by their description, I imagine to be the barracoota, as they attribute to it the same propensity.

Saturday passed without my seeing anything of Tinah the whole day. The next morning, he and Iddeah came to me, and assured me that they had made the strictest enquiries concerning the injury intended us, but had not been able to discover any circumstance which could lead them to suspect who were concerned in it. This was not at all satisfactory, and I behaved towards them with great coolness, at which they were much distressed; and Iddeah, at length, gave vent to her sorrow by tears. I could no longer keep up the appearance of mistrusting them; but I earnestly recommended to them, as they valued the King of England's friendship, that they would exert their utmost endeavours to find out the offenders; which they faithfully promised. Our reconciliation accordingly took place, and messengers were sent to acquaint Otow and Teppahoo, and to invite them to return.

It has since occurred to me, that this attempt to cut the ship adrift, was most probably the act of some of our own people; whose purpose of remaining at Otaheite might have been effectually answered, without danger, if the ship had been driven on shore. At the time, I entertained not the least thought of this kind, nor did the possibility of it enter into my ideas, having no suspicion that so general an inclination, or so strong an attachment to these islands, could prevail among my people, as to induce them to abandon every prospect of returning to their native country.

A messenger came to me this afternoon, from the Earee of Tiarrabou, the S E division of Otaheite, with an invitation for me to visit him. I excused myself on account of the distance, and, at Tinah's request, sent back by the messenger a handsome present, which I hope Tinah will get the credit of. I observed, with much satisfaction, that a great part of what Tinah had received from me, he had distributed; to some, out of friendship and esteem, and to others, from motives of political civility.

Teppahoo and his family left us to-day to go to Tettaha, where a grand *heiva* was to be performed, at which their presence was required.

A small party of *heiva* people passed through Oparre this morning, on their way to Tettaha, where they were going by appointment. They had the civility to send me word, that, if I chose, they would stay to perform a short *heiva* before me; and I immediately attended. It began by a dance of two young girls, to the music of drums and flutes, which lasted no long time; at the conclusion, they suddenly dropped all their dress, which was left as a present for me, and went off without my seeing them any more. After this, the men danced: their performance was more indecent than any I had before seen, but was not the less applauded on that account by the natives, who seemed much delighted.

After this entertainment, I went with Tinah and Iddeah, to pay a visit to an old lady named Wanow-oora, widow to Towah, the late Earee of Tettaha, who conducted the expedition against Eimeo, when Captain Cook was here in 1777. The old lady had just landed, and we found her sitting on the beach, by the head of her canoe. With Tinah, was a priest and three men, who carried a young dog, a fowl, and two young plantain boughs: these were intended for the offering, or present, called Otee. Tinah and his party seated themselves at about ten yards distance from Wanow-oora, and were addressed by her, in short sentences, for a few minutes, and received her Otee, which was exactly the same as his. Tinah's priest, in return, made a short prayer, and his offering was presented to the old lady. Tinah then rose and went to her, and embraced her in a very affectionate manner; and she returned his kindness with tears, and many expressions which I could not understand. Soon after, he conducted her to a shed, and we remained with her till it was time to go on board to dinner. I invited her to be of the party, but she excused herself on account of age and infirmity. Tinah gave directions for her and her attendants to be supplied with whatever they had occasion for, and we went off to the ship.

Friday the 13th. This forenoon, Tinah sent to inform me, that many strangers were arrived from all parts, to be present at a grand *heiva,* which he had prepared in compliment to me. I accordingly went on shore, and found a great crowd of people collected together. A ring was made at a little distance from our post, and Tinah and several other chiefs came to meet me. When we were all seated, the *heiva* began by women dancing; after which a present of cloth, and a *tawme* or breast-plate was laid before me. This ceremony being over, the men began to wrestle, and regularity was no longer preserved. Old Otow came to me, and desired I would help to put a stop to the wrestling, as the people came from different districts, some of which were ill disposed towards others. What Otow had apprehended was not without reason, for in an instant the whole was tumult: every man took to his arms, and, as I found my single interference could be of no service, I retired to our post, and ordered all my people there under arms. At the time the disturbance began, Tinah and Iddeah were absent: their first care was for me, and Iddeah came to see if I was safe at the post. She had a double covering of cloth round her, and her waist was girded with a large rope. I desired her to stay under my protection: this she would not consent to, but said she would return as soon as all was over; and away she went.

I immediately gave orders for two guns to be fired from the ship without shot, which had a good effect: and, as no chief was concerned in the tumult, but, on the contrary, all of them exerted their influence to prevent mischief, every thing was soon quiet, and Tinah and Iddeah returned to let me know that all was settled. They went on board, with some other chiefs, and dined with me.

After dinner, I went on shore with Tinah and his friends; and I found three large hogs dressed, and a quantity of bread-fruit, which he had ordered to be prepared before he went on board, and now desired I would present them to the different parties that had come to see the entertainment:—one to the chief people of Attahooroo, one to the *Arreoys,* and a third to the performers of the *heiva.* I presented them according to his directions, and they were received with thankfulness and pleasure. This I looked upon as very handsomely done on the part of Tinah, and I was glad to see that it was regarded in the same light by his guests. These instances of liberality make full amends for the little slips which I have formerly noticed in Tinah. At this time, a day seldom passed, that he did not give proofs of his hospitality, by entertaining the principal people that came from different parts of the island to visit him, or to see the ship. Some of the chiefs he commonly invited to dine on board, and made provi-

sion for others on shore. Scarce any person of consequence went away without receiving some present from
him. This I encouraged, and was glad it was in my power
to assist him. But, besides the political motives that I have
alluded to, it would be unjust to Tinah not to acknowl-
edge that his disposition seemed improved: he was more
open and unreserved in his manners than formerly, and
his hospitality was natural and without ostentation.

Monday the 16th. I was present this afternoon, at a
wrestling match by women. The manner of challenging,
and method of attack, was exactly the same as among the
men. The only difference that I could observe, was not
in favour of the softer sex; for in these contests they
showed less temper and more animosity than I could have
imagined them capable of. The women, I was told, not
only wrestle with each other, but sometimes with the
men; of this I have never seen an instance, and imagine
it can happen but seldom, as the women in general are
small, and by no means masculine. Iddeah is said to be
very famous at this exercise.

I walked with Tinah towards the hills, to see his country residence, which was at a very neat house, pleasantly
situated, and surrounded with plantations. From this
place we saw the island Tethuroa. The next morning, I
went to Matavai, to look after the Indian corn, which
I judged would be full ripe for gathering; but, on my arrival, I found that the natives had been before hand with
me, the whole being taken away. This I was not at all
sorry for, as it shows that they value it too much to
neglect cultivating it.

Iddeah sent on board, for our dinners to-day, a very
fine tarro pudding; and Tinah brought a bunch of
bananas, that weighed 81 lbs., on which were 286 fine
fruit: ten had broken off in the carriage. The tarro pudding is excellent eating, and easily made: I shall describe
this piece of cookery, as the knowledge of it may be
useful in the West Indies. The tarro being cleared of the
outside skin, is grated down, and made up in rolls of
about half a pound each, which they cover neatly with
leaves, and bake for near half an hour. An equal quantity
of ripe cocoa-nut meat is likewise grated, from which,
through a strainer, the rich milky juice is expressed. This
juice is heated, by putting smooth hot stones in the vessel

that contains it, and the tarro is then mixed with it, and
kept constantly stirring to prevent burning, till it is ready,
which is known by the cocoa-nut juice turning to a clear
oil.

Iddeah was very uneasy to-day, on account of her
youngest child being ill. She would not accept of assistance from our surgeon, but said she had sent to Tettaha
for a man, who she expected would come and tell her
what to do. These physical people are called *Tata rapaow*.

Thursday the 26th. This morning, a man died of a consumption, about two miles from our post. I was informed
of it by Mr. Peckover, the gunner, who I had desired to
look out for such a circumstance. I therefore went, accompanied by Iddeah, in hopes of seeing the funeral
ceremony; but before we arrived, the body was removed
to the Toopapow. It lay bare, except a piece of cloth
round the loins, and another round the neck: the eyes
were closed: the hands were placed, one over the pit of
the stomach, and the other upon his breast. On a finger
of each hand was a ring, made of plaited fibres of the
cocoa-nut tree, with a small bunch of red feathers. Under
the Toopapow a hole was dug, in which, at the end of a
month, the corpse was to be buried. The deceased was of
the lower class; the Toopapow, however, was neat, and
offerings of cocoa-nuts and plaited leaves lay on the
ground.

The dead are sometimes brought to the Toopapow in
wooden coffins, which are not shaped like ours, but are
simply a long box. This custom, Iddeah informed me,
they learnt from the Europeans, and is not very common,
as making plank is a work of great labour.

Monday, March the 2nd. When I landed this morning,
I found the inhabitants, that lived near to us, had left
their houses, and retired towards the mountains; and was
informed that in the night a water cask, part of an azi-
muth compass, and Mr. Peckover's bedding, had been
stolen from the post on shore; the knowledge of which
had caused a general alarm. I sent a message to complain
of this theft to Tinah, who did not come near me. About
two hours elapsed, during which time I went on board to
breakfast, and returned, when I saw Tinah and Oreepyah,
with a number of people, at a house at some distance; and
soon after they all marched to the eastward, passing close

by our post. Oediddee, who was with me, told me that they had intelligence of the thief, and were gone in quest of him: and in less than an hour, news was brought that they had taken him. Shortly after, the whole party appeared, with the water-cask and compass. Tinah had hold of the thief by the arm, and, showing him to me, desired that I would kill him. The bedding, he said, he had not heard of, but would go in search of it. I applauded him for the pains he had taken in this business, and explained, with some success, the injustice of stealing from us: that if any of our people committed the least offence against them, it did not pass unnoticed; and that friendship required on their part, that those who injured us should not be protected by them. Tinah stopped me from saying more by embracing me, and the whole crowd cried out *Tyo mity* (i.e., good friend). Tinah then left me, to enquire after the bedding, and I sent the offender on board, whom I punished with a severe flogging. I was glad to find this man was not of Oparre or Matavai.

The fine fruit, called Avee, was just coming into season: it was likewise in season at the time of our arrival in October. The bread-fruit trees, I have no doubt, bear all the year round: we have seen a scarcity of bread-fruit, but have never been wholly without it. Some fern-root was shown to me, which, in scarce seasons, is used by the natives as bread. It bears a long even-edged leaf, about an inch wide; the taste somewhat resembled that of a yam. I was informed by our people, that in their walks they saw, in many places, patches of Indian corn just making their appearance through the ground. This convinces me that the corn taken from Matavai could not have been better disposed of.

Goats are frequently offered for sale, but I rather discouraged the buying of them, for fear of injuring the breed. The natives will not eat them, neither will they taste the milk; and ask, with some appearance of disgust, why we do not milk the sows? I endeavoured to prevail on Tinah and Iddeah to eat the goats' milk, by mixing it with fruit, but they would only try one spoonful.

We had begun to make preparations for sailing; and Tinah supplied us with a sufficient stock of wood, by ordering trees to be brought down from the country. He had frequently expressed a wish that I would leave some

firearms and ammunition with him, as he expected to be
attacked after the ship sailed; and, perhaps, chiefly on
account of our partiality to him: I, therefore, thought it
but reasonable to attend to his request; and I was the
more readily prevailed on, as he said his intentions were
to act only on the defensive. This indeed seems most
suited to his disposition, which is neither active nor enter-
prising. If Tinah had spirit in proportion to his size and
strength, he would probably be the greatest warrior in
Otaheite: but courage is not the most conspicuous of his
virtues. When I promised to leave with him a pair of
pistols, which they prefer to muskets, he told me, that
Iddeah would fight with one, and Oediddee with the
other. Iddeah has learnt to load and fire a musket with
great dexterity, and Oediddee is an excellent marksman.
It is not common for women in this country to go to war,
but Iddeah is a very resolute woman, of a large make,
and has great bodily strength.

Friday the 6th. I sent Mr. Fryer, the master, to sound
Taowne harbour. The knowledge that we intended shortly
to sail, having spread among the natives, a great many
broken iron tools were brought from all parts of the island, to be repaired at our forge; and this morning, a
messenger arrived from Waheatua, the Earee of Tiarraboo, with several pieces of Spanish iron, which he desired
to have made into small adzes. This request was, of
course, complied with.

CHAPTER XI

FROM the 5th to the 14th of this month, the wind blew constantly from between the N W and S W, with a great deal of rain. This was the longest continuance of westerly winds without interruption that we experienced. On the 13th, several canoes arrived here, and at Matavai, from Tethuroa: in these were a large tribe of the *Arreoys,* and among them Huheine Moyere, the wife of Oreepyah, who is an *Arreoy* woman, and remained at Tethuroa after Oreepyah came away. On her arrival, a ceremony was performed, called Hooepippee, which seemed to be designed as a public visit to all their friends, who are collected on the occasion. In this ceremony, there was nothing remarkable: the *Arreoy* men took their opportunity to plunder the women who were near them, and Iddeah made a present of some cloth to Huheine Moyere, and a baked hog to the *Arreoys.*

After this ceremony, a present was produced from many of the principal people, for young Otoo, the Earee Rahie; which was received by Iddeah, Tinah being absent. This present consisted of five hogs, and forty-eight baskets filled with bread-fruit, cocoa-nuts, tarro, and different kinds of puddings. The baskets were decorated with slips of cloth, stained with variety of colours, and carried by 24 men, each of whom had a pole on his shoulder, at each end of which was a basket.

I have seldom spoken of Otoo, who was too young to have any share in the management of affairs, and with whom we were not permitted to have any intercourse, except speaking to him now and then, across a river; at which times, I did not neglect to send the children some little presents, so that they always rejoiced to see me. I might have been admitted to a nearer acquaintance, if I would have gone with my shoulders uncovered, as his

parents did, but this I declined. The children do not all
live under the same roof, the two sisters eating and sleep-
ing in a separate house, though at other times, they are
generally together.

The island Tethuroa may very properly be compared
to some of our watering places in England, producing a
similar effect upon those who visit it. Many, who went
there covered with scurf, returned plump and fair, and
scarce like the same people. This alteration for the better,
is in a great measure to be attributed to the discontin-
uance of the Ava, which Tethuroa does not produce: the
cocoa-nut trees, likewise, which supply them with their
only beverage, growing on low sandy keys, and having
their roots below the level of the sea, may probably have
qualities different from the cocoa-nuts of Otaheite; which,
with a plenty of fish, that at other times they are not accustomed to, must no doubt contribute to the amendment
described.

Saturday 14th. I was visited to-day by a very old man,
an uncle to Tupia, the person who went from these islands in the *Endeavour,* in the year 1769, and who died
at Batavia. He appeared to be near 70 years old, and was
treated with much respect by the natives. He made several enquiries concerning his nephew, and requested that
when I came again, I would bring his hair. At the time
that Tinah mentioned to me his desire of visiting England,
I asked what account I could give to his friends, if he
should not live to return; to which he replied, that I must
cut off his hair, and carry it to them, and they would be
perfectly satisfied.

On the 16th, I was informed, that a stop was put to
the sale of hogs, in the district of Tettaha. Teppahoo, the
Earee of that district, told me that they had very few hogs
left there, and that it was necessary, for a certain time, to
prohibit every person from killing or selling, that they
might have time to breed. I did not think it reasonable
to solicit any indulgence on this head: my friends at
Matavai and Oparre promised to supply us, as long as we
remained here, though we had considerably thinned their
stock. After our departure, the same restriction was to
take place in these districts, and it being delayed on our
account, certainly deserves to be regarded among their
acts of friendship towards us.

As it was generally known that we were preparing to sail, a number of the natives from other parts of the island were constantly with us, and petty thefts were committed, whenever the negligence of our people afforded an opportunity: but no attempt of any consequence was made.

This evening, Mr. Samuel, my clerk, returned from an excursion to the mountains, having been two days absent. He described the hills to be well clothed with wood, except the tops of the higher mountains, which only produced bushes and fern. The birds he saw, were blue paroquets and green doves, except one, which he found burrowing in the ground, and brought to me. This bird was about the size of a pigeon, and proved to be a white-bellied petterel, of the same kind as those seen in high latitudes, which are called sheerwaters. He likewise brought a branch of a plant, like the New Zealand tea-plant, and which, at Van Diemen's Land, we had made use of for brooms. From the hills he saw the islands Maitea and Huaheine, which are situated nearly in opposite directions from Otaheite, and are 70 leagues distant from each other.

For some days past, Tinah had been busied in getting two *Parais,* or mourning-dresses, made, which he intended as a present to King George. Being finished, they were this morning hung up in his house, as a public exhibition, and a long prayer made on the occasion; the substance of which was, that the King of England might for ever remain his friend, and not forget him. When he presented the *parais* for me to take on board, he could not refrain from shedding tears. During the short remainder of our stay here, there appeared among the natives an evident degree of sorrow, that we were so soon to leave them, which they showed by unusual kindness and attention.

We began, this afternoon, to remove the plants to the ship. They were in excellent order: the roots had appeared through the bottom of the pots, and would have shot into the ground, if care had not been taken to prevent it.

The weather was considerably altered for the better, and the trade-wind appeared settled. The rainy and bad season of the year may be reckoned to begin towards the end of November, and to continue till near the end of March. During this time, the winds are variable, and often westerly, though we seldom found them to blow strong in that direction. We likewise experienced frequent intervals of fine weather; but, during these months, so open a road as Matavai bay is not a safe anchoring-place for ships that intend remaining any length of time at Otaheite.

Tuesday the 31st. To-day, all the plants were on board, being in 774 pots, 39 tubs, and 24 boxes. The number of bread-fruit plants were 1,015: besides which, we had collected a number of other plants. The *avee,* which is one of the finest-flavoured fruits in the world. The *ayyah,* which is a fruit not so rich, but of a fine flavour and very refreshing. The *rattah,* not much unlike a chestnut, which grows on a large tree, in great quantities: they are singly in large pods, from 1 to 2 inches broad; and may be eaten raw, or boiled in the same manner as Windsor beans, and so dressed, are equally good. The *orai-ah,* which is a very superior kind of plantain. All these I was particularly recommended to collect, by my worthy friend, Sir Joseph Banks. I had also taken on board some plants of the *ettow* and *matte,* with which the natives here make a beautiful red colour; and a root called *peeah,* of which they make an excellent pudding.

I now made my last presents to several of my friends, with whom I had been most intimate, particularly to Teppahoo. Several people expressed great desire to go with us to England. Oediddee, who was always very much attached to us, said, he considered it as his right, having formerly left his native place, to sail with Captain Cook. Scarce any man belonging to the ship was without a *tyo,* who brought to him presents, chiefly of provisions for a sea store.

Friday the 3d April. Tinah and his wife, with his parents, brothers, and sister, dined with me to-day, and, as I meant to sail early the next morning, they all remained on board for the night. The ship was crowded the whole day with the natives, and we were loaded with cocoa-nuts, plantains, bread-fruit, hogs, and goats. In the evening, there was no dancing or mirth on the beach, such as we had been accustomed to, but all was silent.

At daylight, we unmoored: the stock of the best bower anchor was so much eaten by the worms, that it broke in stowing the anchor: the small bower had an iron stock;

and in these voyages, it is very necessary that ships should be provided with iron anchor stocks. At half past six, there being no wind, we weighed, and, with our boats and two sweeps, towed the ship out of the harbour. Soon after, the sea breeze came, and we stood off towards the sea.

The outlet of Toahroah harbour being narrow, I could permit only a few of the natives to be on board: many others, however, attended in canoes, till the breeze came, when I was obliged to leave them. We stood off and on, almost all the remainder of the day. Tinah and Iddeah pressed me very strongly to anchor in Matavai Bay, and stay one night longer; but, as I had already taken leave of most of my friends, I thought it better to keep to my intention of sailing. After dinner, I ordered the presents which I had reserved for Tinah and his wife, to be put in one of the ship's boats, and, as I had promised him fire-arms, I gave him two muskets, a pair of pistols, and a good stock of ammunition. I then represented to them, the necessity of their going away, that the boat might return to the ship before it was dark; on which they took a most affectionate leave of me, and went into the boat. One of their expressions, at parting, was *"Yourah no t' Eatua tee eveerah."* "May the Eatua protect you, for ever and ever."

All the time that we remained at Otaheite, the picture of Captain Cook, at the desire of Tinah, was kept on board the ship. On delivering it to him, I wrote on the back, the time of the ship's arrival and departure, with an account of the number of plants on board.

Tinah had desired that I would salute him, at his departure, with the great guns, which I could not comply with, for fear of disturbing the plants; but, as a parting token of our regard, we manned ship with all hands, and gave him three cheers. At sunset, the boat returned, and we made sail, bidding farewell to Otaheite, where for twenty-three weeks we had been treated with the utmost affection and regard, and which seemed to increase in proportion to our stay. That we were not insensible to their kindness, the events which followed more than sufficiently proves: for to the friendly and endearing behaviour of these people, may be ascribed the motives for that event which effected the ruin of an expedition, that there was every reason to·hope, would have been completed in the most fortunate manner.

To enter into a description of the island, or its inhabitants, I look upon as superfluous. From the accounts of former voyages, and the facts which I have related, the character of the people will appear in as true a light, as by any description in my power to give. The length of time that we remained at Otaheite, with the advantage of having been there before, gave me opportunities of making, perhaps, a more perfect vocabulary of the language, than has yet appeared; but I have chosen to defer it for the present, as there is a probability that I may hereafter be better qualified for such a task.

We left Otaheite with only two patients in the venereal list, which shows that the disease has not gained ground. The natives say that it is of little consequence, and we saw several instances of people that had been infected, who, after absenting themselves for 15 or 20 days, made their appearance again, without any visible symptom remaining of the disease. Their method of cure I am unacquainted with; but their customary diet, and mode of living, must contribute towards it. We saw a great many people, however, with scrofulous habits, and bad sores: these they denied to be produced from any venereal cause; and our surgeon was of the same opinion.

The result of the mean of 50 sets of lunar observations, taken by me on shore, gives for the Longitude of Point Venus .... 210 33 57 E
Captain Cook, in 1769, places it in 210 27 30
In 1777, his last voyage 210 22 28

The tide, in Toahroah harbour, was very inconsiderable, and not regular. The greatest rise that I observed, was 11 inches; but, what was most singular, the time of high water did not appear to be governed by the moon, it being at the highest, every day, between noon and two o'clock. The variable winds and weather, at this time of the year, has no doubt an influence on the tides: on some days, scarce any rise was perceptible.

CHAPTER XII

*At the Island Huaheine—A Friend of Omai visits the Ship
—Leave the Society Islands—A Water-spout—The Island
Whytootackee discovered—Anchor in Annamooka Road
—Our Parties on Shore robbed by the Natives—Sail from
Annamooka—The Chiefs detained on board—Part
friendly*

WE steered towards the island Huaheine, which we
got sight of the next morning. At noon we brought
to, near the entrance of Owharre harbour, it not being my
intention to anchor. We could see every part of the harbour distinctly, but my attention was particularly directed
to the spot where Omai's house had stood, no part of
which was now visible. It was near three o'clock before
any canoes came off to us, for the people on shore imagined that the ship was coming into the harbour. The first
that arrived, had three men in it, who brought a few
cocoa-nuts. I enquired about the chief, or Earee Rahie;
and one of the fellows, with great gravity, said, he was
the Earee Rahie, and that he had come to desire I would
bring the ship into the harbour. I could not help laughing
at his impudence: however, I gave him a few nails for his
cocoa-nuts, and he left us. Immediately after, a double
canoe, in which were ten men, came alongside; among
them was a young man, who recollected and called me by
my name. Several other canoes arrived, with hogs, yams,
and other provisions, which we purchased. My acquaintance told me that he had lived with our friend Omai. He
confirmed the account that has already been given, and
informed me, that, of all the animals which had been left
with Omai, the mare only remained alive. He said that
Omai and himself had often rode together; and I
observed, that many of the islanders, who came on board,
had the representation of a man on horseback tattooed on
their legs. After the death of Omai, his house was broken
to pieces, and the materials stolen. The firearms were at
Ulietea, but useless. I enquired after the seeds and plants,
and was informed that they were all destroyed, except one

tree; but of what kind that was, I could not make out
from their description. I was much pressed to take the
ship into the harbour, and Omai's companion requested
me to let him go to England. When they found that I
would not stop among them, they seemed jealous of our
going to Ulietea, and it appeared to give them some satisfaction, when I told them that I should not go near that
island.

The canoes had left us, and we were making sail, when
we discovered an Indian in the water, swimming towards
the shore, which in all probability he would not have been
able to reach. We took him up, and, luckily, another
canoe coming alongside, we put him in her. The people
of the canoe said that the man was insane; but how he
came to be swimming so far from the land, we could not
conjecture. At six o'clock we made sail, and ran all night
to the S W, and S W by S, between the islands Huaheine
and Ulietea. The next morning, I altered the course,
steering more to the westward, for the Friendly Islands.

On the 9th, at nine o'clock in the morning, the weather
became squally, and a body of thick black clouds collected in the E. Soon after, a water-spout was seen at no
great distance from us, which appeared to great advantage
from the darkness of the clouds behind it. As nearly as I
could judge, it was about two feet diameter at the upper
part, and about eight inches at the lower. I had scarce
made these remarks, when I observed that it was advancing rapidly towards the ship. We immediately altered our
course, and took in all the sails, except the fore-sail; soon
after which, it passed within ten yards of our stern, making a rustling noise, but without our feeling the least effect
from its being so near us. The rate at which it travelled,
I judged to be about ten miles per hour, going towards the
W in the direction of the wind. In a quarter of an hour
after passing us, it dispersed. I never was so near a water-
spout before: the connexion between the column, which
was higher than our mast-heads, and the water below, was
no otherwise visible, than by the sea being disturbed in a
circular space of about six yards in diameter, the centre
of which, from the whirling of the water round it, formed
a hollow; and from the outer parts of the circle, the water
was thrown up with much force, in a spiral direction, and
could be traced to the height of 15 or 20 feet. At this ele-

vation we lost sight of it, and could see nothing of its junction with the column above. It is impossible to say what injury we should have suffered, if it had passed directly over us. Masts, I imagine, might have been carried away, but I do not apprehend it would have endangered the loss of a ship.

As we sailed very near the track made in former voyages, I had little reason to expect that we should at this time make any new discovery: nevertheless, on the 11th, at daylight, land was seen to the S S W, at about five leagues distance, which appeared to be an island of a moderate height. On the north part was a round hill: the northwest part was highest and steep: the southeast part sloped off to a low point.

The wind had been westerly since the preceding noon, and at the time we saw the land, the ship was standing to the N W. At six, we tacked to the southward, and, as we advanced in that direction, discovered a number of low keys, of which at noon we counted nine: they were all covered with trees. The large island first seen had a most fruitful appearance, its shore being bordered with flat land, on which grew innumerable cocoa-nut and other trees; and the higher grounds beautifully interspersed with lawns. The wind being light and unfavourable, we endeavoured all day, but without success, to get near the land. In the night we had a heavy squall, which obliged us to clew up all our sails, and soon after it fell calm.

On the 12th, the winds were light and variable all day, with calms. At two in the afternoon, we were within 3 miles of the southernmost key, and could see a number of people within the reefs. Shortly after, a canoe, in which were four men, paddled off to us, and came alongside, without showing any signs of apprehension or surprise. I gave them a few beads, and they came into the ship. One man, who seemed to have an ascendancy over the others, looked about the ship with some appearance of curiosity, but none of them would venture to go below. They asked for some boiled fresh pork, which they saw in a bowl, belonging to one of the seamen, and it was given them to eat, with boiled plantains. Being told that I was the *Earee* or chief of the ship, the principal person came and joined noses with me, and presented to me a large mother of pearl shell, which hung with plaited hair round his neck; this he fastened round my neck, with signs of great satisfaction.

They spoke the same language as at Otaheite, with very little variation, as far as I could judge. In a small vocabulary, that I made whilst conversing with these men, only four words out of twenty-four differed from the Otaheite. The name of the large island, they told me, was Wytootackee, and the Earee was called Lomakkayah. They said that there were no hogs, dogs, or goats upon the island, nor had they yams, or tarro; but that plantains, cocoanuts, fowls, bread-fruit, and avees, were there in great abundance. Notwithstanding they said that no hogs were on the island, it was evident they had seen such animals; for they called them by the same name as is given to them at Otaheite, which made me suspect that they were deceiving me. However, I ordered a young boar and sow to be put into their canoe, with some yams and tarro, as we could afford to part with some of these articles. I also gave to each of them a knife, a small adze, some nails, beads, and a looking-glass. The latter they examined with great curiosity; but with the iron-work they appeared to be acquainted; calling it *aouree,* which is the common name for iron among the islands where it is known.

As they were preparing to leave us, the chief of the canoe took possession of everything that I had given to the others. One of them showed some signs of dissatisfaction; but, after a little altercation, they joined noses, and were reconciled. I now thought they were going to leave the ship; but only two of them went into the canoe, the other two purposing to stay all night with us, and to have the canoe return for them in the morning. I would have treated their confidence with the regard it merited, but it was impossible to say how far the ship might be driven from the island in the night. This I explained to them, and they reluctantly consented to leave us. They were very solicitous that somebody from the ship should go on shore with them; and just before they quitted us, they gave me a wooden spear, which was the only thing, the paddles excepted, they had brought with them in the canoe. It was a common long staff, pointed with the *toa* wood.

The island of Wytootackee is about ten miles in circuit; its latitude from 18° 50′ to 18° 54′ S, and longitude 200° 19′ E. A group of small keys, eight in number, lie to the S E, 4 or 5 miles distant from Whytootackee, and a single one to the W S W; the southernmost of the group is in latitude 18° 58′ S. Variation of the compass 8° 14′ E.

The people that came off to us did not differ in appearance from the natives of Hervey's Islands, seen in Captain Cook's last voyage, though much more friendly and inoffensive in their manners. They were tattooed across the arms and legs, but not on the loins or posteriors, like the people of Otaheite. From their knowledge of iron, they have doubtless communication with Hervey's Islands, which are not more than 18 leagues distant from them.

In the night, a breeze sprung up from the S, and we continued our course to the westward.

On the 18th, at sunset, we saw Savage Island; and in the night, passed by to the southward of it.

At eleven o'clock in the forenoon of the 21st, we saw the island Caow, from the mast-head, bearing N W by W ¾ W. This island is a high mountain, with a sharp-pointed top, and is the northwesternmost of all the Friendly Islands. At noon we saw it very distinctly from the deck, it being then 19 leagues distant from us.

The wind being to the southward, we could not fetch Annamooka, at which island I intended to stop, before the evening of the 23d, when we anchored in the road, in 23 fathoms; the extremes of Annamooka bearing E by N and S by E, our distance from the shore being half a league. In the middle of the day, a canoe had come off to us from the island Mango, in which was a chief, named Latoomy-lange, who dined with me. Immediately on our anchoring, several canoes came alongside, with yams and cocoa-nuts, but none of the natives offered to come on board, without first asking permission. As yet, I had seen no person with whom I could recollect to have been formerly acquainted. I made enquiries after some of our old friends, particularly the chiefs, but I found myself not sufficiently master of the language to obtain the information I wanted.

Friday the 24th. Our station being inconvenient for watering, at daylight we weighed, and worked more to the eastward, where we anchored in 21 fathoms; the extremes of Annamooka bearing N 85° E, and S 33° W; the Sandy bay S 73° E; our distance from the shore, half a league. Sounded all round the ship, and found the ground to be a coarse coral bottom, but with even soundings.

By this time, some large sailing canoes were arrived from different islands in the neighbourhood of Anna-mooka; and an old lame man, named Tepa, whom I had known in 1777, and immediately recollected, came on board. Two other chiefs, whose names were Noocaboo and Kunocappo, were with him. Tepa having formerly been accustomed to our manner of speaking their language, I found I could converse with him tolerably well. He informed me, that Poulaho, Feenow, and Tubow, were alive, and at Tongataboo, and that they would come hither as soon as they heard of our arrival, of which he promised to send them immediate notice. He said that the cattle which we had left at Tongataboo, had all bred, and that the old ones were yet living. He enquired after several people who were here with Captain Cook. Being desirous to see the ship, I took him and his companions below, and showed them the bread-fruit and other plants, at seeing which they were greatly surprised. I made each of them a present; and, when they had satisfied their curiosity, I invited them to go on shore with me in the ship's boat.

I took Nelson with me to procure some bread-fruit plants, one of our stock being dead, and two or three others a little sickly. When we landed, there were about two hundred people on the beach, most of them women and children. Tepa showed me a large boat-house, which, he told me, we might make use of; thinking we should have a party on shore, as our ships had formerly. I went with him in search of water, but could find no better place than where Captain Cook had watered, which is a quarter of a mile inland from the east end of the beach. I next walked to the west point of the bay, where some plants and seeds had been sown by Captain Cook; and had the satisfaction to see, in a plantation close by, about twenty fine pine-apple plants, but no fruit, this not being the proper season. They told me, that they had eaten many of them, that they were fine and large, and that at Tonga-taboo there were great numbers.

When I returned to the landing-place, I was desired to sit down, and a present was brought me, which consisted of some bundles of cocoa-nuts only. This fell short of my expectations; however, I appeared satisfied, and distributed beads and trinkets to the women and children near me.

Numerous were the marks of mourning with which these people disfigure themselves, such as bloody temples, their heads deprived of most of the hair, and, what was worse, almost all of them with the loss of some of their fingers. Several fine boys, not above six years old, had lost both their little fingers; and some of the men, besides these, had parted with the middle finger of the right hand.

The chiefs went off with me to dinner, and I found a brisk trade carrying on at the ship for yams; some plantains and bread-fruit were likewise brought on board, but no hogs. In the afternoon, more sailing canoes arrived, some of which contained not less than ninety passengers. We purchased eight hogs, some dogs, fowls, and shaddocks. Yams were in great abundance, very fine and large; one yam weighed above 45 lbs. Among the people that came this afternoon, were two of the name of Tubow, which is a family of the first distinction among the Friendly Islands; one of them was chief of the island Lefooga; with him and Tepa I went on shore to see the wooding place. I found a variety of sizeable trees; but the kind which I principally pitched upon, was the Barringtonia, of Forster. I acquainted Tepa with my intention of sending people to cut wood, which meeting with his approbation, we parted.

On the 25th, at daylight, the wooding and watering parties went on shore. I had directed them not to cut the kind of tree*, which, when Captain Cook wooded here in 1777, blinded, for a time, many of the wood-cutters. They had not been an hour on shore, before one man had an axe stolen from him, and another an adze. Tepa was applied to, who got the axe restored, but the adze was not recovered. In the evening we completed wooding.

Sunday the 26th. In the morning, Nelson went on shore to get a few plants; but, no principal chief being among the people, he was insulted, and a spade taken from him. A boat's grapnel was likewise stolen from the watering

---

* *Excæcaria Agallocha Linn. Sp. Pl.* called in the Malay language *Caju Mata Boota*, which signifies, the tree that wounds the eyes.

party. Tepa recovered the spade for us; but the crowd of natives was become so great, by the number of canoes that had arrived from different islands, that it was impossible to do anything, where there was such a multitude of people, without a chief of sufficient authority to command the whole. I therefore ordered the watering party to go on board, and determined to sail; for I could not discover that any canoe had been sent to acquaint the chiefs of Tongataboo of our being here. For some time after the thefts were committed, the chiefs kept away, but before noon, they came on board.

At noon, we unmoored, and at one o'clock, got under sail. The two Tubows, Kunocappo, Latoomy-lange, and another chief, were on board, and I acquainted them, that, unless the grapnel was returned, they must remain in the ship. They were surprised, and not a little alarmed. Canoes were immediately dispatched after the grapnel, which, I was informed, could not possibly be brought to the ship before the next day, as those who had stolen it, immediately sailed with their prize to another island. Nevertheless, I detained them till sunset, when their uneasiness and impatience increased to such a degree that they began to beat themselves about the face and eyes, and some of them cried bitterly. As this distress was more than the grapnel was worth, and I had no reason to imagine that they were privy to, or in any manner concerned in, the theft, I could not think of detaining them longer, and called their canoes alongside. I then told them they were at liberty to go, and made each of them a present of a hatchet, a saw, with some knives, gimblets, and nails. This unexpected present, and the sudden change in their situation, affected them not less with joy than they had before been with apprehension. They were unbounded in their acknowledgements; and I have little doubt but that we parted better friends than if the affair had never happened.

We stood to the northward all night, with light winds; and on the next day, the 27th, at noon, were between the islands Tofoa and Kotoo. Latitude observed 19° 18′ S.

Thus far, the voyage had advanced in a course of uninterrupted prosperity, and had been attended with many circumstances equally pleasing and satisfactory. A very different scene was now to be experienced. A conspiracy had been formed, which was to render all our past labour productive only of extreme misery and distress. The means had been concerted and prepared with so much secrecy and circumspection, that no one circumstance appeared to occasion the smallest suspicion of the impending calamity.

CHAPTER XIII

A Mutiny in the Ship

WE kept near the island Kotoo, all the afternoon, in hopes that some canoes would come off to the ship; but in this I was disappointed. The wind being northerly, in the evening, we steered to the westward, to pass to the south of Tofoa. I gave directions for this course to be continued during the night. The master had the first watch; the gunner the middle watch; and Mr. Christian the morning watch. This was the turn of duty for the night.

Tuesday the 28th. Just before sun-rising, while I was yet asleep, Mr. Christian, with the master at arms, gunner's mate, and Thomas Burkitt, seaman, came into my cabin, and seizing me, tied my hands with a cord behind my back, threatening me with instant death, if I spoke or made the least noise: I, however, called as loud as I could, in hopes of assistance; but they had already secured the officers who were not of their party, by placing sentinels at their doors. There were three men at my cabin door, besides the four within; Christian had only a cutlass in his hand, the others had muskets and bayonets. I was hauled out of bed, and forced on deck in my shirt, suffering great pain from the tightness with which they had tied my hands. I demanded the reason of such violence, but received no other answer than abuse, for not holding my tongue. The master, the gunner, the surgeon, Mr. Elphinstone, master's mate, and Nelson, were kept confined below; and the fore hatchway was guarded by sentinels. The boatswain and carpenter, and also the clerk, Mr. Samuel, were allowed to come upon deck, where they saw me standing abaft the mizen-mast, with my hands tied behind my back, under a guard, with Christian at their head. The boatswain was ordered to hoist the launch out, with a threat, if he did not do it instantly, *to take care of himself.*

When the boat was out, Mr. Hayward and Mr. Hallet, two of the midshipmen, and Mr. Samuel, were ordered into it. I demanded what their intention was in giving this order, and endeavoured to persuade the people near me not to persist in such acts of violence; but it was to no effect: "Hold your tongue, Sir, or you are dead this instant," was constantly repeated to me.

The master, by this time, had sent to request that he might come on deck, which was permitted; but he was soon ordered back again to his cabin.

I continued my endeavours to turn the tide of affairs, when Christian changed the cutlass which he had in his hand for a bayonet that was brought to him, and, holding me with a strong grip by the cord that tied my hands, he with many oaths threatened to kill me immediately, if I would not be quiet: the villains round me had their pieces cocked and bayonets fixed. Particular people were called on to go into the boat, and were hurried over the side; whence I concluded that with these people I was to be set adrift: I therefore made another effort to bring about a change, but with no other effect than to be threatened with having my brains blown out.

The boatswain and seamen, who were to go in the boat, were allowed to collect twine, canvas, lines, sails, cordage, an 8 and 20 gallon cask of water, and Mr. Samuel got 150 lbs. of bread, with a small quantity of rum and wine, also a quadrant and compass; but he was forbidden, on pain of death, to touch either map, ephemeris, book of astronomical observations, sextant, time-keeper, or any of my surveys or drawings.

The mutineers having forced those of the seamen whom they meant to get rid of, into the boat, Christian directed a dram to be served to each of his own crew. I then unhappily saw that nothing could be done to effect the recovery of the ship: there was no one to assist me, and every endeavour on my part was answered with threats of death.

The officers were next called upon deck, and forced over the side into the boat, while I was kept apart from every one, abaft the mizen-mast; Christian, armed with a bayonet, holding me by the bandage that secured my hands. The guard round me had their pieces cocked, but on my daring the ungrateful wretches to fire, they uncocked them.

Isaac Martin, one of the guard over me, I saw, had an inclination to assist me, and as he fed me with shaddock, (my lips being quite parched) we explained our wishes to each other by our looks; but this being observed, Martin was removed from me. He then attempted to leave the ship, for which purpose he got into the boat; but with many threats they obliged him to return.

The armourer, Joseph Coleman, and two of the carpenters, M'Intosh and Norman, were also kept contrary to their inclination; and they begged of me, after I was astern in the boat, to remember that they declared they had no hand in the transaction. Michael Byrne, I am told, likewise wanted to leave the ship.

It is of no moment for me to recount my endeavours to bring back the offenders to a sense of their duty: all I could do was by speaking to them in general; but it was to no purpose, for I was kept securely bound, and no one except the guard suffered to come near me.

To Mr. Samuel I am indebted for securing my journals and commission, with some material ship papers. Without these I had nothing to certify what I had done, and my honour and character might have been suspected, without my possessing a proper document to have defended them. All this he did with great resolution, though guarded and strictly watched. He attempted to save the time-keeper, and a box with my surveys, drawings, and remarks for fifteen years past, which were numerous; when he was hurried away, with "Damn your eyes, you are well off to get what you have."

It appeared to me, that Christian was some time in doubt whether he should keep the carpenter, or his mates; at length he determined on the latter, and the carpenter was ordered into the boat. He was permitted, but not without some opposition, to take his tool chest.

Much altercation took place among the mutinous crew during the whole business: some swore "I'll be damned if he does not find his way home, if he gets anything with him" (meaning me); and, when the carpenter's chest was carrying away, "Damn my eyes, he will have a vessel built in a month." While others laughed at the helpless situation of the boat, being very deep, and so little room for those who were in her. As for Christian, he seemed as if meditating destruction on himself and every one else.

I asked for arms, but they laughed at me, and said I was well acquainted with the people among whom I was going, and therefore did not want them; four cutlasses, however, were thrown into the boat, after we were veered astern.

The officers and men being in the boat, they only waited for me, of which the master at arms informed Christian; who then said—"Come, Captain Bligh, your officers and men are now in the boat, and you must go with them; if you attempt to make the least resistance you will instantly be put to death": and, without further ceremony, with a tribe of armed ruffians about me, I was forced over the side, where they untied my hands. Being in the boat, we were veered astern by a rope. A few pieces of pork were thrown to us, and some clothes, also the cutlasses I have already mentioned; and it was then that the armourer and carpenters called out to me to remember that they had no hand in the transaction. After having undergone a great deal of ridicule, and been kept some time to make sport for these unfeeling wretches, we were at length cast adrift in the open ocean.

I had with me in the boat the following persons:

Names	Stations
JOHN FRYER	Master
THOMAS LEDWARD	Acting Surgeon
DAVID NELSON	Botanist
WILLIAM PECKOVER	Gunner
WILLIAM COLE	Boatswain
WILLIAM PURCELL	Carpenter
WILLIAM ELPHINSTON	Master's Mate
THOMAS HAYWARD	} Midshipmen
JOHN HALLET	
JOHN NORTON	} Quarter Masters
PETER LINKLETTER	
LAWRENCE LEBOGUE	Sailmaker
JOHN SMITH	} Cooks
THOMAS HALL	
GEORGE SIMPSON	Quarter Master's Mate
ROBERT TINKLER	A boy
ROBERT LAMB	Butcher
MR. SAMUEL	Clerk

There remained on board the *Bounty,*

FLETCHER CHRISTIAN	Master's Mate
PETER HAYWOOD	
EDWARD YOUNG	Midshipmen
GEORGE STEWART	
CHARLES CHURCHILL	Master at Arms
JOHN MILLS	Gunner's Mate
JAMES MORRISON	Boatswain's Mate
THOMAS BURKITT	Able Seaman
MATTHEW QUINTAL	Ditto
JOHN SUMNER	Ditto
JOHN MILLWARD	Ditto
WILLIAM M'KOY	Ditto
HENRY HILLBRANT	Ditto
MICHAEL BYRNE	Ditto

Names	Stations
WILLIAM MUSPRAT	Able Seaman
ALEXANDER SMITH	Ditto
JOHN WILLIAMS	Ditto
THOMAS ELLISON	Ditto
ISAAC MARTIN	Ditto
RICHARD SKINNER	Ditto
MATTHEW THOMPSON	Ditto
WILLIAM BROWN	Gardener
JOSEPH COLEMAN	Armourer
CHARLES NORMAN	Carpenter's Mate
THOMAS M'INTOSH	Carpenter's Crew

In all 25 hands, and the most able men of the ship's company.

Having little or no wind, we rowed pretty fast towards Tofoa, which bore N E about ten leagues from us. While the ship was in sight she steered to the W N W, but I considered this only as a feint; for when we were sent away—'Huzza for Otaheite,' was frequently heard among the mutineers.

Christian, the chief of the mutineers, is of a respectable family in the north of England. This was the third voyage he had made with me; and, as I found it necessary to keep my ship's company at three watches, I had given him an order to take charge of the third, his abilities being thoroughly equal to the task; and by this means the master and gunner were not at watch and watch.

Haywood is also of a respectable family in the north of England, and a young man of abilities, as well as Christian. These two had been objects of my particular regard and attention, and I had taken great pains to instruct them, having entertained hopes, that, as professional men, they would have become a credit to their country.

Young was well recommended, and had the look of an able stout seaman: he, however, fell short of what his appearance promised.

Stewart was a young man of creditable parents, in the Orkneys; at which place, on the return of the *Resolution* from the South Seas, in 1780, we received so many civilities, that, on that account only, I should gladly have taken him with me: but, independent of his recommendation, he was a seaman, and had always borne a good character.

Notwithstanding the roughness with which I was treated, the remembrance of past kindnesses produced some signs of remorse in Christian. When they were forcing me out of the ship, I asked him if this treatment was a proper return for the many instances he had received of my friendship? he appeared disturbed at my question, and answered with much emotion, "That,— Captain Bligh,—that is the thing;—I am in hell—I am in hell."

As soon as I had time to reflect, I felt an inward satisfaction, which prevented any depression of my spirits: conscious of my integrity, and anxious solicitude for the good of the service in which I had been engaged, I found my mind wonderfully supported, and I began to conceive hopes, notwithstanding so heavy a calamity, that I should one day be able to account to my King and country for the misfortune.—A few hours before, my situation had been peculiarly flattering. I had a ship in the most perfect order, and well stored with every necessary both for service and health: by early attention to those particulars I had, as much as lay in my power, provided against any accident, in case I could not get through Endeavour Straits, as well as against what might befall me in them; add to this, the plants had been successfully preserved in the most flourishing state: so that, upon the whole, the voyage was two-thirds completed, and the remaining part, to all appearance, in a very promising way; every person on board being in perfect health, to establish which was ever amongst the principal objects of my attention.

It will very naturally be asked, what could be the reason for such a revolt? in answer to which I can only conjecture, that the mutineers had flattered themselves with the hopes of a more happy life among the Otaheiteans, than they could possibly enjoy in England; and this, joined to some female connexions, most probably occasioned the whole transaction.

The women at Otaheite are handsome, mild and cheerful in their manners and conversation, possessed of great sensibility, and have sufficient delicacy to make them admired and beloved. The chiefs were so much attached to our people, that they rather encouraged their stay among them than otherwise, and even made them promises of large possessions. Under these, and many other attendant circumstances, equally desirable, it is now perhaps not so much to be wondered at, though scarcely possible to have been foreseen, that a set of sailors, most of them void of connexions, should be led away; especially when, in addition to such powerful inducements, they imagined it in their power to fix themselves in the midst of plenty, on one of the finest islands in the world, where they need not labour, and where the allurements of dissipation are beyond anything that can be conceived. The utmost, however, that any commander could have supposed to have happened is, that some of the people would have been tempted to desert. But if it should be asserted, that a commander is to guard against an act of mutiny and piracy in his own ship, more than by the common rules of service, it is as much as to say that he must sleep locked up, and when awake, be girded with pistols.

Desertions have happened, more or less, from most of the ships that have been at the Society Islands; but it has always been in the commander's power to make the chiefs return their people: the knowledge, therefore, that it was unsafe to desert, perhaps, first led mine to consider with what ease so small a ship might be surprised, and that so favourable an opportunity would never offer to them again.

The secrecy of this mutiny is beyond all conception. Thirteen of the party, who were with me, had always lived forward among the seamen; yet neither they, nor the messmates of Christian, Stewart, Haywood, and Young, had ever observed any circumstance that made them in the least suspect what was going on. To such a close-planned act of villainy, my mind being entirely free from any suspicion, it is not wonderful that I fell a sacrifice. Perhaps, if there had been marines on board, a sentinel at my cabin-door might have prevented it; for I slept with the door always open, that the officer of the watch might have access to me on all occasions, the possibility of such a conspiracy being ever the farthest from my thoughts. Had their mutiny been occasioned by any grievances, either real or imaginary, I must have discovered symptoms of their discontent, which would have put me on my guard: but the case was far otherwise. Christian, in particular, I was on the most friendly terms with: that very day he was engaged to have dined with me: and the preceding night, he excused himself from supping with me, on pretence of being unwell; for which I felt concerned, having no suspicions of his integrity and honour.

CHAPTER XIV

*Proceed in the Launch to the Island Tofoa—Difficulty in ob-
taining Supplies there—Treacherous Attack of the Natives
—Escape to the Sea, and bear away for New Holland*

MY first determination was to seek a supply of
bread-fruit and water at Tofoa, and afterwards to
sail for Tongataboo, and there risk a solicitation to
Poulaho, the king, to equip our boat, and grant us a
supply of water and provisions, so as to enable us to
reach the East Indies.

The quantity of provisions I found in the boat, was
150 lb. of bread, 16 pieces of pork, each piece weighing
2 lb., 6 quarts of rum, 6 bottles of wine, with 28 gallons
of water, and four empty barricoes.

Fortunately it was calm all the afternoon, till about
four o'clock, when we were so far to windward, that,
with a moderate easterly breeze which sprung up, we
were able to sail. It was nevertheless dark when we got
to Tofoa, where I expected to land; but the shore proved
to be so steep and rocky, that we were obliged to give
up all thoughts of it, and keep the boat under the lee
of the island with two oars; for there was no anchorage.
Having fixed on this mode of proceeding for the night,
I served to every person half a pint of grog, and each took
to his rest as well as our unhappy situation would allow.

In the morning, at dawn of day, we rowed along shore
in search of a landing-place, and about ten o'clock we discovered a cove with a stony beach, at the North West
part of the island, where I dropt the grapnel within 20
yards of the rocks. A great surf ran on the shore; but,
as I was unwilling to diminish our stock of provisions, I
landed Mr. Samuel, and some others, who climbed the
cliffs, and got into the country to search for supplies. The
rest of us remained at the cove, not discovering any other
way into the country, than that by which Mr. Samuel
had proceeded. It was great consolation to me to find,
that the spirits of my people did not sink, notwithstanding

our miserable and almost hopeless situation. Towards
noon, Mr. Samuel returned, with a few quarts of water,
which he had found in holes; but he had met with no
spring, or any prospect of a sufficient supply in that
particular, and had seen only the signs of inhabitants.
As it was uncertain what might be our future necessities,
I only issued a morsel of bread, and a glass of wine, to
each person for dinner.

I observed the latitude of this cove to be 19° 41′ S.
This is the N W part of Tofoa, the north-westernmost
of the Friendly Islands.

The weather was fair, but the wind blew so strong from
the E S E that we could not venture to sea. Our deten-
tion made it absolutely necessary to endeavour to obtain
something towards our support; for I determined, if
possible, to keep our first stock entire. We therefore
weighed, and rowed along shore, to see if anything could
be got; and at last discovered some cocoa-nut trees; but
they were on the top of high precipices, and the surf made
it dangerous landing: both one and the other we, however, got the better of. Some of the people, with much
difficulty, climbed the cliffs, and got about 20 cocoa-nuts,
and others slung them to ropes, by which we hauled
them through the surf into the boat. This was all that
could be done here; and, as I found no place so safe as
the one we had left, to spend the night at, I returned to
the cove, and, having served a cocoa-nut to each person,
we went to rest again in the boat.

At daylight, we attempted to put to sea; but the wind
and weather proved so bad, that I was glad to return to
our former station; where, after issuing a morsel of bread
and a spoonful of rum to each person, we landed, and I
went off with Mr. Nelson, Mr. Samuel, and some others,
into the country, having hauled ourselves up the precipice
by long vines, which were fixed there by the natives for
that purpose; this being the only way into the country.

We found a few deserted huts, and a small plantain
walk, but little taken care of; from which we could only
collect three small bunches of plantains. After passing
this place, we came to a deep gully that led towards a
mountain, near a volcano; and, as I conceived that in the
rainy season very great torrents of water must pass
through it, we hoped to find sufficient for our use, re-

maining in some holes of the rocks; but, after all our
search, the whole that we collected was only 9 gallons.
We advanced within two miles of the foot of the highest
mountain in the island, on which is the volcano that is
almost constantly burning. The country near it is covered
with lava, and has a most dreary appearance. As we
had not been fortunate in our discoveries, and saw
nothing to alleviate our distresses, except the plantains
and water abovementioned, we returned to the boat,
exceedingly fatigued and faint. When I came to the
precipice whence we were to descend into the cove, I
was seized with such a dizziness in my head, that I
thought it scarce possible to effect it: however, by the
assistance of Nelson and others, they at last got me down,
in a weak condition. Every person being returned by
noon, I gave about an ounce of pork and two plantains
to each, with half a glass of wine. I again observed the
latitude of this place 19° 41′ S. The people who remained by the boat I had directed to look for fish, or
what they could pick up about the rocks; but nothing
eatable could be found: so that, upon the whole, we
considered ourselves on as miserable a spot of land as
could well be imagined.

I could not say positively, from the former knowledge
I had of this island, whether it was inhabited or not;
but I knew it was considered inferior to the other islands,
and I was not certain but that the Indians only resorted
to it at particular times. I was very anxious to ascertain
this point; for, in case there had been only a few people
here, and those could have furnished us with but very
moderate supplies, the remaining in this spot to have
made preparations for our voyage, would have been preferable to the risk of going amongst multitudes, where
perhaps we might lose everything. A party, therefore,
sufficiently strong, I determined should go another route,
as soon as the sun became lower; and they cheerfully
undertook it.

About two o'clock in the afternoon the party set out;
but, after suffering much fatigue, they returned in the
evening, without any kind of success.

At the head of the cove, about 150 yards from the
water-side, there was a cave; the distance across the stony
beach was about 100 yards, and from the country into

the cove there was no other way than that which I have already described. The situation secured us from the danger of being surprised, and I determined to remain on shore for the night, with a part of my people, that the others might have more room to rest in the boat, with the master; whom I directed to lie at a grapnel, and be watchful, in case we should be attacked. I ordered one plantain for each person to be boiled; and, having supped on this scanty allowance, with a quarter of a pint of grog, and fixed the watches for the night, those whose turn it was, laid down to sleep in the cave, before which we kept up a good fire; yet notwithstanding we were much troubled with flies and mosquitoes.

Friday, May the 1st. At dawn of day, the party set out again in a different route, to see what they could find; in the course of which, they suffered greatly for want of water: they, however, met with two men, a woman, and a child: the men came with them to the cove, and brought two cocoa-nut shells of water. I endeavoured to make friends of these people, and sent them away for bread-fruit, plantains, and water. Soon after, other natives came to us; and by noon there were thirty about us, from whom we obtained a small supply; but I could only afford one ounce of pork, and a quarter of a bread-fruit, to each man for dinner, with half a pint of water; for I was fixed in my resolution not to use any of the bread or water in the boat.

No particular chief was yet among the natives: they were, notwithstanding, tractable, and behaved honestly, exchanging the provisions they brought for a few buttons and beads. The party who had been out, informed me of their having seen several neat plantations; so that it remained no longer a doubt of there being settled inhabitants on the island; for which reason I determined to get what I could, and to sail the first moment that the wind and weather would allow us to put to sea.

I was much puzzled in what manner to account to the natives for the loss of my ship: I knew they had too much sense to be amused with a story that the ship was to join me, when she was not in sight from the hills. I was at first doubtful whether I should tell the real fact, or say that the ship had overset and sunk, and that we only were saved: the latter appeared to be the most proper and advantageous for us, and I accordingly instructed my people, that we might all agree in one story. As I expected, inquiries were made about the ship, and they seemed readily satisfied with our account; but there did not appear the least symptom of joy or sorrow in their faces, although I fancied I discovered some marks of surprise. Some of the natives were coming and going the whole afternoon, and we got enough of bread-fruit, plantains, and cocoa-nuts for another day; but of water they only brought us about five pints. A canoe also came in with four men, and brought a few cocoa-nuts and bread-fruit, which I bought as I had done the rest. Nails were much inquired after, but I would not suffer any to be shown, as they were wanted for the use of the boat.

Towards evening, I had the satisfaction to find our stock of provisions somewhat increased; but the natives did not appear to have much to spare. What they brought was in such small quantities, that I had no reason to hope we should be able to procure from them sufficient to stock us for our voyage. At sunset, all the natives left us in quiet possession of the cove. I thought this a good sign, and made no doubt that they would come again the next day with a better supply of food and water, with which I hoped to sail without further delay: for if, in attempting to get to Tongataboo, we should be driven to leeward of the islands, there would be a larger quantity of provisions to support us against such a misfortune.

At night, I served a quarter of a bread-fruit and a cocoa-nut to each person for supper; and, a good fire being made, all but the watch went to sleep.

At day-break, the next morning, I was pleased to find every one's spirits a little revived, and that they no longer regarded me with those anxious looks, which had constantly been directed towards me since we lost sight of the ship: every countenance appeared to have a degree of cheerfulness, and they all seemed determined to do their best.

As there was no certainty of our being supplied with water by the natives, I sent a party among the gullies in the mountains, with empty shells, to see what could be found. In their absence the natives came about us, as I expected, and in greater numbers; two canoes also came in from round the north side of the island. In one of them was an elderly chief, called Macca-ackavow. Soon after, some of our foraging party returned, and with them came a good-looking chief, called Egijeefow, or perhaps more properly Eefow, Egij or Eghee, signifying a chief. To each of these men I made a present of an old shirt and a knife, and I soon found they either had seen me, or had heard of my being at Annamooka. They knew I had been with Captain Cook, who they inquired after, and also Captain Clerk. They were very inquisitive to know in what manner I had lost my ship. During this conversation, a young man, named Nageete, appeared, whom I remembered to have seen at Annamooka: he expressed much pleasure at our meeting. I inquired after Poulaho and Feenow, who, they said, were at Tongataboo; and Eefow agreed to accompany me thither, if I would wait till the weather moderated. The readiness and affability of this man gave me much satisfaction.

This, however, was but of short duration, for the natives began to increase in number, and I observed some symptoms of a design against us. Soon after they attempted to haul the boat on shore, on which I brandished my cutlass in a threatening manner, and spoke to Eefow to desire them to desist; which they did, and everything became quiet again. My people, who had been in the mountains, now returned with about three gallons of water. I kept buying up the little bread-fruit that was brought to us, and likewise some spears to arm my men with, having only four cutlasses, two of which were in the boat. As we had no means of improving our situation, I told our people I would wait till sunset, by which time, perhaps, something might happen in our favour: for if we attempted to go at present, we must fight our way through, which we could do more advantageously at night; and that in the meantime we would endeavour to get off to the boat what we had bought. The beach was lined with the natives, and we heard nothing but the knocking of stones together, which they had in each hand. I knew very well this was the sign of an attack. At noon, I served a cocoa-nut and a bread-fruit to each person for dinner, and gave some to the chiefs, with whom I continued to appear intimate and friendly. They frequently importuned me to sit down, but I as constantly refused: for it occurred both to Nelson and myself, that they intended to seize hold of me, if I gave

them such an opportunity. Keeping, therefore, constantly
on our guard, we were suffered to eat our uncomfortable
meal in some quietness.

After dinner, we began by little and little to get our
things into the boat, which was a troublesome business,
on account of the surf. I carefully watched the motions
of the natives, who continued to increase in number; and
found that, instead of their intention being to leave us,
fires were made, and places fixed on for their stay during
the night. Consultations were also held among them,
and everything assured me we should be attacked. I sent
orders to the master, that when he saw us coming down,
he should keep the boat close to the shore, that we might
the more readily embark.

I had my journal on shore with me, writing the occurrences in the cave, and in sending it down to the boat, it
was nearly snatched away, but for the timely assistance of
the gunner.

The sun was near setting, when I gave the word, on
which every person, who was on shore with me, boldly
took up his proportion of things, and carried them to the
boat. The chiefs asked me if I would not stay with them
all night, I said, "No, I never sleep out of my boat; but in
the morning we will again trade with you, and I shall
remain till the weather is moderate, that we may go,
as we have agreed, to see Poulaho, at Tongataboo."
Macca-ackavow then got up, and said, "You will not sleep
on shore? then Mattie" (which directly signifies we
will kill you), and he left me. The onset was now preparing; every one, as I have described before, kept knocking
stones together, and Eefow quitted me. All but two or
three things were in the boat, when I took Nageete by the
hand, and we walked down the beach, every one in a
silent kind of horror.

While I was seeing the people embark, Nageete wanted
me to stay to speak to Eefow; but I found he was encouraging them to the attack, and it was my determination, if they had then began, to have killed him for his
treacherous behaviour. I ordered the carpenter not to
quit me till the other people were in the boat. Nageete,
finding I would not stay, loosed himself from my hold and
went off, and we all got into the boat except one man,
who, while I was getting on board, quitted it, and ran up

the beach to cast the stern fast off, notwithstanding the master and others called to him to return, while they were hauling me out of the water.

I was no sooner in the boat than the attack began by about 200 men; the unfortunate poor man who had run up the beach was knocked down, and the stones flew like a shower of shot. Many Indians got hold of the stern rope, and were near hauling the boat on shore; which they would certainly have effected, if I had not had a knife in my pocket, with which I cut the rope. We then hauled off to the grapnel, every one being more or less hurt. At this time, I saw five of the natives about the poor man they had killed, and two of them were beating him about the head with stones in their hands.

We had no time to reflect, for to my surprise, they filled their canoes with stones, and twelve men came off after us to renew the attack, which they did so effectually as nearly to disable us all. Our grapnel was foul, but Providence here assisted us; the fluke broke, and we got to our oars, and pulled to sea. They, however, could paddle round us, so that we were obliged to sustain the attack without being able to return it, except with such stones as lodged in the boat, and in this I found we were very inferior to them. We could not close, because our boat was lumbered and heavy, of which they well knew how to take advantage: I therefore adopted the expedient of throwing overboard some clothes, which, as I expected, they stopped to pick up; and, as it was by this time almost dark, they gave over the attack, and returned towards the shore, leaving us to reflect on our unhappy situation.

The poor man killed by the natives was John Norton: this was his second voyage with me as a quarter master, and his worthy character made me lament his loss very much. He has left an aged parent, I am told, whom he supported.

I once before sustained an attack of a similar nature, with a smaller number of Europeans, against a multitude of Indians: it was after the death of Captain Cook, on the Morai at Owhyhee, where I was left by Lieutenant King. Yet, notwithstanding this experience, I had not an idea that the power of a man's arm could throw stones, from 2 to 8 lbs. weight, with such force and exactness as these people did. Here unhappily we were without firearms, which the Indians knew; and it was a fortunate circumstance that they did not begin to attack us in the cave; for in that case our destruction must have been inevitable, and we should have had nothing left for it but to sell our lives as dearly as we could; in which I found every one cheerfully disposed to concur. This appearance of resolution deterred them, supposing that they could effect their purpose without risk after we were in the boat.

Taking this as a sample of the disposition of the natives, there was but little reason to expect much benefit by persevering in the intention of visiting Poulaho; for I considered their good behaviour formerly to have proceeded from a dread of our firearms, and which, therefore, was likely to cease, as they knew we were now destitute of them: and, even supposing our lives not in danger, the boat and everything we had, would most probably be taken from us, and thereby all hopes precluded of ever being able to return to our native country.

We set our sails, and steered along shore by the west side of the island Tofoa; the wind blowing fresh from the eastward. My mind was employed in considering what was best to be done, when I was solicited by all hands to take them towards home: and, when I told them that no hopes of relief for us remained (except what might be found at New Holland) till I came to Timor, a distance of full 1,200 leagues, where there was a Dutch settlement, but in what part of the island I knew not; they all agreed to live on 1 ounce of bread, and a quarter of a pint of water, per day. Therefore, after examining our stock of provisions, and recommending to them, in the most solemn manner, not to depart from their promise, we bore away across a sea, where the navigation is but little known, in a small boat, 23 feet long from stem to stern, deep laden with eighteen men. I was happy, however, to see that every one seemed better satisfied with our situation than myself.

Our stock of provisions consisted of about 150 lbs. of bread, 28 gallons of water, 20 lbs. of pork, three bottles of wine, and 5 quarts of rum. The difference between this and the quantity we had on leaving the ship, was principally owing to our loss in the bustle and confusion of the attack. A few cocoa-nuts were in the boat, and some bread-fruit, but the latter was trampled to pieces.

CHAPTER XV

Passage towards New Holland—Islands discovered in our Route—Our great Distresses—See the Reefs of New Holland, and find a Passage through them

IT was about eight o'clock at night when we bore away under a reefed lug fore-sail: and, having divided the people into watches, and got the boat in a little order, we returned God thanks for our miraculous preservation, and, fully confident of His gracious support, I found my mind more at ease than it had been for some time past.

At day-break, the gale increased; the sun rose very fiery and red, a sure indication of a severe gale of wind. At eight it blew a violent storm, and the sea ran very high, so that between the seas the sail was becalmed, and when on the top of the sea it was too much to have set: but we could not venture to take in the sail, for we were in very imminent danger and distress, the sea curling over the stern of the boat, which obliged us to bail with all our might. A situation more distressing has, perhaps, seldom been experienced.

Our bread was in bags, and in danger of being spoiled by the wet: to be starved to death was inevitable, if this could not be prevented: I therefore began to examine what clothes there were in the boat, and what other things could be spared; and, having determined that only two suits should be kept for each person, the rest was thrown overboard, with some rope and spare sails, which lightened the boat considerably, and we had more room to bail the water out. Fortunately the carpenter had a good chest in the boat, in which we secured the bread the first favourable moment. His tool chest also was cleared, and the tools stowed in the bottom of the boat, so that this became a second convenience.

I served a teaspoonful of rum to each person (for we were very wet and cold), with a quarter of a bread-fruit, which was scarce eatable, for dinner: our engagement was now strictly to be carried into execution, and I was fully determined to make our provisions last eight weeks, let the daily proportion be ever so small.

At noon, I considered our course and distance from Tofoa to be W N W ¾ W 86 miles, latitude 19° 27′ S. I directed the course to the W N W, that we might get a sight of the islands called Feejee, if they lay in the direction the natives had pointed out to me.

The weather continued very severe, the wind veering from N E to E S E. The sea ran higher than in the forenoon, and the fatigue of bailing, to keep the boat from filling, was exceedingly great. We could do nothing more than keep before the sea; in the course of which the boat performed so well, that I no longer dreaded any danger in that respect. But among the hardships we were to undergo, that of being constantly wet was not the least: the night was very cold, and at daylight our limbs were so benumbed, that we could scarce find the use of them. At this time I served a teaspoonful of rum to each person, from which we all found great benefit.

As I have mentioned before, I determined to keep to the W N W, till I got more to the northward; for I not only expected to have better weather, but to see the Feejee Islands, as I have often understood, from the natives of Annamooka, that they lie in that direction. Captain Cook likewise considered them to be N W by W from Tongataboo. Just before noon, we discovered a small flat island, of a moderate height, bearing W S W, 4 or 5 leagues. I observed our latitude to be 18° 58′ S; our longitude was, by account, 3° 4′ W from the island Tofoa, having made a N 72° W course, distance 95 miles, since yesterday noon. I divided five small cocoa-nuts for our dinner, and every one was satisfied.

A little after noon, other islands appeared, and at a quarter past three o'clock we could count eight, bearing from S round by the W to N W by N; those to the S, which were the nearest, being 4 leagues distant from us.

I kept my course to the N W by W, between the islands, the gale having considerably abated. At six o'clock, we discovered three other small islands to the N W, the westernmost of them bore N W ½ W 7 leagues. I steered to the southward of these islands, a W N W course for the night, under a reefed sail.

Served a few broken pieces of bread-fruit for supper, and performed prayers.

The night turned out fair, and, having had tolerable rest, every one seemed considerably better in the morning, and contentedly breakfasted on a few pieces of yams that were found in the boat. After breakfast we examined our bread, a great deal of which was damaged and rotten; this, nevertheless, we were glad to keep for use.

I had hitherto been scarcely able to keep any account of our run; but we now equipped ourselves a little better, by getting a log-line marked, and, having practised at counting seconds, several could do it with some degree of exactness.

The islands we had passed, lie between the latitude of 19° 5′ S and 18° 19′ S, and, according to my reckoning, from 3° 17′ to 3° 46′ W longitude from the island Tofoa: the largest may be about 6 leagues in circuit; but it is impossible for me to be very correct. To show where they are to be found again is the most my situation enabled me to do. The sketch I have made, will give a comparative view of their extent. I believe all the larger islands are inhabited, as they appeared very fertile.

At noon I observed, in latitude 18° 10′ S, and considered my course and distance from yesterday noon, N W by W ½ W, 94 miles; longitude, by account, from Tofoa 4° 29′ W.

For dinner, I served some of the damaged bread, and a quarter of a pint of water.

About six o'clock in the afternoon, we discovered two islands, one bearing W by S 6 leagues, and the other N W by N 8 leagues; I kept to windward of the northernmost, and passing it by ten o'clock, I resumed our course to the N W and W N W for the night.

Wednesday the 6th. The weather was fair and the wind moderate all day from the E N E. At day-light, a number of other islands were in sight from S S E to the W, and round to N E by E; between those in the N W I determined to pass. At noon a small sandy island or key 2 miles distant from me, bore from E to S ¾ W. I had passed ten islands, the largest of which I judged to be 6 or 8 leagues in circuit. Much larger lands appeared in the S W and N N W, between which I directed my course. Latitude observed 17° 17′ S; course since yes-

terday noon N 50° W; distance 84 miles; longitude
made, by account, 5° 37′ W.

Our allowance for the day was a quarter of a pint of
cocoa-nut milk, and the meat, which did not exceed 2
ounces to each person: it was received very contentedly,
but we suffered great drought. I durst not venture to
land, as we had no arms, and were less capable of defending ourselves than we were at Tofoa.

To keep an account of the boat's run was rendered difficult, from being constantly wet with the sea breaking
over us; but, as we advanced towards the land, the sea
became smoother, and I was enabled to form a sketch of
the islands, which will serve to give a general knowledge
of their extent and position. Those we were near, appeared fruitful and hilly, some very mountainous, and all
of a good height.

To our great joy we hooked a fish, but we were miserably disappointed by its being lost in trying to get it into
the boat.

We continued steering to the N W, between the islands,
which, by the evening, appeared of considerable extent,
woody and mountainous. At sunset, the southernmost
bore from S to S W by W and the northernmost from
N by W ½ W to N E ½ E. At 6 o'clock we were
nearly mid-way between them, and about six leagues distant from each shore, when we fell in with a coral bank,
on which we had only 4 feet of water, without the least
break on it, or ruffle of the sea to give us warning. I
could see that it extended about a mile on each side of us;
but, as it is probable that it may extend much farther,
I have laid it down so in my sketch.

I directed the course W by N for the night, and served
to each person an ounce of the damaged bread, and a
quarter of a pint of water, for supper.

As our lodgings were very miserable, and confined for
want of room, I endeavoured to remedy the latter defect,
by putting ourselves at watch and watch; so that one half
always sat up while the other lay down on the boat's
bottom, or upon a chest, with nothing to cover us but the
heavens. Our limbs were dreadfully cramped, for we
could not stretch them out; and the nights were so cold,
and we so constantly wet, that, after a few hours sleep,
we could scarce move.

At dawn of day, we again discovered land from W S W to W N W, and another island N N W, the latter a high round lump of but little extent: the southern land that we had passed in the night was still in sight. Being very wet and cold, I served a spoonful of rum and a morsel of bread for breakfast.

The land in the west was distinguished by some extraordinary high rocks, which, as we approached them, assumed a variety of forms. The country appeared to be agreeably interspersed with high and low land, and in some places covered with wood. Off the N E part lay some small rocky islands, between which and an island 4 leagues to the N E, I directed my course; but a lee current very unexpectedly set us very near to the rocky isles, and we could only get clear of it by rowing, passing close to the reef that surrounded them. At this time we observed two large sailing canoes coming swiftly after us along shore, and, being apprehensive of their intentions, we rowed with some anxiety, fully sensible of our weak and defenceless state. At noon it was calm and the weather cloudy; my latitude is therefore doubtful to 3 or 4 miles. Our course since yesterday noon N W by W, distance 79 miles; latitude by account, 16° 29′ S, and longitude by account, from Tofoa, 6° 46′ W. Being constantly wet, it was with the utmost difficulty I could open a book to write, and I am sensible that what I have done can only serve to point out where these lands are to be found again, and give an idea of their extent.

All the afternoon, we had light winds at N N E; the weather was very rainy, attended with thunder and lightning. Only one of the canoes gained upon us, which by three o'clock in the afternoon was not more than 2 miles off, when she gave over chase.

If I may judge from the sail of these vessels, they are of a similar construction with those at the Friendly Islands, which, with the nearness of their situation, gives reason to believe that they are the same kind of people. Whether these canoes had any hostile intention against us must remain a doubt: perhaps we might have benefited by an intercourse with them; but in our defenceless situation, to have made the experiment would have been risking too much.

I imagine these to be the islands called Feejee, as their

extent, direction, and distance from the Friendly Islands, answers to the description given of them by those Islanders. Heavy rain came on at four o'clock, when every person did their utmost to catch some water, and we increased our stock to 34 gallons, besides quenching our thirst for the first time since we had been at sea; but an attendant consequence made us pass the night very miserably, for being extremely wet, and having no dry things to shift or cover us, we experienced cold and shiverings scarce to be conceived. Most fortunately for us, the forenoon turned out fair, and we stripped and dried our clothes. The allowance I issued to-day, was an ounce and a half of pork, a teaspoonful of rum, half a pint of cocoa-nut milk, and an ounce of bread. The rum, though so small in quantity, was of the greatest service. A fishing-line was generally towing from the stern of the boat, but though we saw great numbers of fish, we could never catch one.

At noon, I observed, in latitude 16° 4′ S, and found we had made a course, from yesterday noon, N 62° W, distance 62 miles; longitude, by account, from Tofoa, 7° 42′ W.

The land passed yesterday, and the day before, is a group of islands, fourteen or sixteen in number, lying between the latitude of 16° 26′ S and 17° 57′ S, and in longitude, by my account, 4° 47′ to 7° 17′ W from Tofoa. Three of these islands are very large, having from 30 to 40 leagues of sea-coast.

In the afternoon we cleaned out the boat, and it employed us till sunset to get everything dry and in order. Hitherto I had issued the allowance by guess, but I now made a pair of scales, with two cocoa-nut shells; and, having accidentally some pistol-balls in the boat, twenty-five of which weighed 1 lb., or 16 ounces, I adopted one,* as the proportion of weight that each person should receive of bread at the times I served it. I also amused all hands, with describing the situation of New Guinea and New Holland, and gave them every information in my power, that in case any accident happened to me, those who survived might have some idea of what they were about, and be able to find their way to Timor,

---

* It weighed 272 grains.

which at present they knew nothing of, more than the name, and some not even that. At night, I served a quarter of a pint of water, and half an ounce of bread, for supper.

Saturday, May the 9th. In the morning, a quarter of a pint of cocoa-nut milk, and some of the decayed bread, was served for breakfast; and for dinner, I divided the meat of four cocoa-nuts, with the remainder of the rotten bread, which was only eatable by such distressed people.

At noon, I observed the latitude to be 15° 47′ S; course since yesterday N 75° W, distance 64 miles; longitude made, by account, 8° 45′ W.

In the afternoon, I fitted a pair of shrouds for each mast, and contrived a canvas weather cloth round the boat, and raised the quarters about 9 inches, by nailing on the seats of the stern sheets, which proved of great benefit to us.

The wind had been moderate all day, in the S E quarter, with fine weather; but, about nine o'clock in the evening, the clouds began to gather, and we had a prodigious fall of rain, with severe thunder and lightning. By midnight we caught about 20 gallons of water. Being miserably wet and cold, I served to the people a tea-spoonful of rum each, to enable them to bear with their distressed situation. The weather continued extremely bad, and the wind increased; we spent a very miserable night, without sleep, except such as could be got in the midst of rain. The day brought no relief but its light. The sea broke over us so much, that two men were constantly bailing; and we had no choice how to steer, being obliged to keep before the waves for fear of the boat filling.

The allowance now regularly served to each person was one twenty-fifth of a pound of bread, and a quarter of a pint of water, at eight in the morning, at noon, and at sunset. To-day I gave about half an ounce of pork for dinner, which, though any moderate person would have considered only as a mouthful, was divided into three or four.

The rain abated towards noon, and I observed the latitude to be 15° 17′ S; course N 67° W, distance 78 miles; longitude made 10° W.

The wind continued strong from S S E to S E, with

very squally weather, and a high breaking sea, so that we
were miserably wet, and suffered great cold in the night.

Monday the 11th. In the morning at day-break, I
served to every person a teaspoonful of rum, our limbs
being so cramped that we could scarce move them. Our
situation was now extremely dangerous, the sea frequently running over our stern, which kept us bailing
with all our strength.

At noon, the sun appeared, which gave us as much
pleasure as in a winter's day in England. I issued the
twenty-fifth of a pound of bread, and a quarter of a pint
of water, as yesterday. Latitude observed 14° 50′ S;
course N 71° W, distance 102 miles; and longitude, by
account, 11° 39′ W from Tofoa.

In the evening it rained hard, and we again experienced a dreadful night. At length the day came, and
showed to me a miserable set of beings, full of wants,
without anything to relieve them. Some complained of
great pain in their bowels, and every one of having almost
lost the use of his limbs. The little sleep we got was no
ways refreshing, as we were covered with sea and rain.
I served a spoonful of rum at day-dawn, and the usual
allowance of bread and water, for breakfast, dinner, and
supper.

At noon it was almost calm, no sun to be seen, and
some of us shivering with cold. Course since yesterday
W by N, distance 89 miles; latitude, by account, 14° 33′
S; longitude made 13° 9′ W. The direction of our course
was to pass to the northward of the New Hebrides.

The wet weather continued, and in the afternoon the
wind came from the southward, blowing fresh in squalls.
As there was no prospect of getting our clothes dried,
I recommended to every one to strip, and wring them
through the salt water, by which means they received a
warmth, that, while wet with rain, they could not have.

This afternoon, we saw a kind of fruit on the water,
which Nelson told me was the Barringtonia of Forster;
and, as I saw the same again in the morning, and some
men of war birds, I was led to believe that we were not
far from land.

We continued constantly shipping seas, and bailing,
and were very wet and cold in the night; but I could not
afford the allowance of rum at day-break.

Wednesday the 13th. At noon I had a sight of the sun, latitude 14° 17′ S; course W by N 79 miles; longitude made 14° 28′ W. All this day, we were constantly shipping water, and suffered much cold and shiverings in the night.

Thursday the 14th. Fresh gales at S E, and gloomy weather, with rain, and a high sea. At six in the morning, we saw land, from S W by S 8 leagues, to N W by W ¾ W 6 leagues, which soon after appeared to be four islands, one of them much larger than the others, and all of them high and remarkable. At noon, we discovered a small island and some rocks, bearing N W by N 4 leagues, and another island W 8 leagues, so that the whole were six in number; the four I had first seen bearing from S ½ E to S W by S; our distance 3 leagues from the nearest island. My latitude observed was 13° 29′ S, and longitude, by account, from Tofoa, 15° 49′ W; course since yesterday noon N 63° W, distance 89 miles. At four in the afternoon, we passed the westernmost island.

Friday the 15th. At one in the morning, another island was discovered, bearing W N W, 5 leagues distance, and at eight o'clock we saw it for the last time, bearing N E 7 leagues. A number of gannets, boobies, and men of war birds were seen.

These islands lie between the latitude of 13° 16′ and 14° 10′ S: their longitude, according to my reckoning, 15° 51′ to 17° 6′ W from the island Tofoa.* The largest island I judged to be about 20 leagues in circuit, the others 5 or 6. The easternmost is the smallest island, and most remarkable, having a high sugar-loaf hill.

The sight of these islands served only to increase the misery of our situation. We were very little better than starving, with plenty in view; yet to attempt procuring any relief was attended with so much danger, that prolonging of life, even in the midst of misery, was thought preferable, while there remained hopes of being able to surmount our hardships. For my own part, I consider the general run of cloudy and wet weather to be a blessing of providence. Hot weather would have caused

* By making a proportional allowance for the error afterwards found in the dead reckoning, I estimate the longitude of these islands to be from 167° 17′ E to 168° 34′ E from Greenwich.

us to have died with thirst; and probably being so constantly covered with rain or sea protected us from that dreadful calamity.

As I had nothing to assist my memory, I could not then determine whether these islands were a part of the New Hebrides or not: I believed them to be a new discovery, which I have since found true; but, though they were not seen either by Monsieur Bougainville or Captain Cook, they are so nearly in the neighbourhood of the New Hebrides, that they must be considered as part of the same group. They are fertile, and inhabited, as I saw smoke in several places.

The wind was at S E, with rainy weather all day. The night was very dark, not a star could be seen to steer by, and the sea broke continually over us. I found it necessary to counteract as much as possible the effect of the southerly winds, to prevent being driven too near New Guinea; for in general we were forced to keep so much before the sea, that if we had not, at intervals of moderate weather, steered a more southerly course, we should inevitably, from a continuance of the gales, have been thrown in sight of that coast: in which case there would mostly probably have been an end to our voyage.

Saturday the 16th. In addition to our miserable allowance of one twenty-fifth of a pound of bread, and a quarter of a pint of water, I issued for dinner about an ounce of salt pork to each person. I was often solicited for this pork, but I considered it more proper to issue it in small quantities than to suffer it to be all used at once or twice, which would have been done if I had allowed it.

At noon I observed, in 13° 33′ S; longitude made from Tofoa, 19° 27′ W; course N 82° W, distance 101 miles. The sun breaking out through the clouds, gave us hopes of drying our wet clothes; but the sunshine was of short duration. We had strong breezes at S E by S, and dark gloomy weather, with storms of thunder, lightning, and rain. The night was truly horrible, and not a star to be seen; so that our steerage was uncertain.

Sunday the 17th. At dawn of day, I found every person complaining, and some of them solicited extra allowance; which I positively refused. Our situation was miserable; always wet, and suffering extreme cold in the night, without the least shelter from the weather. Being constantly obliged to bail, to keep the boat from filling, was, perhaps, not to be reckoned an evil, as it gave us exercise.

The little rum we had was of great service: when our nights were particularly distressing, I generally served a teaspoonful or two to each person: and it was always joyful tidings when they heard of my intentions.

At noon, a water-spout was very near on board of us. I issued an ounce of pork, in addition to the allowance of bread and water; but before we began to eat, every person stripped, and having wrung their clothes through the sea-water, found much warmth and refreshment. Course since yesterday noon W S W, distance 100 miles; latitude, by account, 14° 11′ S, and longitude made 21° 3′ W.

The night was dark and dismal; the sea constantly breaking over us, and nothing but the wind and waves to direct our steerage. It was my intention, if possible, to make New Holland, to the southward of Endeavour Straits, being sensible that it was necessary to preserve such a situation as would make a southerly wind a fair one; that we might range along the reefs till an opening should be found into smooth water, and we the sooner be able to pick up some refreshments.

Monday, May the 18th. In the morning, the rain abated, when we stripped, and wrung our clothes through the sea-water, as usual, which refreshed us greatly. Every person complained of violent pain in their bones: I was only surprised that no one was yet laid up. The customary allowance of one twenty-fifth of a pound of bread, and a quarter of a pint of water, was served at breakfast, dinner, and supper.

At noon, I deduced my situation, by account, for we had no glimpse of the sun, to be in latitude 14° 52′ S; course since yesterday noon, W S W 106 miles; longitude made from Tofoa 22° 45′ W. Saw many boobies and noddies, a sign of being in the neighbourhood of land. In the night, we had very severe lightning, with heavy rain; and were obliged to keep bailing without intermission.

Tuesday the 19th. Very bad weather and constant rain. At noon, latitude, by account, 14° 37′ S; course since yesterday N 81° W, distance 100 miles; longitude made 24° 30′ W. With the allowance of bread and water, served half an ounce of pork to each person, for dinner.

Wednesday, May the 20th. Fresh breezes E N E with constant rain; at times a deluge. Always bailing.

At dawn of day, some of my people seemed half dead: our appearances were horrible; and I could look no way, but I caught the eye of some one in distress. Extreme hunger was now too evident, but no one suffered from thirst, nor had we much inclination to drink, that desire, perhaps, being satisfied through the skin. The little sleep we got was in the midst of water, and we constantly awoke with severe cramps and pains in our bones. This morning I served about two teaspoonfuls of rum to each person, and the allowance of bread and water, as usual. At noon the sun broke out, and revived every one. I found we were in latitude 14° 49' S; longitude made 25° 46' W; course S 88° W, distance 75 miles.

All the afternoon, we were so covered with rain and salt water, that we could scarcely see. We suffered extreme cold, and every one dreaded the approach of night. Sleep, though we longed for it, afforded no comfort: for my own part, I almost lived without it. About two o'clock in the morning we were overwhelmed with a deluge of rain. It fell so heavy that we were afraid it would fill the boat, and were obliged to bail with all our might. At dawn of day, I served a larger allowance of rum. Towards noon, the rain abated and the sun shone, but we were miserably cold and wet, the sea breaking constantly over us; so that, notwithstanding the heavy rain, we had not been able to add to our stock of fresh water. Latitude, by observation, 14° 29' S, and longitude made, by account, from Tofoa, 27° 25' W; course since yesterday noon, N 78° W, 99 miles. I now considered myself nearly on a meridian with the east part of New Guinea.

Friday, May the 22nd. Strong gales from E S E to S S E, a high sea, and dark dismal night.

Our situation this day was extremely calamitous. We were obliged to take the course of the sea, running right before it, and watching with the utmost care, as the least error in the helm would in a moment have been our destruction.

At noon it blew very hard, and the foam of the sea

kept running over our stern and quarters; I however got propped up, and made an observation of the latitude, in 14° 17′ S; course N 85° W, distance 130 miles; longitude made 29° 38′ W.

The misery we suffered this night exceeded the preceding. The sea flew over us with great force, and kept us bailing with horror and anxiety. At dawn of day I found every one in a most distressed condition, and I began to fear that another such night would put an end to the lives of several, who seemed no longer able to support their sufferings. I served an allowance of two teaspoonfuls of rum; after drinking which, having wrung our clothes, and taken our breakfast of bread and water, we became a little refreshed.

Towards noon, the weather became fair, but with very little abatement of the gale, and the sea remained equally high. With some difficulty I observed the latitude to be 13° 44′ S: course since yesterday noon N 74° W, distance 116 miles; longitude made 31° 32′ W from Tofoa.

The wind moderated in the evening, and the weather looked much better, which rejoiced all hands, so that they ate their scanty allowance with more satisfaction than for some time past. The night also was fair; but being always wet with the sea, we suffered much from the cold. A fine morning, I had the pleasure to see, produced some cheerful countenances; and, the first time for 15 days past, we experienced comfort from the warmth of the sun. We stripped, and hung our clothes up to dry, which were by this time become so thread-bare, that they would not keep out either wet or cold.

At noon, I observed in latitude 13° 33′ S; longitude, by account, from Tofoa 33° 28′ W; course N 84° W, distance 114 miles. With the usual allowance of bread and water for dinner, I served an ounce of pork to each person. This afternoon we had many birds about us, which are never seen far from land, such as boobies and noddies.

As the sea began to run fair, and we shipped but little water, I took the opportunity to examine into the state of our bread, and found, that, according to the present mode of issuing, there was a sufficient quantity remaining for 29 days' allowance; by which time I hoped we should be able to reach Timor. But as this was very uncertain,

and it was possible that, after all, we might be obliged to
go to Java, I determined to proportion the allowance so
as to make our stock hold out 6 weeks. I was apprehensive that this would be ill received, and that it would
require my utmost resolution to enforce it; for, small as
the quantity was which I intended to take away, for our
future good, yet it might appear to my people like robbing
them of life; and some, who were less patient than their
companions, I expected would very ill brook it. However, on my representing the necessity of guarding
against delays that might be occasioned in our voyage
by contrary winds, or other causes, and promising to
enlarge upon the allowance as we got on, they cheerfully
agreed to my proposal. It was accordingly settled, that
every person should receive one twenty-fifth of a pound
of bread for breakfast, and the same quantity for dinner;
so that by omitting the proportion for supper, we had
43 days' allowance.

Monday the 25th. At noon some noddies came so
near to us, that one of them was caught by hand. This
bird was about the size of a small pigeon. I divided it,
with its entrails, into 18 portions, and by a well-known
method at sea, of, *Who shall have this?** it was distributed,
with the allowance of bread and water for dinner, and
eat up bones and all, with salt water for sauce. I observed
the latitude 13° 32' S; longitude made 35° 19' W;
course N 89° W, distance 108 miles.

In the evening, several boobies flying very near to us,
we had the good fortune to catch one of them. This bird
is as large as a duck: like the noddy, it has received its
name from seamen, for suffering itself to be caught on
the masts and yards of ships. They are the most pre-
sumptive proofs of being in the neighbourhood of land of
any seafowl we are acquainted with. I directed the bird
to be killed for supper, and the blood to be given to three
of the people who were the most distressed for want of
food. The body, with the entrails, beak and feet, I
divided into 18 shares, and with an allowance of bread,

---

* One person turns his back on the object that is to be divided: another then points separately to the portions, at each of them asking
aloud, "Who shall have this?" to which the first answers by nam-
ing somebody. This impartial method of division gives every
man an equal chance of the best share.

which I made a merit of granting, we made a good supper, compared with our usual fare.

Tuesday the 26th. Fresh breezes from the S E, with fine weather. In the morning we caught another booby, so that Providence appeared to be relieving our wants in an extraordinary manner. Towards noon, we passed a great many pieces of the branches of trees, some of which appeared to have been no long time in the water. I had a good observation for the latitude, and found our situation to be in 13° 41′ S; longitude, by account, from Tofoa, 37° 13′ W; course S 85° W, 112 miles. The people were overjoyed at the addition to their dinner, which was distributed in the same manner as on the preceding evening; giving the blood to those who were the most in want of food.

To make the bread a little savoury, most of the people frequently dipped it in salt water; but I generally broke mine into small pieces, and eat it in my allowance of water, out of a cocoa-nut shell, with a spoon; economically avoiding to take too large a piece at a time, so that I was as long at dinner as if it had been a much more plentiful meal.

The weather was now serene, which, nevertheless, was not without its inconveniences, for we began to feel distress of a different kind from that which we had lately been accustomed to suffer. The heat of the sun was so powerful, that several of the people were seized with a languor and faintness, which made life indifferent. We were so fortunate as to catch two boobies in the evening: their stomachs contained several flying-fish and small cuttlefish, all of which I saved to be divided for dinner the next day.

Wednesday the 27th. A fresh breeze at E S E, with fair weather. We passed much driftwood this forenoon, and saw many birds; I therefore did not hesitate to pronounce that we were near the reefs of New Holland. From my recollection of Captain Cook's survey of this coast, I considered the direction of it to be N W, and I was therefore satisfied that, with the wind to the southward of E, I could always clear any dangers.

At noon, I observed in latitude 13° 26′ S; course since yesterday N 82° W, distance 109 miles; longitude made 39° 4′ W. After writing my account, I divided the two birds with their entrails, and the contents of their maws, into 18 portions, and, as the prize was a very valuable one, it was divided as before, by calling out *Who shall have this?* so that to-day with the allowance of a twenty-fifth of a pound of bread at breakfast, and another at dinner, with the proportion of water, I was happy to see that every person thought he had feasted.

In the evening, we saw a gannet; and the clouds remained so fixed in the W, that I had little doubt of our being near the land. The people, after taking their allowance of water for supper, amused themselves with conversing on the probability of what we should find.

Thursday the 28th. At one in the morning, the person at the helm heard the sound of breakers, and I no sooner lifted up my head, than I saw them close under our lee, not more than a quarter of a mile distant from us. I immediately hauled on a wind to the N N E, and in ten minutes time we could neither see nor hear them.

I have already mentioned my reason for making New Holland so far to the southward: for I never doubted of numerous openings in the reef, through which I could have access to the shore: and, knowing the inclination of the coast to be to the N W, and the wind mostly to the southward of E, I could with ease range such a barrier of reefs till I should find a passage, which now became absolutely necessary, without a moment's loss of time. The idea of getting into smooth water, and finding refreshments, kept my people's spirits up: their joy was very great after we had got clear of the breakers, to which we had approached much nearer than I thought was possible, without first discovering them.

In the morning, at day-light, we could see nothing of the land or of the reefs. We bore away again, and at nine o'clock, saw the reefs. The sea broke furiously over every part, and we had no sooner got near to them, than the wind came at E, so that we could only lie along the line of the breakers; within which we saw the water so smooth, that every person already anticipated the heartfelt satisfaction he should receive, as soon as we could get within them. I now found we were embayed, for we could not lie clear with sails, the wind having backed against us; and the sea set in so heavy towards the reef, that our situation was become unsafe. We could effect but little with the oars, having scarce strength to pull them; and I began to apprehend that we should be obliged to attempt pushing over the reef. Even this I did not despair of effecting with success, when happily we discovered a break in the reef, about one mile from us, and at the same time an island of a moderate height within it, nearly in the same direction, bearing W ½ N. I entered the passage with a strong stream running to the westward, and found it about a quarter of a mile broad, with every appearance of deep water.

On the outside, the reef inclined to the N E for a few miles, and from thence to the N W: on the south side of the entrance, it inclined to the S S W as far as I could see it; and I conjecture that a similar passage to this which we now entered, may be found near the breakers that I first discovered, which are 23 miles S of this channel.

I did not recollect what latitude Providential Channel* lies in, but I considered it to be within a few miles of this, which is situate in 12° 51′ S latitude.

Being now happily within the reefs, and in smooth water, I endeavoured to keep near them to try for fish; but the tide set us to the N W, I therefore bore away in that direction, and, having promised to land on the first convenient spot we could find, all our past hardships seemed already to be forgotten.

At noon, I had a good observation, by which our latitude was 12° 46′ S, whence the foregoing situations may be considered as determined with some exactness. The island first seen bore W S W 5 leagues. This, which I have called the island Direction, will in fair weather always show the channel, from which it bears due W, and may be seen as soon as the reefs, from a ship's masthead: it lies in the latitude of 12° 51′ S. These, however, are marks too small for a ship to hit, unless it can hereafter be ascertained that passages through the reef are numerous along the coast, which I am inclined to think they are, in which case there would be little risk, even if the wind was directly on the shore.

My longitude, made by dead reckoning, from the island Tofoa to our passage through the reef, is 40° 10′

* Providential Channel is laid down by Captain Cook, in 12° 34′ S, longitude 143° 33′ E.

W. Providential Channel, I imagine, must lie very nearly under the same meridian with our passage; by which it appears we had outrun our reckoning 1° 9'.

We now returned God thanks for His gracious protection, and with much content took our miserable allowance of a twenty-fifth of a pound of bread, and a quarter of a pint of water, for dinner.

CHAPTER XVI

*Progress to the Northward, along the Coast of New Holland
—Land on different Islands, in search of Supplies*

As we advanced within the reefs, the coast began to show itself very distinctly, in a variety of high and low land; some parts of which were covered with wood. In our way towards the shore, we fell in with a point of a reef which is connected with that towards the sea, and here we came to a grapnel, and tried to catch fish, but had no success. The island Direction at this time bore S 3 or 4 leagues. Two islands lay about four miles to the W by N, and appeared eligible for a resting-place, if for nothing more; but on our approach to the nearest island, it proved to be only a heap of stones, and its size too inconsiderable to shelter the boat. We therefore proceeded to the next, which was close to it and towards the main. On the northwest side of this, I found a bay and a fine sandy point to land at. Our distance was about a quarter of a mile from a projecting part of the main, which bore from S W by S, to N N W ¾ W. We landed to examine if there were any signs of the natives being near us: we saw some old fireplaces, but nothing to make me apprehend that this would be an unsafe situation for the night. Every one was anxious to find something to eat, and it was soon discovered that there were oysters on the rocks, for the tide was out; but it was nearly dark, and only a few could be gathered. I determined therefore to wait till the morning, when I should better know how to proceed, and I directed that one half of our company should sleep on shore, and the other half in the boat. We would gladly have made a fire, but, as we could not accomplish it, we took our rest for the night, which happily was calm and undisturbed.

Friday the 29th. The dawn of day brought greater strength and spirits to us than I expected; for, notwithstanding every one was very weak, there appeared strength sufficient remaining to make me conceive the most favourable hopes of our being able to surmount the difficulties we might yet have to encounter.

As there were no appearances to make me imagine that any of the natives were near us, I sent out parties in search of supplies, while others of the people were putting the boat in order, that we might be ready to go to sea in case any unforeseen cause should make it necessary. One of the gudgeons of the rudder had come out in the course of the night, and was lost. This, if it had happened at sea, might have been attended with the most serious consequences, as the management of the boat could not have been so nicely preserved as these very heavy seas required. I had been apprehensive of this accident, and had in some measure prepared for it, by having grummets fixed on each quarter of the boat for oars; but our utmost readiness in using them would not probably have saved us. It appears, therefore, a providential circumstance, that it happened in a place of safety, and that it was in our power to remedy the defect; for by great good luck we found a large staple in the boat, which answered the purpose.

The parties returned, highly rejoiced at having found plenty of oysters and fresh water. I had also made a fire, by the help of a small magnifying glass; and, what was still more fortunate, we found among the few things which had been thrown into the boat and saved, a piece of brimstone and a tinder-box, so that I secured fire for the future.

One of the people had been so provident as to bring away with him from the ship, a copper pot: by being in possession of this article we were enabled to make a proper use of the supply we now obtained; for, with a mixture of bread, and a little pork, we made a stew that might have been relished by people of far more delicate appetites, and of which each person received a full pint.

The general complaints of disease among us, were a dizziness in the head, great weakness of the joints, and violent tenesmus; most of us having had no evacuation by stool since we left the ship. I had constantly a severe pain at my stomach; but none of our complaints were alarming: on the contrary, every one retained marks of strength, that, with a mind possessed of a tolerable share of fortitude, seemed able to bear more fatigue than I imagined we should have to undergo in our voyage to Timor.

As I would not allow the people to expose themselves to the heat of the sun, it being near noon, every one took his allotment of earth where it was shaded by the bushes, for a short sleep.

The oysters which we found, grew so fast to the rocks, that it was with difficulty they could be broken off; and at length we discovered it to be the most expeditious way to open them where they were fixed. They were of a good size, and well tasted. To add to this happy circumstance, in the hollow of the land there grew some wire grass, which indicated a moist situation. On forcing a stick, about three feet long, into the ground, we found water, and with little trouble dug a well, which produced as much as our occasions required. It was very good, but I could not determine if it was a spring or not. We were not obliged to make the well deep, for it flowed as fast as we emptied it; which, as the soil was apparently too loose to retain water from the rains, renders it probable to be a spring. On the south side of the island likewise, we found a small run of good water.

Besides places where fires had been made, there were other signs of the natives sometimes resorting to this island. I saw two ill-constructed huts or wigwams, which had only one side loosely covered; and a pointed stick was found, about three feet long, with a slit in the end of it, to sling stones with; the same as the natives of Van Diemen's Land use.

The track of some animal was very discernible, and Nelson agreed with me that it was the Kanguroa, but whether these animals swim over from the mainland, or are brought here by the natives to breed, it is impossible to determine. The latter is not improbable; as they may be taken with less difficulty in a confined spot like this, than on the continent.

The island is about a league in circuit: it is a high lump of rocks and stones covered with wood; but the trees are small, the soil, which is very indifferent and sandy, being barely sufficient to produce them. The trees that came within our knowledge were the manchineal and a species of purow: also some palm-trees, the tops of which we cut down, and the soft interior part or heart of them was so palatable that it made a good addition to our mess. Nelson discovered some fern-roots, which I thought might be good roasted, as a substitute for bread, but in this I was mistaken: it however was very serviceable in its natural state to allay thirst, and on that account I directed a quantity to be collected to take into the boat. Many pieces of cocoa-nut shells and husks were found about the shore, but we could find no cocoa-nut trees, neither did I see any on the main.

I had cautioned the people not to touch any kind of berry or fruit that they might find; yet they were no sooner out of my sight than they began to make free' with three different kinds, that grew all over the island, eating without any reserve. The symptoms of having eaten too much, began at last to frighten some of them; but on questioning others, who had taken a more moderate allowance, their minds were a little quieted. The others, however, became equally alarmed in their turn, dreading that such symptoms would come on, and that they were all poisoned, so that they regarded each other with the strongest marks of apprehension, uncertain what would be the issue of their imprudence. Fortunately the fruit proved wholesome and good. One sort grew on a small delicate kind of vine; they were the size of a large gooseberry, and very like in substance, but had only a sweet taste; the skin was a pale red, streaked with yellow the long way of the fruit: it was pleasant and agreeable. Another kind grew on bushes, like that which is called the seaside grape in the West Indies; but the fruit was very different, being more like elderberries, and grew in clusters in the same manner. The third sort was a blackberry; this was not in such plenty as the others, and resembled a bullace, or large kind of sloe, both in size and taste. When I saw that these fruits were eaten by the birds, I no longer doubted of their being wholesome, and those who had already tried the experiment, not finding any bad effect, made it a certainty that we might eat of them without danger.

Wild pigeons, parrots, and other birds, were about the summit of the island, but, having no firearms, relief of that kind was not to be expected, unless we should find some unfrequented spot where the birds were so tame that we might take them with our hands.

The shore of this island is very rocky, except the place at which we landed, and here I picked up many pieces of pumice-stone. On the part of the main nearest to us, were several sandy bays, which at low-water became an extensive rocky flat. The country had rather a barren appearance, except in a few places where it was covered with wood. A remarkable range of rocks lay a few miles to the S W, and a high peaked hill seemed to terminate the coast towards the sea, with islands to the southward. A high fair cape showed the direction of the coast to the N W, about 7 leagues distant; and two small isles lay 3 or 4 leagues to the northward of our present station.

I saw a few bees or wasps, and several lizards; and the blackberry bushes were full of ants' nests webbed like a spider's, but so close and compact as not to admit the rain. A trunk of a tree, about fifty feet long, lay on the beach; from which I conclude that a heavy sea sets in here, with a northerly wind.

This day being the anniversary of the restoration of King Charles the Second, and the name not being inapplicable to our present situation (for we were restored to fresh life and strength), I named this Restoration Island; for I thought it probable that Captain Cook might not have taken notice of it. The other names which I have presumed to give the different parts of the coast, are meant only to show my route more distinctly.

At noon, I observed the latitude of the island to be 12° 39' S; our course having been N 66° W, distance 18 miles from yesterday noon. The wind was at E S E, with very fine weather.

In the afternoon, I sent parties out again to gather oysters, with which and some of the inner part of the palm-top, we made another good stew for supper, each person receiving a full pint and a half; but I refused bread to this meal, for I considered that our wants might yet be very great, and was intent on saving our principal support whenever it was in my power. After supper, we again divided, and those who were on shore slept by a good fire.

Saturday, May the 30th. In the morning, I discovered a visible alteration in our company for the better, and I sent them away again to gather oysters. We had now only 2 lbs. of pork left. This article, which I could not keep under lock and key as I did the bread, had been pilfered by some inconsiderate person, but every one denied having any knowledge of this act; I therefore resolved to put it out of their power for the future, by sharing what remained, for our dinner. While the party was out picking up oysters, I got the boat in readiness for sea, and filled all our water vessels, which amounted to nearly 60 gallons.

The party being returned, dinner was soon ready, which was as plentiful a meal as the supper on the preceding evening, and with the pork I gave an allowance of bread. As it was not yet noon, I sent the people once more to gather oysters for a sea store, recommending to them to be as diligent as possible, for that I was determined to sail in the afternoon.

At noon, I again observed the latitude 12° 39′ S; it was then high-water, the tide had risen 3 feet, but I could not be certain from whence the flood came. I deduce the time of high-water at full and change to be ten minutes past seven in the morning.

Early in the afternoon, the people returned with the few oysters that they had collected, and everything was put into the boat. I then examined the quantity of bread remaining, and found 38 days' allowance, according to the last mode of issuing a twenty-fifth of a pound at breakfast and at dinner.

Fair weather, and moderate breezes at E S E and S E.

Being ready for sea, I directed every person to attend prayers. At four o'clock we were preparing to embark; when about twenty of the natives appeared, running and hallooing to us, on the opposite shore. They were each armed with a spear or lance, and a short weapon which they carried in their left hand: they made signs for us to come to them. On the top of the hills we saw the heads of many more: whether these were their wives and children, or others who waited for our landing, meaning not to show themselves, lest we might be intimidated, I cannot say; but, as I found we were discovered to be on the coast, I thought it prudent to make the best of our way, for fear of being pursued by canoes; though, from the accounts of Captain Cook, the chance was that there were very few if any of consequence on any part of the coast. I passed these people as near as I could with safety: they were naked, and apparently black, and their hair or wool bushy and short.

I directed my course within two small islands that lie to the north of Restoration Island, passing between them and the mainland, towards Fair Cape, with a strong tide in my favour; so that I was abreast of it by eight o'clock. The coast we passed was high and woody. As I could see no land without Fair Cape, I concluded that the coast inclined to the N W and W N W: I therefore steered more towards the W; but by eleven o'clock at night, we met with low land, which inclined to the N E; and at three o'clock in the morning I found that we were embayed, which obliged us to stand back for a short time to the southward.

Sunday the 31st. At day-break, I was exceedingly surprised to find the appearance of the country entirely changed, as if in the course of the night we had been transported to another part of the world; for we had now a low sandy coast in view, with very little verdure, or anything to indicate that it was at all habitable to a human being, except a few patches of small trees or brushwood.

Many small islands were in sight to the N E, about six miles distant. The east part of the main bore N 4 miles, and Fair Cape S S E 5 or 6 leagues. I took the channel between the nearest island and the mainland, which were about one mile apart, leaving all the islands on the starboard side. Some of these were very pretty spots, covered with wood, and well situated for fishing: large shoals of fish were about us, but we could not catch any. In passing this strait we saw another party of Indians, seven in number, running towards us, shouting and making signs for us to land. Some of them waved green branches of the bushes which were near them, as a token of friendship; but some of their other motions were less friendly. A little farther off, we saw a larger party, who likewise came towards us. I therefore determined not to land, though I much wished to have had some intercourse with these people. Nevertheless I laid the boat close to the rocks, and beckoned to them to approach; but none of them would come within 200 yards of us. They were armed in the same manner as the people we had seen from Restoration Island; they were stark naked, their colour black, with short bushy hair or wool, and in their appearance were similar to them in every respect. An island of a good height bore N ½ W, 4 miles from us, at which I resolved to land, and from thence to take a look at the coast. At this isle we arrived about eight o'clock in the morning. The shore was rocky, but the water was smooth, and we landed without difficulty. I sent two parties out, one to the northward, and the other to the southward, to seek for supplies, and others I ordered to stay by the boat. On this occasion, fatigue and weakness so far got the better of their sense of duty, that some of the people expressed their discontent at having worked harder than their companions, and declared that they would rather be without their dinner than go in search of it. One person, in particular, went so far as to tell me, with a mutinous look, that he was as good a man as myself. It was not possible for me to judge where this might have an end, if not stopped in time; therefore to prevent such disputes in future, I determined either to preserve my command, or die in the attempt: and, seizing a cutlass, I ordered him to take hold of another and defend himself; on which he called out that I was going to kill him, and immediately made concessions. I did not allow this to interfere further with the harmony of the boat's crew, and everything soon became quiet.

The parties continued collecting what they could find, which were some fine oysters and clams, and a few small dog-fish that were caught in the holes of the rocks. We also found some rain-water in the hollow of the rocks, on the north part of the island, so that of this essential article we were again so fortunate as to obtain a full supply.

After regulating the mode of proceeding, I walked to the highest part of the island, to consider our route for the night. To my surprise, no more of the mainland could be seen here than from below, the northernmost part in sight, which was full of sandhills, bearing W by N, about three leagues. Except the isles to the E S E and S, that we had passed, I could only discover a small key N W by N. As this was considerably farther from the main than the spot on which we were at present, I judged it would be a more secure resting-place for the night; for here we were liable to an attack, if the Indians had canoes, as they undoubtedly must have observed our landing. My mind being made up on this point, I returned, after taking a particular look at the island we were on, which I found only to produce a few bushes, and some coarse grass; the extent of the whole not being two miles in circuit. On the north side, in a sandy bay, I saw an old canoe, about thirty-three feet long, lying bottom upwards, and half buried in the beach. It was made of three pieces, the bottom entire, to which the sides were sewed in the common way. It had a sharp projecting prow rudely carved, in resemblance of the head of a fish; the extreme breadth was about three feet, and I imagine it was capable of carrying twenty men. The discovery of so large a canoe, confirmed me in the purpose of seeking a more retired place for our night's lodging.

At noon, the parties were all returned, but had found much difficulty in gathering the oysters, from their close adherence to the rocks, and the clams were scarce: I therefore saw, that it would be of little use to remain longer in this place, as we should not be able to collect more than we could eat. I named this Sunday Island: it lies N by W ¾ W from Restoration Island; the latitude, by a good observation, 11° 58′ S.

We had a fresh breeze at S E by S, with fair weather. At two o'clock in the afternoon, we dined; each person having a full pint and a half of stewed oysters and clams, thickened with small beans, which Nelson informed me were a species of Dolichos. Having eaten heartily, and completed our water, I waited to determine the time of high-water, which I found to be at three o'clock, and the rise of the tide about five feet. According to this, it is high-water on the full and change at nineteen minutes past nine in the morning: I observed the flood to come from the southward, though at Restoration Island, I thought it came from the northward. I think Captain Cook mentions that he found great irregularity in the set of the flood on this coast.

We steered for the key seen in the N W by N, where we arrived just at dark, but found it so surrounded by a reef of rocks, that I could not land without danger of staving the boat; and on that account we came to a grapnel for the night.

Monday, June the 1st. At dawn of day, we got on shore, and tracked the boat into shelter; for the wind blowing fresh without, and the ground being rocky, it was not safe to trust her at a grapnel, lest she should be blown to sea: I was, therefore, obliged to let her ground in the course of the ebb. From appearances, I expected that if we remained till night we should meet with turtle, as we discovered recent tracks of them. Innumerable birds of the noddy kind made this island their resting-place; so that we had reason to flatter ourselves with hopes of getting supplies in greater abundance than it had hitherto been in our power. Our situation was at least 4 leagues distant from the main. We were on the north-westernmost of four small keys, which were surrounded by a reef of rocks connected by sand-banks, except between the two northernmost; and there likewise it was dry at low-water; the whole forming a lagoon island, into which the tide flowed: at this entrance I kept the boat.

As usual, I sent parties away in search of supplies, but, to our great disappointment, we could only get a few clams and some dolichos: with these, and the oysters we had brought from Sunday Island, I made up a mess for dinner, with the addition of a small quantity of bread.

Towards noon, Nelson, and some others, who had been to the easternmost key, returned; but Nelson was in so weak a condition that he was obliged to be supported by two men. His complaint was a violent heat in his bowels, a loss of sight, much drought, and an inability to walk. This I found was occasioned by his being unable to support the heat of the sun, and that, when he was fatigued and faint, instead of retiring into the shade to rest, he had continued to attempt more than his strength was equal to. I was glad to find that he had no fever; and it was now that the little wine, which I had so carefully saved, became of real use. I gave it in very small quantities, with some pieces of bread soaked in it; and he soon began to recover. The boatswain and carpenter also were ill, and complained of headache, and sickness of the stomach. Others, who had not had any evacuation by stool, became shockingly distressed with the tenesmus; so that there were but few without complaints. An idea prevailed, that the sickness of the boatswain and carpenter was occasioned by eating the dolichos. Myself, however, and some others, who had taken the same food, felt no inconvenience; but the truth was, that many of the people had eaten a large quantity of them raw, and Nelson informed me, that they were constantly teasing him, whenever a berry was found, to know if it was good to eat; so that it would not have been surprising if many of them had been really poisoned.

Our dinner was not so well relished as at Sunday Island, because we had mixed the dolichos with our stew. The oysters and soup, however, were eaten by every one, except Nelson, whom I fed with a few small pieces of bread soaked in half a glass of wine, and he continued to mend.

In my walk round the island, I found several cocoa-nut shells, the remains of an old wigwam, and the backs of two turtle, but no sign of any quadruped. One of the people found three sea-fowl's eggs.

As is common on such spots, the soil is little other than sand, yet it produced small toa-trees, and some others, that we were not acquainted with. There were fish in the lagoon, but we could not catch any. Our wants, therefore, were not likely to be supplied here, not even with water for our daily expense: nevertheless, I determined to wait till the morning, that we might try our success in the night for turtle and birds. A quiet night's rest also, I conceived, would be of essential service to those who were unwell.

The wigwam and turtle shell were proofs that the natives at times visited this place; and that they had canoes, the remains of the large canoe that we saw at Sunday Island left no room to doubt: but I did not apprehend that we ran any risk by remaining here a short time. I directed our fire, however, to be made in the thicket, that we might not be discovered by its light.

At noon, I observed the latitude of this island to be 11° 47′ S. The mainland extended towards the N W, and was full of white sand-hills: another small island lay within us, bearing W by N ¼ N, 3 leagues distant. Our situation being very low, we could see nothing of the reef towards the sea.

The afternoon was advantageously spent in sleep. There were, however, a few not disposed to it, and those were employed in dressing some clams to take with us for the next day's dinner: others we cut up in slices to dry, which I knew was the most valuable supply we could find here; but they were very scarce.

Towards evening, I cautioned every one against making too large a fire, or suffering it after dark to blaze up. Mr. Samuel and Mr. Peckover had the superintendence of this business, while I was strolling about the beach to observe if I thought it could be seen from the main. I was just satisfied that it could not, when on a sudden the island appeared all in a blaze, that might have been discerned at a much more considerable distance. I ran to learn the cause, and found that it was occasioned by the imprudence and obstinacy of one of the party, who, in my absence, had insisted on having a fire to himself; in making which the flames caught the neighbouring grass and rapidly spread. This misconduct might have produced very serious consequences, by discovering our situation to the natives; for, if they had attacked us, we had neither arms nor strength to oppose an enemy. Thus the relief which I expected from a little sleep was totally lost, and I anxiously waited for the flowing of the tide, that we might proceed to sea.

It was high-water at half past five this evening, whence I deduced the time, on the full and change of the moon, to be fifty-eight minutes past ten in the morning: the rise was nearly five feet. I could not observe the set of the flood; but imagined it to come from the southward, and that I was mistaken at Restoration Island, as I found the time of high-water gradually later the more we advanced to the northward.

At Restoration Island, high-water, full and change,	7ʰ	10′
Sunday Island, ...	9	19
Here, ...	10	58

After eight o'clock, Mr. Samuel and Mr. Peckover went out to watch for turtle, and three men went to the east key to endeavour to catch birds. All the others complaining of being sick, took their rest, except Mr. Hayward and Mr. Elphinston, whom I directed to keep watch. About midnight the bird party returned, with only twelve noddies, birds which I have already described to be about the size of pigeons: but if it had not been for the folly and obstinacy of one of the party, who separated from the other two, and disturbed the birds, they might have caught a great number. I was so much provoked at my plans being thus defeated, that I gave this offender* a good beating. I now went in search of the turtling party, who had taken great pains, but without success. This did not surprise me, as it was not to be expected that turtle would come near us, after the noise which had been made at the beginning of the evening in extinguishing the fire. I therefore desired them to come back, but they requested to stay a little longer, as they still hoped to find some before daylight: however, they returned by three o'clock, without any reward for their labour.

The birds we half dressed, that they might keep the better: and these, with a few clams, made the whole of the supply procured here. I tied a few gilt buttons and some pieces of iron to a tree, for any of the natives that might come after us; and, finding my invalids much better for their night's rest, we embarked, and departed by dawn of day. Wind at S E; course to the N by W.

When we had run 2 leagues to the northward, the sea suddenly became rough, which not having before experienced since we were within the reefs, I concluded to be occasioned by an open channel to the ocean. Soon afterwards, we met with a large shoal, on which were two sandy keys; between these and two others, 4 miles to the W, I passed on to the northward, the sea still continuing to be rough.

Towards noon, I fell in with six other keys, most of which produced some small trees and brushwood. These formed a pleasing contrast with the mainland we had passed, which was full of sand-hills. The country continued hilly, and the northernmost land, the same we had seen from the lagoon island, appeared like downs, sloping towards the sea. Nearly abreast of us, was a flat-topped hill, which, on account of its shape, I called Pudding-pan Hill; and a little to the northward were two other hills,

---

* Robert Lamb.—This man, when he came to Java, acknowledged he had eaten nine birds raw, after he separated from his two companions.

which we called the Paps; and here was a small tract of country without sand, the eastern part of which forms a cape, whence the coast inclines to the N W by N.

At noon, I observed in the latitude of 11° 18′ S, the cape bearing W, distant 10 miles. Five small keys bore from N E to S E, the nearest of them about 2 miles distant, and a low sandy key between us and the cape bore W, distant 4 miles. My course from the lagoon island had been N ½ W, distant 30 miles.

I am sorry it was not in my power to obtain a sufficient knowledge of the depth of water; but in our situation nothing could be undertaken that might have occasioned delay. It may however be understood, that, to the best of my judgement, from appearances, a ship may pass wherever I have omitted to represent danger.

I divided six birds, and issued one twenty-fifth of a pound of bread, with half a pint of water, to each person for dinner, and I gave half a glass of wine to Nelson, who was now so far recovered as to require no other indulgence.

The gunner, when he left the ship, brought his watch with him, by which we had regulated our time till to-day, when unfortunately it stopped; so that noon, sun-rise, and sunset, are the only parts of the twenty-four hours of which from henceforward I can speak with certainty, as to time.

The wind blew fresh from the S S E and S E all the afternoon, with fair weather. As we stood to the N by W, we found more sea, which I attributed to our receiving less shelter from the reefs to the eastward: it is probable they do not extend so far north as this; at least, it may be concluded that there is not a continued barrier to prevent shipping having access to the shore. I observed that the stream set to the N W, which I considered to be the flood. In some places along the coast, we saw patches of wood. At five o'clock, steering to the N W, we passed a large and fair inlet, into which, I imagine, there is a safe and commodious entrance; it lies in latitude 11° S. About 3 leagues to the northward of this is an island, at which we arrived about sunset, and took shelter for the night under a sandy point, which was the only part we could land at. This being rather a wild situation, I thought it best to sleep in the boat:

nevertheless I sent a party away to see if anything could be got, but they returned without success. They saw a great number of turtle bones and shells, where the natives had been feasting, and their last visit seemed to be of late date. The island was covered with wood, but in other respects, it was a lump of rocks.

Wednesday the 3rd. We lay at a grapnel till daylight, with a very fresh gale and cloudy weather. The main bore from S E by S to N N W ½ W, 3 leagues; and a mountainous island, with a flat top, N by W, 4 or 5 leagues; between which and the mainland were several other islands. The spot we were at, which I call Turtle Island, lies in latitude, by account, 10° 52′ S; and 42 miles W from Restoration Island. Abreast of it, the coast has the appearance of a sandy desert, but improves about 3 leagues farther to the northward, where it terminates in a point, near to which are many small islands. I sailed between these islands, where I found no bottom at 12 fathoms; the high mountainous island with a flat top, and four rocks to the S E of it, that I call the Brothers, being on my starboard hand. Soon after, an extensive opening appeared in the mainland in which were a number of high islands. I called this the Bay of Islands. We continued steering to the N W. Several islands and keys were in sight to the northward: the most northerly island was mountainous, having on it a very high round hill; and a smaller was remarkable for a single peaked hill.

The coast to the northward and westward of the Bay of Islands is high and woody, and has a broken appearance, with many islands close to it; among which there are fine bays, and convenient places for shipping. The northernmost of these islands I call Wednesday Island: to the N W of this we fell in with a large reef, which I believe joins a number of keys that were in sight from the N W to the E N E. We therefore stood to the S W half a league, when it was noon, and I had a good observation of the latitude in 10° 31′ S. Wednesday Island bore E by S 5 miles; the westernmost land in sight S W 2 or 3 leagues; the islands to the northward, from N W by W, to N E, and the reef from W to N E, distant 1 mile. I was now tolerably certain that we should be clear of New Holland in the afternoon.

I know not how far this reef extends. It may be a continuation, or a detached part of the range of shoals that surround the coast. I believe the mountainous island to be separate from the shoals; and have no doubt that near them may be found good passages for ships. But I rather recommend to those who are to pass this strait from the eastward, to take their direction from the coast of New Guinea: yet, I likewise think that a ship coming from the southward, will find a fair strait in the latitude of 10° S. I much wished to have ascertained this point; but in our distressful situation, any increase of fatigue, or loss of time, might have been attended with the most fatal consequences. I therefore determined to pass on without delay.

As an addition to our dinner of bread and water, I served to each person six oysters.

At two o'clock in the afternoon, as we were steering to the S W, towards the westernmost part of the land in sight, we fell in with some large sand-banks that run off from the coast: I therefore called this Shoal Cape. We were obliged to steer to the northward again, till we got round the shoals, when I directed the course to the W.

At four o'clock, the westernmost of the islands to the northward bore N 4 leagues; Wednesday Island E by N 5 leagues; and Shoal Cape S E by E 2 leagues. A small island was seen bearing W, at which we arrived before dark, and found that it was only a rock, where boobies resort, for which reason I called it Booby Island. Here terminated the rocks and shoals of the north part of New Holland, for, except Booby Island, no land was seen to the westward of S, after three o'clock this afternoon.

I find that Booby Island was seen by Captain Cook, and, by a remarkable coincidence of ideas, received from him the same name: but I cannot with certainty reconcile the situation of some parts of the coast that I have seen, to his survey. I ascribe this to the various forms in which land appears, when seen from the different heights of a ship and a boat. The chart I have given, is by no means meant to supersede that made by Captain Cook, who had better opportunities than I had, and was in every respect properly provided for surveying. The intention of mine is chiefly to render this narrative more intelligible, and to show in what manner the coast appeared to me from an open boat. I have little doubt but that the opening, which I named the Bay of Islands, is Endeavour Straits; and that our track was to the northward of Prince of Wales's Isles. Perhaps, by those who shall hereafter navigate these seas, more advantage may be derived from the possession of both our charts, than from either of them singly.

CHAPTER XVII

Passage from New Holland to the Island Timor—Arrive at Coupang—Reception there

AT eight o'clock in the evening, we once more launched into the open ocean. Miserable as our situation was in every respect, I was secretly surprised to see that it did not appear to affect any one so strongly as myself; on the contrary, it seemed as if they had embarked on a voyage to Timor, in a vessel sufficiently calculated for safety and convenience. So much confidence gave me great pleasure, and I may venture to assert, that to this cause our preservation is chiefly to be attributed.

I encouraged every one with hopes that eight or ten days would bring us to a land of safety; and, after praying to God for a continuance of His most gracious protection, I served an allowance of water for supper, and directed our course to the W S W, to counteract the southerly winds, in case they should blow strong.

We had been just six days on the coast of New Holland, in the course of which we found oysters, a few clams, some birds, and water. But perhaps a benefit nearly equal to this we received, by having been relieved from the fatigue of being constantly in the boat, and enjoying good rest at night. These advantages certainly preserved our lives; and, small as the supply was, I am very sensible how much it alleviated our distresses. By this time, nature must have sunk under the extremes of hunger and fatigue. Some would have ceased to struggle for a life that only promised wretchedness and misery; and others, though possessed of more bodily strength, must soon have followed their unfortunate companions. Even in our present situation, we were most deplorable objects; but the hopes of a speedy relief kept up our spirits. For my own part, incredible as it may appear, I felt neither extreme hunger nor thirst. My allowance contented me, knowing that I could have no more.

Thursday the 4th. I served one twenty-fifth of a pound of bread, and an allowance of water, for breakfast, and the same for dinner, with an addition of six oysters to each person. At noon, latitude observed 10° 48′ S; course since yesterday noon S 81° W, distance 111 miles; longitude, by account, from Shoal Cape, 1° 45′ W. A strong trade wind at E S E, with fair weather.

This day, we saw a number of water-snakes, that were ringed yellow and black, and towards noon we passed a great deal of rock-weed. Though the weather was fair, we were constantly shipping water, which kept two men always employed to bail the boat.

Friday the 5th. At noon, I observed in latitude 10° 45′ S; our course since yesterday W ¼ N, 108 miles; longitude made 3° 35′ W. Six oysters were, as yesterday, served to each man, in addition to the usual allowance of bread and water.

In the evening, a few boobies came about us, one of which I caught with my hand. The blood was divided among three of the men who were weakest, but the bird I ordered to be kept for our dinner the next day. Served a quarter of a pint of water for supper, and to some, who were most in need, half a pint. In the course of the night, being constantly wet with the sea, we suffered much cold and shiverings.

Saturday the 6th. At day-light, I found that some of the clams, which had been hung up to dry for sea-store, were stolen; but every one solemnly denied having any knowledge of it. This forenoon we saw a gannet, a sand-lark, and some water-snakes, which in general were from 2 to 3 feet long.

The usual allowance of bread and water was served for breakfast, and the same for dinner, with the bird, which I distributed in the usual way, of Who shall have this? I proposed to make Timor about the latitude of 9° 30′ S, or 10° S. At noon I observed the latitude to be 10° 19′ S; course N 77° W, distance 117 miles; longitude made from the Shoal Cape, the north part of New Holland, 5° 31′ W.

In the afternoon, I took an opportunity of examining our store of bread, and found remaining 19 days' allowance, at the former rate of serving one twenty-fifth of a pound three times a day: therefore, as I saw every prospect of a quick passage, I again ventured to grant an allowance for supper, agreeable to my promise at the time it was discontinued.

We passed the night miserably wet and cold, and in the morning I heard heavy complaints. The sea was high and breaking over us. I could only afford the allowance of bread and water for breakfast; but for dinner I gave out an ounce of dried clams to each person, which was all that remained.

At noon, I altered the course to the W N W, to keep more from the sea, as the wind blew strong. Latitude observed 9° 31′ S; course N 57° W, distance 88 miles; longitude made 6° 46′ W.

The sea ran very high all this day, and we had frequent showers of rain, so that we were continually wet, and suffered much cold in the night. Mr. Ledward, the surgeon, and Lawrence Lebogue, an old hardy seaman, appeared to be giving way very fast. I could only assist them by a teaspoonful or two of wine, which I had carefully saved, expecting such a melancholy necessity.

Monday the 8th. Wind at S E. The weather was more moderate than it had been for some days past. A few gannets were seen. At noon, I observed in 8° 45′ S; course W N W ¼ W, 106 miles; longitude made 8° 23′ W. The sea being smooth, I steered W by S.

At four in the afternoon, we caught a small dolphin, which was the first relief of the kind that we obtained. I issued about two ounces to each person, including the offals, and saved the remainder for dinner the next day. Towards evening the wind freshened, and it blew strong all night, so that we shipped much water, and suffered greatly from the wet and cold.

Tuesday the 9th. At daylight, as usual, I heard much complaining, which my own feeling convinced me was too well founded. I gave the surgeon and Lebogue a little wine, but I could afford them no further relief, except encouraging them with hopes that a very few days longer, at our present fine rate of sailing, would bring us to Timor.

Gannets, boobies, men of war and tropic birds, were constantly about us. Served the usual allowance of bread and water, and at noon we dined on the remains of the dolphin, which amounted to about an ounce per man.

I observed the latitude to be 9° 9′ S; longitude made 10° 8′ W; course since yesterday noon S 76° W; distance 107 miles.

This afternoon, I suffered great sickness from the nature of part of the stomach of the fish, which had fallen to my share at dinner. At sun-set I served an allowance of bread and water for supper.

Wednesday the 10th. In the morning, after a very comfortless night, there was a visible alteration for the worse in many of the people; which gave me great apprehensions. An extreme weakness, swelled legs, hollow and ghastly countenances, a more than common inclination to sleep, with an apparent debility of understanding, seemed to me the melancholy presages of an approaching dissolution. The surgeon and Lebogue, in particular, were most miserable objects. I occasionally gave them a few teaspoonfuls of wine, out of the little that remained, which greatly assisted them. The hopes of being able to accomplish the voyage, was our principal support. The boatswain very innocently told me, that he really thought I looked worse than any one in the boat. The simplicity with which he uttered such an opinion amused me, and I returned him a better compliment.

Our latitude at noon was 9° 16′ S. Longitude from the north part of New Holland, 12° 1′ W. Course since yesterday noon, W ½ S, 111 miles. Birds and rock-weed showed that we were not far from land; but I expected such signs here, as there are many islands between the east part of Timor and New Guinea. The night was more moderate than the last.

Thursday the 11th. Every one received the customary allowance of bread and water, and an extra allowance of water was given to those who were most in need. At noon I observed in latitude 9° 41′ S; course S 77° W, distance 109 miles; longitude made 13° 49′ W. I had little doubt of having now passed the meridian of the eastern part of Timor, which is laid down in 128° E. This diffused universal joy and satisfaction.

In the afternoon, we saw gannets, and many other birds, and at sun-set we kept a very anxious look-out. In the evening we caught a booby, which I reserved for our dinner the next day.

Friday the 12th. At three in the morning, with an
excess of joy, we discovered Timor bearing from W S W
to W N W, and I hauled on a wind to the N N E till daylight, when the land bore from S W by S to N E by N.
Our distance from the shore, 2 leagues.

It is not possible for me to describe the pleasure which
the blessing of the sight of this land diffused among us. It
appeared scarce credible to ourselves, that in an open
boat, and so poorly provided, we should have been able
to reach the coast of Timor in forty-one days after leaving
Tofoa, having in that time run, by our log, a distance of
3,618 miles; and that, not withstanding our extreme distress, no one should have perished in the voyage.

I have already mentioned, that I knew not where the
Dutch settlement was situated; but I had a faint idea that
it was at the S W part of the island. I therefore, after daylight, bore away along shore to the S S W, which I was
the more readily induced to do, as the wind would not
suffer us to go towards the N E without great loss of time.

The day gave us a most agreeable prospect of the land,
which was interspersed with woods and lawns; the interior
part mountainous, but the shore low. Towards noon, the
coast became higher, with some remarkable headlands.
We were greatly delighted with the general look of the
country, which exhibited many cultivated spots and beautiful situations; but we could only see a few small huts,
whence I concluded that no European resided in this part
of the island. Much sea ran on the shore, which made
landing impracticable. At noon, we were abreast of a high
headland; the extremes of the land bore S W ½ W, and
N N E ½ E; our distance off shore being 3 miles; latitude,
by observation, 9° 59′ S; and my longitude, by dead
reckoning from the north part of New Holland, 15° 6′ W.

With the usual allowance of bread and water for dinner, I divided the bird we had caught the night before, and
to the surgeon and Lebogue I gave a little wine.

The wind blew fresh at E, and E S E, with very hazy
weather. During the afternoon, we continued our course
along a low shore, covered with innumerable palm-trees,
called the Fan Palm from the leaf spreading like a fan;
but here we saw no signs of cultivation, nor had the country so fine an appearance as to the eastward. This, however, was only a small tract, for by sunset it improved

again, and I saw several great smokes where the inhabitants were clearing and cultivating their grounds. We had now run 25 miles to the W S W since noon, and were W 5 miles from a low point, which, in the afternoon, I imagined had been the southernmost land; and here the coast formed a deep bend, with low land in the bight that appeared like islands. The west shore was high; but from this part of the coast to the high cape which we were abreast of at noon, the shore is low, and I believe shoal. I particularly remark this situation, because here the very high ridge of mountains, that run from the east end of the island, terminate, and the appearance of the country changes for the worse.

That we might run past any settlement in the night, I determined to preserve my station till the morning, and therefore brought to under a close-reefed fore-sail. We were here in shoal water, our distance from the shore being half a league, the westernmost land in sight bearing W S W ½ W. Served bread and water for supper, and the boat lying to very well, all but the officer of the watch endeavoured to get a little sleep.

Saturday the 13th. At two in the morning, we wore, and stood in shore till daylight, when I found we had drifted, during the night, about 3 leagues to the W S W, the southernmost land in sight bearing W. On examining the coast, and not seeing any sign of a settlement, we bore away to the westward, having a strong gale, against a weather current, which occasioned much sea. The shore was high and covered with wood; but we did not run far, before low land again formed the coast, the points of which opening at W, I once more fancied we were on the south part of the island; but at ten o'clock we found the coast again inclining towards the south, part of it bearing W S W ½ W. At the same time, high land appeared in the S W; but the weather was so hazy, that it was doubtful whether the two lands were separated, the opening only extending one point of the compass. For this reason I stood towards the outer land, and found it to be the island Roti.

I returned to the shore we had left, and brought to a grapnel in a sandy bay, that I might more conveniently calculate my situation. In this place, we saw several smokes, where the natives were clearing their grounds.

During the little time we remained here, the master and carpenter very much importuned me to let them go in search of supplies; to which, at length, I assented; but, not finding any other person willing to be of their party, they did not choose to quit the boat. I stopped here no longer than for the purpose just mentioned, and we continued steering along shore. We had a view of a beautiful-looking country, as if formed by art into lawns and parks. The coast is low and covered with woods, in which are innumerable fan palm-trees, that look like cocoa-nut walks. The interior part is high land, but very different from the more eastern parts of the island, where it is exceedingly mountainous, and to appearance, the soil better.

At noon, the island Roti bore S W by W 7 leagues. I had no observation for the latitude, but by account, we were in 10° 12′ S; our course since yesterday noon being S 77° W, 54 miles. The usual allowance of bread and water was served for breakfast and dinner, and to the surgeon and Lebogue I continued to give wine.

We had a strong breeze at E S E, with hazy weather, all the afternoon. At two o'clock, having run through a very dangerous breaking sea, the cause of which I attributed to be a strong tide setting to windward, and shoal water, we discovered a spacious bay or sound, with a fair entrance about two or three miles wide. I now conceived hopes that our voyage was nearly at an end, as no place could appear more eligible for shipping, or more likely to be chosen for a European settlement: I therefore came to a grapnel near the east side of the entrance, in a small sandy bay, where we saw a hut, a dog, and some cattle; and I immediately sent the boatswain and gunner away to the hut, to discover the inhabitants.

The S W point of the entrance bore W ½ S 3 miles; the S E point S by W ¾ mile; and the island Roti from S by W ¼ W to S W ¼ W, about 5 leagues.

While we lay here, I found the ebb came from the northward, and before our departure the falling of the tide discovered to us a reef of rocks, about two cables length from the shore: the whole being covered at high-water, renders it dangerous. On the opposite shore also appeared very high breakers; but there is nevertheless plenty of room, and certainly a safe channel for a first-rate man of war.

The bay or sound within, seemed to be of a considerable extent; the northern part being about 5 leagues distant. Here the land made in moderate risings joined by lower grounds. But the island Roti, to the southward, is the best mark by which to know this place.

I had just time to make these remarks, when I saw the boatswain and gunner returning with some of the natives: I therefore no longer doubted of our success, and that our expectations would be fully gratified. They brought five Indians, and informed me that they had found two families, where the women treated them with European politeness. From these people I learned, that the governor resided at a place called Coupang, which was some distance to the N E. I made signs for one of them to go in the boat, and show us the way to Coupang, intimating that I would pay him for his trouble: the man readily complied, and came into the boat.

These people were of a dark tawny colour, had long black hair, and chewed a great deal of betel. Their dress was a square piece of cloth round the hips, in the folds of which was stuck a large knife; a handkerchief wrapped round the head; and another hanging by the four corners from the shoulders, which served as a bag for their betel equipage. They brought us a few pieces of dried turtle, and some ears of Indian corn. This last was the most welcome; for the turtle was so hard, that it could not be eaten without being first soaked in hot water. They offered to bring us some other refreshments if I would wait; but, as the pilot was willing, I determined to push on. It was about half an hour past four when we sailed.

By direction of the pilot, we kept close to the east shore under all our sail; but as night came on, the wind died away, and we were obliged to try at the oars, which I was surprised to see we could use with some effect. At ten o'clock, finding we advanced but slowly, I came to a grapnel, and for the first time I issued double allowance of bread and a little wine to each person.

Sunday the 14th. At one o'clock in the morning, after the most happy and sweet sleep that ever men enjoyed, we weighed, and continued to keep the east shore on board, in very smooth water; when at last I found we were again open to the sea; the whole of the land to the westward, that we had passed, being an island, which the pilot called Pulo Samow. The northern entrance of this channel is about a mile and a half or two miles wide, and I had no ground at 10 fathoms.

The report of two cannon that were fired, gave new life to every one; and soon after we discovered two square-rigged vessels and a cutter at anchor to the eastward. We endeavoured to work to windward, but were obliged to take to our oars again, having lost ground on each tack. We kept close to the shore, and continued rowing till four o'clock, when I brought to a grapnel, and gave another allowance of bread and wine to all hands. As soon as we had rested a little, we weighed again, and rowed till near daylight, when we came to a grapnel, off a small fort and town, which the pilot told me was Coupang.

Among the things which the boatswain had thrown into the boat before we left the ship, was a bundle of signal flags that had been used by the boats to show the depth of water in sounding: with these we had, in the course of the passage, made a small jack, which I now hoisted in the main shrouds, as a signal of distress; for I did not think proper to land without leave.

Soon after day-break, a soldier hailed us to land, which I immediately did, among a crowd of Indians, and was agreeably surprised to meet with an English sailor, who belonged to one of the vessels in the road. His captain, he told me, was the second person in the town; I therefore desired to be conducted to him, as I was informed the governor was ill, and could not then be spoken with.

Captain Spikerman received me with great humanity. I informed him of our distressed situation; and requested that care might be taken of those who were with me, without delay. On which he gave directions for their immediate reception at his own house, and went himself to the governor, to know at what time I could be permitted to see him; which was fixed to be at eleven o'clock.

I now desired my people to come on shore, which was as much as some of them could do, being scarce able to walk: they, however, were helped to the house, and found tea with bread and butter provided for their breakfast.

The abilities of a painter, perhaps, could seldom have been displayed to more advantage, than in the delineation of the two groups of figures, which at this time presented themselves to each other. An indifferent spectator would have been at a loss which most to admire; the eyes of famine sparkling at immediate relief, or the horror of their preservers at the sight of so many spectres, whose ghastly countenances, if the cause had been unknown, would rather have excited terror than pity. Our bodies were nothing but skin and bones, our limbs were full of sores, and we were clothed in rags: in this condition, with the tears of joy and gratitude flowing down our cheeks, the people of Timor beheld us with a mixture of horror, surprise, and pity.

The Governor, Mr. William Adrian Van Este, notwithstanding extreme ill-heath, became so anxious about us, that I saw him before the appointed time. He received me with great affection, and gave me the fullest proofs that he was possessed of every feeling of a humane and good man. Sorry as he was, he said, that such a calamity could ever have happened to us, yet he considered it as the greatest blessing of his life that we had fallen under his protection; and, though his infirmity was so great that he could not do the office of a friend himself, he would give such orders as I might be certain would procure us every supply we wanted. A house should be immediately prepared for me, and, with respect to my people, he said, that I might have room for them either at the hospital or on board of Captain Spikerman's ship, which lay in the road; and he expressed much uneasiness that Coupang could not afford them better accommodations, the house assigned to me being the only one uninhabited, and the situation of the few families that lived at this place such, that they could not conveniently receive strangers. For the present, till matters could be properly regulated, he gave directions that victuals for my people should be dressed at his own house.

On returning to Captain Spikerman's house, I found that every kind of relief had been given to my people. The surgeon had dressed their sores, and the cleaning of their persons had not been less attended to, several friendly gifts of apparel having been presented to them.

I desired to be shown to the house that was intended for me, which I found ready, with servants to attend. It consisted of a hall, with a room at each end, and a loft overhead; and was surrounded by a piazza, with an outer apartment in one corner, and a communication from the

back part of the house to the street. I therefore determined, instead of separating from my people, to lodge
them all with me; and I divided the house as follows: One
room I took to myself, the other I allotted to the master,
surgeon, Mr. Nelson, and the gunner; the loft to the other
officers; and the outer apartment to the men. The hall was
common to the officers, and the men had the back piazza.
Of this disposition I informed the governor, and he sent
down chairs, tables, and benches, with bedding and other
necessaries for the use of every one.

The governor, when I took my leave, had desired me to
acquaint him with everything of which I stood in need;
but it was only at particular times that he had a few
moments of ease, or could attend to anything; being in a
dying state, with an incurable disease. On this account, I
transacted whatever business I had, with Mr. Timotheus
Wanjon, the second of this place, who was the governor's
son-in-law; and who also contributed everything in his
power to make our situation comfortable. I had been,
therefore, misinformed by the seaman, who told me that
Captain Spikerman was the next person in command to
the governor.

At noon, a dinner was brought to the house, sufficiently
good to make persons, more accustomed to plenty, eat too
much. Yet I believe few in such a situation would have
observed more moderation than my people did. My greatest apprehension was, that they would eat too much fruit,
of which there was great variety in season at this time.

Having seen every one enjoy this meal of plenty, I dined
myself with Mr. Wanjon; but I felt no extraordinary inclination to eat or drink. Rest and quiet, I considered, as
more necessary to the re-establishment of my health, and
therefore retired soon to my room, which I found furnished with every convenience. But, instead of rest, my
mind was disposed to reflect on our late sufferings, and
on the failure of the expedition; but, above all, on the
thanks due to Almighty God, who had given us power to
support and bear such heavy calamities, and had enabled
me at last, to be the means of saving eighteen lives.

In times of difficulty, there will generally arise circumstances that bear particularly hard on a commander. In
our late situation, it was not the least of my distresses, to
be constantly assailed with the melancholy demands of my

people for an increase of allowance, which it grieved me
to refuse. The necessity of observing the most rigid econ-
omy in the distribution of our provisions, was so evident,
that I resisted their solicitations, and never deviated from
the agreement we made at setting out. The consequence
of this care was, that at our arrival we had still remaining
sufficient for eleven days, at our scanty allowance: and if
we had been so unfortunate as to have missed the Dutch
settlement at Timor, we could have proceeded to Java,
where I was certain that every supply we wanted could be
procured.

Another disagreeable circumstance, to which my situation exposed me, was the caprice of ignorant people. Had
I been incapable of acting, they would have carried the
boat on shore as soon as we made the island of Timor,
without considering that landing among the natives, at a
distance from the European settlement, might have been
as dangerous as among any other Indians.

The quantity of provisions with which we left the ship,
was not more than we should have consumed in five days,
had there been no necessity for husbanding our stock. The
mutineers must naturally have concluded, that we could
have no other place of refuge than the Friendly Islands;
for it was not likely they should imagine, that, so poorly
equipped as we were in every respect, there could have
been a possibility of our attempting to return homewards:
much less can they suspect that the account of their villainy has already reached their native country.

When I reflect how providentially our lives were saved
at Tofoa, by the Indians delaying their attack; and that,
with scarce anything to support life, we crossed a sea of
more than 1,200 leagues, without shelter from the inclem-
ency of the weather; when I reflect that in an open boat,
with so much stormy weather, we escaped foundering,
that not any of us were taken off by disease, that we had
the great good fortune to pass the unfriendly natives of
other countries without accident, and at last happily to
meet with the most friendly and best of people to relieve
our distresses; I say, when I reflect on all these wonderful
escapes, the remembrance of such great mercies enables
me to bear, with resignation and cheerfulness, the failure
of an expedition, the success of which I had so much at
heart, and which was frustrated at a time when I was con-

gratulating myself on the fairest prospect of being able to complete it in a manner that would fully have answered the intention of his Majesty, and the humane promoters of so benevolent a plan.

With respect to the preservation of our health, during a course of sixteen days of heavy and almost continual rain, I would recommend to every one in a similar situation, the method we practised, which is, to dip their clothes in the salt-water, and wring them out, as often as they become filled with rain: it was the only resource we had, and I believe was of the greatest service to us, for it felt more like a change of dry clothes than could well be imagined. We had occasion to do this so often, that at length all our clothes were wrung to pieces: for, except the few days we passed on the coast of New Holland, we were continually wet either with rain or sea.

Thus, through the assistance of Divine Providence, we surmounted the difficulties and distresses of a most perilous voyage, and arrived safe in a hospitable port, where every necessary and comfort were administered to us with a most liberal hand.

CHAPTER XVIII

At Coupang

FROM the great humanity and attention of the Governor, and the gentlemen, at Coupang, we received every kind of assistance, and were not long without evident signs of returning health. Shortly after our arrival, I presented to the Governor a formal account of the loss of the *Bounty;* and a requisition, in his Majesty's name, that instructions might be sent to all the Dutch settlements, to stop the ship if she made her appearance. With this a complete descriptive list of the mutineers was given.

I likewise requested, in one of my first visits to the Governor, that Nelson might have permission to walk about the country in search of plants, which was readily granted, with an offer of whatever assistance I should think necessary: and the Governor assured me that the country was well worth examination, as it abounded with many curious and medicinal plants. From this indulgence I derived no benefit; for Nelson, who, since we left New Holland, had been but in a weak condition, about this time was taken ill, in consequence of a cold caused by imprudently leaving off warm clothing.

To secure our arrival at Batavia, before the October fleet sailed for Europe, I gave public notice of my intention to hire a vessel to carry us to Batavia. In consequence of this notice, several offers were made, but none that I thought reasonable; which determined me to purchase a small schooner in the road, that was 34 feet long; for which I gave 1,000 rix-dollars, and fitted her for sea, under the name of his Majesty's schooner *Resource*. As the coast of Java is frequently infested with small piratical vessels, it was necessary that we should be provided with the proper means of defence. In this I was assisted by the friendship of Mr. Wanjon, who supplied me with four brass swivels, fourteen stand of small arms, and ammunition, which he obligingly let me have as a loan, to be returned at Batavia.

On the 20th of July, I had the misfortune to lose Mr. David Nelson: he died of an inflammatory fever. The loss of this honest man I very much lamented: he had, with great care and diligence, attended to the object for which he was sent, and had always been ready to forward every plan that was proposed, for the good of the service in which we were engaged. He was not less useful in our voyage hither, in the course of which he gave me great satisfaction, by the patience and fortitude with which he conducted himself.

July 21st. This day, I was employed attending the funeral of Mr. Nelson. The corpse was carried by twelve soldiers dressed in black, preceded by the minister; next followed myself and the second governor; then ten gentlemen of the town and the officers of the ships in the harbour; and after them my own officers and people.

After reading our burial-service, the body was interred behind the chapel, in the burying-ground appropriated to the Europeans of the town. I was sorry I could get no tombstone to place over his remains.

This was the second voyage Mr. Nelson had undertaken to the South Seas, having been sent out by Sir Joseph Banks, to collect plants, seeds, &c., in Captain Cook's last voyage. And now, after surmounting so many difficulties, and in the midst of thankfulness for his deliverance, he was called upon to pay the debt of nature, at a time least expected.

Our schooner being victualled and ready for sea; on the 20th of August, I took an affectionate leave of the hospitable and friendly inhabitants of Coupang, and embarked. In the afternoon we sailed, having the launch, which had so much contributed to our preservation, in tow. We exchanged salutes with the fort and shipping as we ran out of the harbour.

The town of Coupang is situated in a great bay, which is an excellent road for shipping. The latitude of the town is 10° 12′ S. According to the Dutch charts, it is in 121° 51′ E longitude. Taking the mean between the longitude by my reckoning on our arrival at Coupang, and the longitude afterwards calculated from our run to Batavia, gives me for the longitude of Coupang 124° 41′ E.

This settlement was formed in the year 1630, and is the only one the Dutch have on the island Timor. They have residents in different parts of the country. On the north side of Timor, there is a Portuguese settlement. The produce of the island is chiefly sandalwood and bees-wax: the former article is now scarce. Wax they have in great plenty. The bees build their nests in bushes, and in the boughs of trees, to which the natives cannot approach but with fire. The honey is put into jars, and the wax is run into blocks of 3 feet in length, and from 12 to 15 inches square. The natives, at least those who live in the neighbourhood of Coupang, are of a very indolent disposition, of which the Chinese have taken advantage; for though the Malays are very fond of traffic, most of their trade is carried on in small Chinese vessels, of from 10 to 30 tons burthen. There is a market at Coupang for the country people, in which, however, there is little business done. I have seen a man from the country come to market with two potatoes: and this is not unusual. These being sold for 2 doits (equal to a halfpenny English) serve to supply him with betel to chew; and the remainder of the day is passed in lounging about the town. The inland people, who live at a distance from the Europeans, are strong and active; but their want of cleanliness subjects them to filthy diseases.

The chief of the natives, or king of the island, is by the Dutch styled Keyser (Emperor). This prince lives at a place called Backennaffy, about four miles distant from Coupang. His authority over the natives is not wholly undisputed; which is by the Dutch attributed to the intrigues of the Portuguese, who are on the north part of Timor. The island has lately suffered much by a competition between the present king and one of his nephews, which caused a civil war, that lasted from the beginning of the year 1786 to 1788, when their differences were settled by a treaty, chiefly in favour of the king. The ravages committed in these disputes have occasioned a scarcity of provisions, that probably, from the want of industry in the natives, will not soon be remedied. I had an opportunity of making a visit to the king. His dwelling was a large house, which was divided into only three apartments, and surrounded by a piazza: agreeably situated, but very dirty, as was all the furniture. The king, who is an elderly man, received me with much civility, and ordered refreshments to be set before me, which were

tea, rice cakes, roasted Indian corn, and dried buffalo
flesh, with about a pint of arrack, which I believe was all
he had. His dress was, a check wrapper girded round his
waist with a silk and gold belt, a loose linen jacket, and a
coarse handkerchief about his head. A few of his chiefs
were with him, who partook of our repast; after which,
the king retired with three of them for a short time, and
when he returned, presented me with a round plate of
metal, about four inches diameter, on which was stamped
the figure of a star. As I had been informed that arrack
would be an acceptable present, I was prepared to make
a return, which was well received. They never dilute their
liquor, and, from habit, are able to drink a large quantity
of spirits at a time, without being intoxicated.

When a king dies, a large feast is made, to which all the
inhabitants are invited. The body, after a few days, is put
into a coffin, which is closed up and kept three years
before it is interred.

The Dutch have been at some pains to establish Chris-
tianity among the natives: but it has not gained much
ground, except in the neighbourhood of Coupang. The
present king was christened by the name of Barnardus.
His Indian name is *Bacchee Bannock*. The scriptures are
translated into the Malay language, and prayers are performed, in the church at Coupang, by a Malay clergyman,
in that language.

I met, at Timor, with most of the fruits that are described in Captain Cook's first voyage, as natives of
Batavia, except the Mongostan. The bread-fruit tree,
called by the Malays *Soccoom,* likewise grows here with
great luxuriance, and appears to be as much a native of
this island as it is of Otaheite. The fruit is exactly of the
same kind, but not so good. A bread-fruit of Timor weighs
half as much more as one of equal size at Otaheite. It is
not used here as bread, but generally eaten with milk and
sugar. At Backennaffy I saw about twenty of the trees,
larger than any I have seen at Otaheite. Here is also a
sort of bread-fruit tree, that produces seeds, not unlike
Windsor beans, and equally palatable, either boiled or
roasted. No other part of the fruit is eatable; and though
the tree, I am told, is to all appearance the same as the
other, the fruits have but little resemblance; the fruit of

this being covered with projecting points, nearly half an inch in length.

I received a present of some fine plants, from the Governor, which I was afterwards unfortunately obliged to leave at Batavia, for want of proper room to take care of them, in the packet by which I returned to Europe. Mr. Wanjon likewise favoured me with some seeds for his Majesty's garden at Kew, which I had the good fortune to deliver safe, on my return: and some of the mountain rice, cultivated at Timor, on the dry land, which was forwarded to his Majesty's botanic garden at St. Vincent, and to other parts in the West Indies.

A resemblance of language between the people of the South Sea Islands and the inhabitants of many of the islands in the East Indies, has been remarked in Captain Cook's first voyage. Here, the resemblance appeared stronger than has yet been noticed; particularly in their numerals. But besides the language, I observed some customs among the people of Timor, still more striking for their similarity. They practise the *Tooge-tooge** of the Friendly Islands, which they call *Toombock*: and the *Roomee* of Otaheite, which they call *Ramas*. I likewise saw, placed on their graves, offerings of baskets with tobacco and betel.

I left the Governor, Mr. Van Este, at the point of death. To this gentleman our most grateful thanks are due, for the humane and friendly treatment that we received from him. His ill state of health only prevented him from showing us more particular marks of attention. Unhappily, it is to his memory only that I now pay this tribute. It was a fortunate circumstance for us, that Mr. Wanjon, the next in place to the Governor, was equally humane and ready to relieve us. His attention was unremitting, and, when there was a doubt about supplying me with money, to enable me to purchase a vessel, he cheerfully took it upon himself; without which, it was evident, I should have been too late at Batavia to have sailed for Europe with the October fleet. I can only return such services by ever retaining a grateful remembrance of them.

Mr. Max, the town surgeon, likewise behaved to us

* The *Tooge-tooge* is described in Captain Cook's last voyage, Vol. I, page 323; and the *Ramas,* in the same voyage, Vol. II, page 64.

with the most disinterested humanity; he attended every one with the utmost care; for which I could not prevail on him to receive any payment, or to render me any account, or other answer, than that it was his duty.

CHAPTER XIX

From Timor to Batavia

FROM Coupang, we steered N W by W, having a moderate breeze at S E with fair weather.

Saturday the 22nd. At day-light, we saw the island Flores to the northward. At noon, latitude observed 9° 27′ S, and longitude by account, from Coupang, 2° 10′ W. Our distance from the coast of Flores was about 10 leagues; and two high peaked mountains bore N ½ E and N N W. These two mountains resemble each other in shape, and the westernmost is a volcano. The interior parts of Flores are mountainous and woody: but near the sea-coast is a fine open country. A Dutch map, with which I was provided, places the south part of Flores in 9° 3′ S, which I am of opinion is too far south. We steered along the south side of Flores, mostly with light winds and hazy weather, so that we did not constantly keep sight of the coast.

Tuesday the 25th. At noon, we were off Toorns Island, which bore N W by N, 3 or 4 leagues distant. Our latitude observed, was 8° 57′ S, and longitude made by dead reckoning from Coupang, 3° 27′ W. Toorns Island is about 4 leagues in circuit, and has a craggy and uneven appearance. There is a curious high peak on the S W part: the land near the shore is low and woody.

On the 27th, at noon, we were near the entrance of the Straits of Mangaryn, which not appearing so open and clear as represented in the map, I steered for the Straits of Sapi, intending to pass through; but was obliged to give up this plan, by strong currents setting to the S E, which there was not sufficient wind to enable us to stem. I therefore again stood for the Straits of Mangaryn, which we ran through in the afternoon of the 29th, being favoured with a fresh breeze from the S S E. On our first entering the straits, we got close to the Flores shore: our course through was N ½ E. We tried for soundings, but could not any where find bottom at 25 and 30 fathoms depth.

On the Flores side, there are many good harbours and bays, where vessels may anchor; but the country hereabouts appears burnt up and desolate.

I had no azimuth-compass, and consequently could not observe very accurately the variation; but I believe there is so little in Mangaryn Straits, that no great error will be occasioned by considering the true and magnetic bearings to be the same.

When we had passed the straits, we kept to the westward, running along the north side of the island Sumbawa, where there is a very high mountain near the coast; at the foot of which, I am informed, are many runs of good water, conveniently situated for ships to supply themselves. The latitude of the north part of Sumbawa I make, by my observations and bearings, to be 8° 6′ S, which differs very little from the Dutch charts.

In the night of the 31st, several prows were rowing about us, on which account, we kept all night under arms.

Thursday the 3rd. This and the two following days, we were sailing along the north side of the island Lombock, on which is a high mountain. Most of the islands in this route are distinguished by high mountains. Lombock appears to be well clothed with wood. In the nights, we saw fires upon the high lands, at a distance from the coast.

Sunday the 6th. In the afternoon, we saw the high land of Cape Sandana, which is the northeast part of Java.

The next day, we were off Cape Sandana, which is a low cape, projecting from the high land already mentioned. This cape is placed by the Dutch maps in 7° 52′ S. But according to my observation, and our estimated distance from the land, I make it in 7° 46′ S latitude. The longitude, by my dead reckoning, from Coupang to Cape Sandana, was 11° 33′ W.

We steered to the westward, along the coast of Java; and on the 10th, at noon, we anchored off Passourwang, a Dutch settlement on the coast of Java, in 2 fathoms; distant from the shore half a league; the entrance of the river bearing S W. The coast hereabouts is so shoal, that large ships are obliged to anchor 3 or 4 miles from the land. As soon as we were at anchor, I got in my boat and went on shore. The banks of the river, near the entrance, were mud, on which grew a few mangrove bushes. Among them we saw hogs running, and many were lying

dead in the mud, which caused a most intolerable stench
and made me heartily repent having come here; but after
proceeding about a mile up the river, the course of which
was serpentine, we found a very pleasant country, and
landed at a small and well-constructed fort; where I was
received in a friendly and polite manner by M. Adrian
Van Rye, the commandant. By the return of the boat, I
sent on board a small bullock, and other provisions. I
likewise took a pilot to conduct us to Sourabya.

The houses at Passourwang are neatly built, and the
country appears to be well cultivated. The produce of this
settlement is rice, of which they export large quantities.
There are but few Dutch here: the Javanese are numerous, and their chief lives with considerable splendour.
They have good roads, and posts are established along the
coast; and it appears to be a busy and well-regulated
settlement. Latitude 7° 36′ S. Longitude 1° 44′ W of
Cape Sandana.

The next day, about noon, we sailed; and on the 12th,
in the evening, anchored in Sourabya road, in 7 fathoms:
the flag-staff bearing S ¼ W; distance from the shore 1
mile. We found riding here, seven square-rigged and several smaller vessels.

It was too late, when we anchored, to send a boat on
shore. The next morning, before daylight, three guard-
boats stationed themselves near us, and I was informed,
that I must not land or send a boat on shore. This restriction, I learnt from the officer of the guard-boats, was
in conformity to general orders concerning all strange
vessels on their first arrival. At nine in the forenoon, leave
came off for us to land, and soon after the guard-boats
quitted us.

I was received on shore with great civility and friendship by the Governor, or Opperhooft, M. Ant. Barkay,
and the commandant of the troops, M. de Bose. By these
gentlemen I was hospitably entertained, and advised to
remain til the 16th, when some vessels were to sail, with
whom I might keep company, which they recommended
on account of pirates.

Sourabya is one of the most pleasant places I ever saw.
It is situated on the banks of a river, and is a mile and a
half distant from the sea-shore, so that only the flag-staff
can be seen from the road. The river is navigable up to

the town for vessels of 100 tons burthen, and the bank on one side is made convenient for tracking. The Chinese carry on a considerable trade here, and have a town or camp on the side of the river opposite to Sourabya. The country near the town is flat, and the soil light, so that they plough with a single bullock or buffalo *(Karrabow)*. The interior parts of the country, near the mountains, are infested with a breed of fierce tigers, which makes travelling inland very dangerous. They have here a breed of horses, which are small, but they are handsome and strong.

The Javanese in this neighbourhood are numerous. M. Barkay and M. de Bose took me with them to pay a visit to two of the principal natives, whom we found attended by a number of men armed with pikes, in great military order. We were entertained with a concert of music; the instruments were gongs, drums, and a fiddle with two strings. I hired a pilot here to carry us to Batavia. Our latitude observed in Sourabya road was 7° 11′ S. Longitude made from Cape Sandana 1° 52′ W.

On the 17th, we sailed from Sourabya, in company with three prows. At noon, we anchored at Crissey, which is a town with a small fort, belonging to the Dutch. We remained here about two hours, and then weighed. Latitude of Crissey 7° 9′ S. Longitude from Cape Sandana 1° 55′ W.

The navigation through the Straits of Madura is so intricate, that, with the little opportunity I had, I am unable to undertake a description of it. The next day, (September 18th) having passed the straits, we bore away to the westward, along the coast of Java, in company with the prows before mentioned. We had regular soundings all the way to Samarang, off which place we anchored on the 22nd in the afternoon; the church bearing S E; distance from the shore half a league: depth of water 2 fathoms. The shoalness of the coast here makes the road of Samarang very inconvenient, both on account of the great distance that large ships (of which there were several in the road) are obliged to lay from the shore, and of the landing, which is in a river that cannot be entered before half-flood. This river resembles the one at Passourwang, the shores being low, with offensive dead animals lying about. I was met at the landing-place by the equipage-master, and he furnished me with a carriage to carry me to the Governor, whose residence is about two miles from the town of Samarang. I requested, and obtained leave to have our wants supplied, which were, to recruit our provisions, and to get a new main-mast, having sprung ours in the passage from Sourabya.

Samarang is a fortified town, surrounded by a wall and ditch; and is the most considerable settlement, next to Batavia, that the Dutch have in Java. Here is a very good hospital, and a public school, chiefly for teaching the mathematics. They have likewise a theatre. Provisions are remarkably cheap here, beef being at 10 doits per lb., and the price of a fowl 12 doits.

I experienced great civility from some of the gentlemen at Samarang, particularly from M. Le Baron de Bose, a merchant, brother to the M. de Bose, commandant of the troops at Sourabya: and from M. Abegg, the surgeon of the hospital, to whom we were indebted for advice and medicines, for which he would not consent to receive payment.

The latitude of Samarang is 6° 57′ S. Longitude, by my reckoning, from Cape Sandana, 4° 7′ W.

On the 26th, we sailed from Samarang; and with us, a galley mounting six swivels, which the Governor had directed to accompany us to Batavia.

On the 1st of October we anchored in Batavia road, where we found riding, a Dutch ship of war, and twenty sail of Dutch East India ships, besides many smaller vessels.

CHAPTER XX

Occurrences at Batavia, and Passage thence to England

IN the afternoon, at four o'clock, I went on shore, and landed at a house by the river, where strangers first stop and give an account who they are, whence they came, &c. From this place, a Malay gentleman took me in a carriage to the Sabandar, Mr. Englehard, whose house was in the environs of the city, on the side nearest the shipping. The Sabandar is the officer with whom all strangers are obliged to transact their business: at least, the whole must go through his hands. With him, I went to pay my respects to the Governor-General, who received me with great civility. I acquainted his excellency with my situation, and requested my people might be taken care of, and that we should be allowed to take a passage to Europe in the first ship that sailed. I likewise desired permission to sell the schooner and launch. All this his excellency told me should be granted. I then took leave, and returned with the Sabandar, who wrote down the particulars of my wants, in order to form from them a regular petition, to be presented to the council the next day. I had brought from the Governor of Coupang, directed for the Governor-General at Batavia, the account of my voyage and misfortune, translated into Dutch, from an account that I had given to Mr. Van Este. So attentive had they been at Timor to everything that related to us.

There is a large hotel at Batavia, fitted up purposely for the accommodation of strangers, who are not allowed to reside at any other place. It is situated near the great river, in a part of the city that is reckoned the most airy and healthy. Nevertheless, I found the air hot and suffocating, and was taken ill in the night with a violent pain in my head. The next morning, at nine, the council sat, and I attended, accompanied by the Sabandar; and was informed that the council had complied with all I had requested.

When I returned to the hotel, my headache increased,

and a violent fever came on. I sent to acquaint the Sabandar of my situation, and was soon after attended by the head surgeon of the town hospital, Mr. Aansorp; by whose care and skill, in less than twenty-four hours, the fever considerably abated, but a severe headache continued. I had an invitation from the Governor-General to dine with him; which, of course, I was obliged to decline.

I hired a carriage, which cost three dollars per day, for the benefit of taking an airing. My lodgings at the hotel were so close and hot, that I desired the Sabandar to apply to the Governor-General, for leave to hire a house in the country; which request his excellency not only immediately complied with, but gave directions for my being accommodated at the house of the physician or surgeon-general, Mr. Sparling.

One of my people, Thomas Hall, being ill with a flux, I obtained leave for him to be sent to the country hospital, which is a convenient airy building.

Tuesday the 6th. This morning, at sunrise, I left the hotel, and was carried to Mr. Sparling's house, about four miles distant from the city, and near the convalescent hospital, which at this time had also sick men in it, the whole number of patients amounting to 800. I found everything prepared for my comfort and convenience. Mr. Sparling would suffer me to take no medicine, though I had still considerable fever with headache: but I found so much relief from the difference of the air, that in the evening I was able to accompany Mr. Sparling on a visit to the Governor-General, at one of his country seats; where we found many ladies, all dressed in the Malay fashion, some of them richly ornamented with jewels. I had invitations from several gentlemen, and some very kindly pressed me to make their country houses my abode, till my health should be re-established.

My indisposition increasing, Mr. Sparling advised me to quit Batavia as speedily as possible, and represented the necessity of it to the Governor-General. I was informed from his excellency, that the homeward-bound ships were so much crowded, that there would be no possibility of all my people going in one ship, and that they could be accommodated no other way than by dividing them into different ships. Seeing, therefore, that a separation was unavoidable, I determined to follow the advice

of the physician, and, as a packet was appointed to sail
for Europe on the 16th instant, I sent to request of the
Governor that I might be allowed to take a passage in her
for myself, and as many of my people as they were able
to receive. In answer to this, I was acquainted that myself
and two more could be accommodated in the packet, she
being too small to admit a greater number; but that I
might rest assured of passages being provided for those
that remained, by the earliest opportunities.

Friday the 9th. This day, anchored in the road, the
General Elliot, an English ship, commanded by Captain
Lloyd. In the Straits of Banca, he had met with some
boats belonging to the East India Company's ship *Vansittart,* that was lost in the Straits of Billaton, by having
struck on a rock that went through her bottom. Captain
Wilson, who commanded the *Vansittart,* I was informed,
had just finished a survey of those Straits, and was hoist-
ing his boat in, when the ship struck. Immediately on receiving the intelligence, Captain Lloyd, in the *General
Elliot,* and another ship in company, called the *Nonsuch,*
sailed for the wreck. They found the ship had been burnt
down to the water's edge by the Malays. They however
saved forty chests of treasure out of fifty-five, which were
said to have been on board. Most of the ship's company
were saved: one man only was lost in the ship, and five
others in a small boat were missing, who were supposed
to have taken some of the treasure.—The greater part of
the people went with Captain Wilson to China, and some
were with Captain Lloyd.

Saturday the 10th. This morning, the *Resource* was
sold by public auction: the custom at Batavia, is to begin
high, and to lower the price, till some person bids; and the
first bidder is the buyer. She was accordingly put up at
2,000 rix-dollars, but, to my great disappointment, no one
offered to purchase before the auctioneer had lowered the
demand to 295 rix-dollars, for which price she was sold;
the purchaser being an Englishman, Captain John Eddie,
who commanded an English ship from Bengal. If no
strangers had been present at the sale, I imagine they
would have let her run down to 200 dollars, in which case
I should have had no alternative.

The launch likewise was sold. The services she had
rendered us, made me feel great reluctance at parting with

her; which I would not have done, if I could have found a convenient opportunity of getting her conveyed to Europe.

Little as the schooner had sold for, I found I was in danger of having the sum lessened; for the Sabandar informed me, that, by an order of the council, there was a duty on the sale of all vessels. With this demand I would by no means comply; for I thought I had sufficiently suffered, in sustaining a loss of 705 rix-dollars out of 1,000, by the purchase and sale of the vessel, she having cost 1,000 rix-dollars.

This day, Thomas Hall, whom I had sent to be taken care of at the hospital, died. He had been ill of a flux from the time of our arrival at Timor.

I agreed with the captain of the packet for a passage to Europe, for myself, my clerk, and a servant. The Sabandar informed me, it was necessary that my officers and people should be examined before a notary, respecting the loss of the *Bounty,* as otherwise the Governor and council were not legally authorized to detain her, if she should be found in any of the Dutch settlements. They were therefore, at my desire, examined; and afterwards made affidavit before the Governor and council at the Stadthouse.

My officers complaining to me of the unreasonableness of some tradesmen's bills, I spoke to the Sabandar. A bill of 51 dollars for five hats, he reduced to 30 dollars, and in other articles made proportionable deductions.

Paper money is the currency of Batavia, and is so understood in all bargains. At this time, paper was at 28 per cent discount: there is likewise a difference in the value of the ducatoon, which at Batavia is 80 stivers, and in Holland is 63 stivers: this occasions a loss of 21¼ per cent on remittance of money. It therefore follows, that if any person at Batavia remits money by bills of exchange to Europe, they lose by the discount and the exchange 49¼ per cent.

Those who have accounts to pay, and can give unexceptionable bills on Europe, will find a considerable saving by negotiating their bills with private people; who are glad to give for them a premium of 20 per cent at the least. This discovery I made somewhat too late to profit by.

One of the greatest difficulties that strangers have to encounter, is, their being obliged to live at the hotel. This hotel was formerly two houses, which by doors of communication have been made one. It is in the middle of a range of buildings, more calculated for a cold country than for such a climate as Batavia. There is no free circulation of air, and what is equally bad, it is always very dirty; and there is great want of attendance. What they call cleaning the house, is another nuisance; for they never use any water to cool it or to lay the dust, but sweep daily with brooms, in such a manner, that those in the house are almost suffocated by a cloud of dust.

The months of December and January are reckoned the most unhealthy of the year, the heavy rains being then set in.—The account of the seasons, as given to me here, I believe may be relied on.

The middle of November, the west monsoon begins, and rain.

December and January. Continual rain with strong westerly wind.

February. Westerly wind. Towards the end of this month the rain begins to abate.

March. Intervals of fine weather. Wind westerly.

April. In this month the east monsoon begins. Weather generally fine with showers of rain.

May. East moonsoon fixed. Showery.

June and July. Clear weather. Strong east wind.

August and September. Wind more moderate.

October. In this month, the wind begins to be variable, with showers of rain.

The current is said always to run with the wind. Nevertheless, I found the reverse in sailing from Timor to Java. Between the end of October and the beginning of the ensuing year, no Dutch ship bound for Europe is allowed to sail from Batavia, for fear of being near the Mauritius, at the time of the hurricanes, which are frequent there in December and January.

My illness prevented me from gaining much knowledge of Batavia. Of their public buildings, I saw nothing that gave me so much satisfaction as their country hospital for seamen. It is a large commodious and airy building, about four miles from the town, close to the side of the river, or rather in the river: for the ground on which it stands has, by labour, been made an island of, and the sick are carried there in a boat: each ward is a separate dwelling, and the different diseases are properly classed. They have sometimes 1,400 patients in it: at this time there were 800, but more than half of these were recovered, and fit for service, of whom 300 were destined for the fleet that was to sail for Europe. I went through most of the wards, and there appeared great care and attention. The sheets, bedding, and linen of the sick were perfectly neat and clean. The house of the physician, Mr. Sparling, who has the management of the hospital, is at one extremity of the building: and here it was that I resided. To the attention and care of this gentleman, for which he would receive no payment, I am probably indebted for my life.

The hospital in the town is well attended; but the situation is so ill chosen, that it certainly would be the saving of many lives, to build one in its stead up the river; which might be done with great advantage, as water carriage is so easy and convenient. A great neglect in some of the commanders of the shipping here, was, suffering their people to go dirty, and frequently without frock, shirt, or anything to cover their bodies; which, besides being a public nuisance, must probably be productive of ill health in the most robust constitution.

The Governor-General gave me leave to lodge all my people at the country hospital, which I thought a great advantage, and with which they were perfectly satisfied. The officers, however, at their own request, remained in the town.

The time fixed for the sailing of the packet approaching, I settled my accounts with the Sabandar, leaving open the victualling account, to be closed by Mr. Fryer, the master, previous to his departure; who I likewise authorized to supply the men and officers left under his command, with one month's pay, to enable them to purchase clothing for their passage to England.

I had been at great pains to bring living plants from Timor, in six tubs; which contained jacks, nancas, karambolas, namnams, jambos, and three thriving breadfruit plants. These I thought might be serviceable at the Cape of Good Hope, if brought no farther: but I had the mortification of being obliged to leave them all at Batavia. I took these plants on board at Coupang, on the 20th of August: they had experienced a passage of forty-two days to my arrival here. The bread-fruit plants died to the root, and sprouted afresh from thence. The karambolas, jacks, nancas, and namnams, I had raised from the seed, and they were in fine order. No judgement can hence be formed of the success of transporting plants, as in the present trial, they had many disadvantages.

This morning, before sun-rise, I embarked on board the Vlydte packet, commanded by Captain Peter Couvret, bound for Middelburgh. With me likewise embarked Mr. John Samuel, clerk, and John Smith, seaman. Those of our company who stayed behind, the Governor promised me should follow in the first ships, and be as little divided as possible.—At seven o'clock, the packet weighed, and sailed out of the road.

On the 18th, we spoke the *Rambler,* an American brig, belonging to Boston, bound to Batavia. After passing the Straits of Sunda, we steered to the north of the Cocos Isles. These islands, Captain Couvret informed me, are full of cocoa-nut trees: there is no anchorage near them, but good landing for boats. Their latitude 12° 0′ S. Longitude 96° 5′ E.

In the passage to the Cape of Good Hope, there occurred nothing worth remark. I cannot however forbear noticing the Dutch manner of navigating. They steer by true compass, or rather endeavour so to do, by means of a small moveable central card, which they set to the meridian: and whenever they discover the variation has altered 2½° since the last adjustment, they again correct the central card. This is steering within a quarter of a point, without aiming at greater exactness. The officer of the watch likewise corrects the course for lee-way, by his own judgement, before it is marked down in the log board. They heave no log: I was told that the company do not allow it. Their manner of computing their run, is by means of a measured distance of 40 feet, along the ship's side: they take notice of any remarkable patch of froth, when it is abreast the foremost end of the measured distance, and count half seconds till the mark

of froth is abreast the after end. With the num.
half seconds thus obtained, they divide the number
taking the product for the rate of sailing in geographical
miles in one hour, or the number of Dutch miles in four
hours.

It is not usual to make any allowance to the sun's
declination, on account of being on a different meridian
from that for which the tables are calculated: they, in
general, compute with the numbers just as they are found
in the table. From all this, it is not difficult to conceive
the reason why the Dutch are frequently above 10° out
in their reckoning. Their passages likewise are considerably lengthened, by not carrying a sufficient quantity of
sail.

December the 16th, in the afternoon, we anchored in
Table Bay. The next morning, I went on shore, and
waited on His Excellency M. Vander Graaf, who re-
ceived me in the most polite and friendly manner. The
Guardian, commanded by Lieutenant Riou, had left the
Cape about eight days before, with cattle and stores for
Port Jackson. This day, anchored in Table Bay, the
Astrée, a French frigate, commanded by the Count de
St. Rivel, from the Isle of France, on board of which
ship was the late governor, the Chevalier d'Entre-
casteaux. Other ships that arrived during my stay at
the Cape, were, a French forty-gun frigate, an East
India ship, and a brig, of the same nation: likewise two
other French ships, with slaves, from the coast of Mozam-
bique, bound to the West Indies: a Dutch packet from
Europe, after a four months' passage: and the *Harpy,* a
South Sea whaler, with 500 barrels of spermaceti, and
400 of seal, and other oils. There is a standing order
from the Dutch East India Company, that no person who
takes a passage from Batavia for Europe, in any of their
ships, shall be allowed to leave the ship before she arrives
at her intended port. According to which regulation, I
must have gone to Holland in the packet. Of this, I was
not informed till I was taking leave of the Governor-
General, at Batavia, when it was too late for him to give
the Captain an order to permit me to land in the channel.
He however desired I would make use of his name to
Governor Vander Graaf, who readily complied with my

request, and gave the necessary orders to the Captain of the packet, a copy of which His Excellency gave to me; and at the same time, recommendatory letters to people of consequence in Holland, in case I should be obliged to proceed so far.

I left a letter at the Cape of Good Hope, to be forwarded to Governor Phillips, at Port Jackson, by the first opportunity; containing a short account of my voyage, with a descriptive list of the pirates: and from Batavia I had written to Lord Cornwallis; so that every part of India will be prepared to receive them.

We sailed from the Cape, in company with the *Astrée* French frigate. The next morning, neither ship nor land were in sight. On the 15th, we passed in sight of the island St. Helena. The 21st, we saw the island Ascension. On the 10th of February, the wind being at N E, blowing fresh, our sails were covered with a fine orange-coloured dust. Fuego, the westernmost of the Cape de Verde Islands, and the nearest land to us, on that day at noon bore N E by E ½ E, distance 140 leagues. When we had passed the latitude of the Western Islands, a look-out was kept for some rocks, which Captain Couvret had been informed lay in latitude 44° 25′ N, and 2° 50′ E longitude from the east end of St. Michael. This information, Captain Couvret had received from a person that he knew, and who said he had seen them. On the 13th of March, we saw the Bill of Portland, and on the evening of the next day, Sunday, March the 14th, I left the packet, and was landed at Portsmouth, by an Isle of Wight boat.

Those of my officers and people whom I left at Batavia, were provided with passages in the earliest ships; and at the time we parted, were apparently in good health. Nevertheless, they did not all live to quit Batavia. Mr. Elphinstone, master's mate, and Peter Linkletter, seaman, died within a fortnight after my departure; the hardships they had experienced having rendered them unequal to cope with so unhealthy a climate as that of Batavia. The remainder embarked on board the Dutch fleet for Europe, and arrived safe at this country, except Robert Lamb, who died on the passage, and Mr. Ledward, the surgeon, who has not yet been heard of. Thus, of nineteen who were forced by the mutineers into the launch, it has pleased God that twelve should surmount the difficulties and dangers of the voyage, and live to revisit their native country.

AFTERWORD

UNTIL the 1930's it was common for critics and biographers to treat Captain William Bligh as a tyrant and a brutal bully. His detractors declared that he was subject to insane rages, that he oppressed and cheated his men, and was a coward to boot. They described Fletcher Christian as a finely tempered, mettlesome young man, and John Macarthur, who engineered the rebellion against Bligh in New South Wales, as a pillar of society and a man of courage and conviction.

Then, in the 1930's, with the publication of studies of Bligh by George Mackaness, Geoffrey Rawson, Herbert Vere Evatt, Owen Rutter, and H. S. Montgomerie, there came a reaction—sometimes perhaps excessive, as reactions tend to be. Bligh was hailed as a master navigator who helped chart the South Seas, a brave naval officer, a conscientious governor of New South Wales, a stern but just man who raged only against lawlessness and incompetence. On the other hand Christian was seen as blindly impetuous and Macarthur as scheming and rapacious.

But the most popular version of the Bligh story in the 1930's was the trilogy of novels by Charles Nordhoff and James Norman Hall. The first volume, *Mutiny on the Bounty,* hewed to the basic facts but, by adopting the point of view of a young midshipman whom Bligh had allegedly done an injustice and by idealizing Christian, it made Bligh seem a merciless scourge of spirited youth. It prepared the way for a motion picture, starring Charles Laughton, which completed the conversion of Bligh into an ogre and of Christian into a hero of romance.

As is so often the case where a man's character and personality are concerned, the truth is more complex than any extreme view will allow. Judging from the number of sensational episodes in his career, Bligh was obviously no ordinary man. But he was neither angel nor devil, not a hero or a villain.

Well before William Bligh went to sea in 1771 at the age of sixteen, the British navy had made England Queen of the Seas; from North America to India it had helped establish the greatest maritime empire in history. Despite this, and its pride in its tradition, the navy was hardly a charming institution. It winked at corruption and favoritism; for crews it drew heavily on riffraff and sometimes resorted to the infamous "press gangs" to bring them in by force. On board ship the life was usually one of severe discipline, hard work, vile quarters, wretched food, abuse, and, not infrequently, scurvy, shipwreck and death. For the average seaman, even a battle, always with the possibility of prize money afterward, was a welcome change from his daily lot.

It was under such conditions that Bligh spent five years learning his calling. He must have learned it well, for when he was twenty-two years old the celebrated Captain Cook selected him as sailing-master to assist in making charts on his third and—as it proved—last voyage.

The purpose of the expedition was the old one of finding a "northwest passage" to the Indies. But instead of trying to sail north and west around North America, Cook took his two vessels south around Cape Horn, touched at Tasmania, New Zealand, Otaheite (later Tahiti), and the Sandwich (later Hawaiian) Islands and then pushed boldly north through the Bering Sea until stopped by ice. It was on the return journey, in February 1779, on an island beach—uncannily echoing Magellan's fate in the Philippines some 250 years before—that Cook was beaten to death by natives.

The expedition continued on into the Indian Ocean and around the Cape of Good Hope and arrived back in England after more than four years at sea. Although he is neglected in Captain King's official account of the voyage, it is generally acknowledged that Bligh worked closely with Cook in making the charts and observations that distinguished the expedition's great contribution to the knowledge of the South Pacific.

A few months after his return Bligh married Elizabeth Betham. She was an accomplished woman, the daughter of a scholarly official on the Isle of Man, and their correspondence over the years reveals a deep and affectionate relationship. Bligh himself came of a respectable family and appears to have had a good education.

Bligh returned to find England at war not only with her American colonies but with France, Spain and, shortly afterward, Holland. He was appointed master of a frigate and soon tasted action in an engagement between an English and a Dutch squadron near the Dogger Bank in the North Sea. The battle was a violent one and after four hours both fleets broke off the fighting and retired. Two months later Bligh was made a lieutenant and thus became, at the relatively late age of twenty-seven, a commissioned officer eligible for the highest commands.

But the nations were weary of war: peace was quickly concluded and Bligh found himself without a post and called upon to support his family on half pay—about two shillings a day. But he soon secured the command of a merchant ship in the West Indian trade and continued for four years there.

He had thus had sixteen years of the most varied and responsible maritime service when some West Indian planters decided that breadfruit plants from the South Seas (where it was a staple of the islanders), would provide a cheap, nourishing food for their Negro slaves. Sir Joseph Banks, a leading figure in science—he had been the naturalist on Cook's first voyage—became interested in the project and at his suggestion Bligh was given command of the vessel that was to bring the breadfruit from Tahiti to the West Indies.

Out of this rather modest, partly commercial undertaking was to come a series of the strangest and most dramatic incidents in the annals of the seas.

The vessel chosen for the task, the *Bounty*, was only 215 tons and 90 feet long; moreover, a large compartment below had been set aside for the plants. With a crew of forty-six, the *Bounty* sailed on Christmas Eve, 1787.

After a journey into the South Atlantic that took three months, the ship faced the task of rounding Cape Horn in the heavy seas and furious gales of the southern winter. The vessel was not only overcrowded but leaky; and after it had been battered for almost a month, Bligh relented, made about and bore away for Africa and the Cape of Good Hope.

According to Bligh's account, he husbanded the provisions because the voyage might have turned out to be longer than anticipated. Although he thought the crew an inefficient and worthless lot, he did not note any particular signs of unrest. But our other main source of information, the diary kept by the boatswain's mate, James Morrison, asserts that there was much murmuring over Bligh's frequent bad temper, the poor food, and the belief that Bligh had appropriated some of the ship's provisions.

A letter Bligh wrote shortly before they had struck the storm area off Cape Horn describes the ship as fit, the men as being in good spirits, and the "officers and young gentlemen" as "tractable." Only one man had received major punishment: Matthew Quintal (who later became one of the most active mutineers) had been given twenty-four lashes for insolence to the ship's Master. Despite the fact that a dozen lashes left a man's back in ribbons, fifty bared the bone, and two hundred could kill, flogging was a normal part of discipline, and nothing indicates that Bligh was unusual in his resort to it.

In an age when entire crews were sometimes laid low by scurvy, it is noteworthy that not a single man was ill when the *Bounty* arrived at the Cape of Good Hope. Indeed, it is characteristic of Bligh that he punished any man who did not dance to the fiddle for two hours every night. After repairs had been made, the vessel set sail again and reached Matavai Bay, Tahiti, in the middle of October 1788.

The island of Tahiti had first been reported only twenty-one years earlier, and with its charming and pleasure-loving natives—and especially its amorous women—and its natural riches, it was as near a paradise as European sailors had ever come upon. To men who had been penned up for ten long months—and more than 27,000 miles—in a crowded vessel, subject to ship's food, murderous weather, and Bligh's temper, it must have seemed like a dream, a vision of Eden—too good, indeed, to be forsaken. It is impossible to imagine the effect it must have had on a seaman who came perhaps from some city slum or country hovel and faced the prospect on his return of being shanghaied aboard other vessels for other interminable voyages.

The *Bounty* stayed on for almost six months; and probably even at the end of that time no one except Bligh was
ready to leave. Many of the men had formed alliances
with native women and had sunk into the luxuriously
indolent life of the islanders. Three men deserted but
after a few weeks were caught and flogged. Even here, his
critics claim, Bligh harried his crew, having one man
whipped for neglect of duty and another for striking a
native, and taking for the ship the presents of hogs that
natives made to individual crewmen. For many of the men
(such as Fletcher Christian, who is said to have dallied
with several damsels), the thought of leaving the island,
with no likelihood of ever returning, must have been
nearly intolerable. It should be added that although there
was not a single case of venereal disease on the *Bounty*
when it arrived, many of the crew, including Christian,
were on the V.D. list at various times. And Bligh in
his private log (which is much more detailed than the
published *Narrative*) makes clear that he had the utmost
difficulty in getting the officers to fulfill their duties. If it
seems surprising that Bligh did not publish such facts, the
explanation offered by his defenders is that he was too
proud to reveal the demoralization in his command.

More than one thousand breadfruit plants having at last
been stowed on board, the *Bounty* left Tahiti on April 4,
1789. The ship was on her way for fully a month before
the eruption came. Bligh later contended that it had long
been planned but all the evidence indicates that Christian
decided to seize command only a few hours before he did
so. The disorderly way the mutiny was carried out and
the subsequent indecision suggest that it was not only
unplanned but reckless.

The incident that precipitated the crisis occurred the
day before the mutiny. As Morrison relates it in his journal, Bligh had flown into a rage because a few coconuts
had disappeared from the ship's store. Although he had
just appointed Christian acting-lieutenant, Bligh included
him among those whom he cross-questioned. When
Christian answered, ". . . I hope you don't think me so
mean as to be guilty of stealing yours," Bligh shouted,
"Yes, you damned hound, I do." Christian turned and
went below without answering.

The curious fact is that Christian, who was about

twenty-six (roughly eight years younger than Bligh), had served with Bligh twice before, that Bligh had taught and befriended him, and that although he repeatedly abused the younger man during the voyage, Christian was the only one besides the Master whom he constantly invited to dine with him. Bligh was plainly one of those men who never allow personal feeling to interfere with discipline. Like many autocrats, he evidently thought himself privileged to abuse those serving under him, especially if he had favored them.

But Christian, well-born and proud, was not one to relish such an attitude—and least of all after having been wrenched from Eden. He has been variously described as impetuous, passionate (Bligh reports that he was subject to such outbursts of perspiration, especially in his hands, that he soiled whatever he touched), moody, and inordinately fond of women—all of which goes far toward explaining what happened during the evening of April 27, 1789, and the following morning.

After Bligh's outburst against him, Christian decided to desert. Finding the *Bounty* only a few miles from the island of Tofoa, he first thought he could put together a raft and make land with it. But as the night was a fine one, men kept turning up on deck, and, becoming desperate, he hit on the scheme of taking over the vessel. As officer of the early morning watch, he was able to go around and recruit a major part of the crew, and especially those who had at some time been severely punished. They armed themselves, seized Bligh and forced him on deck. Bligh's description of the climax of this episode is given in his *Narrative*. Here is the version left by Morrison, who remained on the *Bounty*:

> . . . when Mr. Bligh found that he must go, he begged of Mr. Christian to desist, saying "I'll pawn my honor. I'll give my bond, Mr. Christian, never to think of this if you'll desist"; and urged his wife and family, to which Mr. Christian replied, "No, Captain Bligh, if you had any honor, things had not come to this; and if you had any regard for your wife and family, you should have thought on them before, and not behaved so much like a villain!" Lieutenant Bligh attempted again to speak, but was ordered to be silent. The boatswain also tried to pacify him, to which he replied, " 'Tis too late; I have

been in hell for this fortnight past and am determined
to bear it no longer, and you know, Mr. Cole, that I
have been used like a dog all the voyage."

After he left Tahiti there is no indication that Bligh
was any harsher than before. So we must assume that the
"fortnight of hell" Christian refers to is that into which
he was plunged by the necessity of leaving the island and
its lovely maidens.

As the launch pulled away, the last cries that Bligh
claimed he heard from the mutineers were "Huzza for
Otaheite!"

It has been said in extenuation of Christian's act that
he was reasonably sure that Bligh and his companions
could reach an island. But he must also have realized that
if any of the nineteen jettisoned men did live to tell the
tale, the mutineers would be hunted to the ends of the
earth. The craft Christian gave them was, moreover, the
Bounty's cutter, such a "rotten carcass of a boat" that if
the nineteen men had used it, it would have soon gone
down. Only the pleas of the boatswain and others moved
a few of the mutineers to lower the launch in its stead.

It may seem to Bligh's discredit that twenty-five out of
a crew of forty-three mutinied even though they must have
known that if caught they would swing from the highest
yardarm. But they also knew how dark was the prospect
faced by those in the launch. (Several, it should be noted,
were detained by force because they were needed, and a
few were apparently so confused as not to be responsible
for their acts.)

Resentment against Bligh was certainly a factor: thus,
all of the nine men who had been flogged or otherwise
severely punished were among the most active mutineers.
And even five of those who accompanied Bligh gave him
serious trouble.

The situation of Bligh and his companions was unimag-
inably desperate. They had been dropped into the middle
of a vast, unmapped sea; the few islands nearby were
either uninhabitable or peopled by savages who were
friendly only as long as they thought the visitors were
strongly armed and had goods to exchange; their boat
was tiny, open, and so overloaded that the water came

within seven inches of the gunwales and only half the men could lie down at a time; they had only 150 pounds of bread, 32 pounds of pork, 28 gallons of water and a little rum and wine, normally enough for only a few days. Their only instruments were a quadrant and a compass. Furthermore, the best of the able-bodied seamen had remained with Christian.

What they did have was a leader who was a master navigator, with a will of iron and a supreme capacity for discipline. After one attempt to land on an island, which ended when the natives attacked them and killed one man, Bligh decided they must make for the nearest settlement, Timor, in the Dutch East Indies. He correctly estimated that it was 3,600 miles to the west.

Although the voyage took forty-seven days and the men ate little more per day than an ounce or two of bread, a gill of water and occasionally a bite of pork; although they were repeatedly attacked by savages and were alternately drenched by rains, battered by storms and broiled by the sun; although they had to make their way through the dreadful shoals of the Great Barrier Reef and were, at the end, no more than skin and bones covered with sores and rags, they lost only the one man slain by the savages.

On Timor, the Dutch governor treated them well, but their trials were far from over. After nine weeks, during which Nelson, a good man and an able botanist, sickened and died, Bligh secured a schooner and set sail for Java. During a stop at Surabaya, five of the men proved so troublesome that Bligh had two of them, Purcell the carpenter and Fryer the master, arrested. At Batavia, an unwholesome place, Bligh and several of the men came down with fever and three of the men died. Lamb the butcher and Ledward the acting surgeon remained behind when Bligh left, but both perished on the way home. As a parting thrust, Ledward wrote to an uncle complaining that Bligh was putting difficulties in the way of his collecting money due him.

Bligh finally got passage on a Dutch vessel and reached England on March 14, 1790, two years and three months after setting out. Of the eighteen men who had gone with him in the launch, only eleven lived to see England again.

Bligh's story, which he soon published in book form,

caused a sensation in London. In the autumn he was acquitted by a court martial of the charge of losing the *Bounty* and at the same time was made a post-captain. Having heard only his side of the story, the public was convinced that he was nearly blameless, and his tireless patron, Sir Joseph Banks, had no trouble persuading the authorities to send him back on another breadfruit expedition.

Meanwhile, the Admiralty had despatched the *Pandora*, under a Captain Edwards, to capture the mutineers.

Extraordinary as is Bligh's story, it is, for strangeness, drama and violence, nothing as compared to that of the mutineers.

After throwing the breadfruit plants overboard and having been driven off the island of Tubuai, the mutineers made for Tahiti. There they took on food and livestock and returned to Tubuai, but again the natives drove them out and again they had to return to Tahiti. This time Christian vowed he would seek out an uninhabited island where they would never be found. Only eight of the twenty-five mutineers accompanied him but they took with them nineteen natives, including twelve women and a baby girl. For many weeks they wandered in the southern seas until they came upon Pitcairn (or Pitcairn's) Island, a thousand miles southeast of Tahiti—barely two square miles of fertile earth amidst the vast emptiness of the South Pacific. They beached the boat there on September 23, 1789.

It was not until February 1808, when an American trading ship, the *Topaz*, happened on the island, that the world learned of the bizarre fate of the *Bounty*'s strange crew. The story came largely from the one mutineer who had survived, John Adams (known on the *Bounty* by the assumed name of Alexander Smith), supplemented by somewhat different versions Adams himself gave to other visitors in 1814 and 1825, and by the recollections of one of the native women. So turbulent and filled with horror were the events they recalled, especially of the early years, that some of it sounds like the memory of a nightmare.

The trouble began only two years after they arrived, when a mutineer named Williams lost his native wife and took the wife of one of the native men. This native, together with another, threatened revenge, but both were killed by the other Tahitians. Two years later the remaining native men slew Williams, Christian (there is no completely reliable account of how this happened), and three other mutineers, and seriously wounded Adams. Infuriated, the widows of the white men—still primitive in matters of passion—murdered the two remaining Tahitian men and thereafter lived promiscuously with the white men. Then one of the remaining mutineers, McKoy, drank himself into a delirium from the product of a still he had built and threw himself from a cliff. About 1799, Matthew Quintal's wife died from a fall, and when the surviving white men, Adams and Young, refused to yield their wives to him, he threatened to kill them; to forestall him they slew him. About a year later Young died of asthma.

Thus from about 1793 to about 1800 the tiny community on the lonely island was riddled by an incredible series of gruesome crimes. The cause must be sought in a combination of circumstances: nine seamen—at least seven of them of dubious character—who had committed the crime of mutiny and of casting adrift nineteen of their fellow men, had fled with a cortege of native women and found themselves on an island, without responsibility, free of law and restraint, beset by sensual temptation, and, most corrupting of all, without hope of ever returning to civilization.

By 1800 only Adams, surrounded by ten or eleven native women and a host of children, remained of the nine original mutineers. When the American captain first saw him in 1808 he had become a kind of patriarchal figure, although not yet forty-five years old. He had instituted daily prayers and other religious observances and had tried to educate the ever-increasing group of children. He died in 1829, by which time peace and plenty had reigned so long that the horrors of the first decade had receded into the realm of legend. Descendants of Adams, Christian, and their Tahitian companions still live on Pitcairn Island.

The *Pandora,* sent out to apprehend the mutineers, reached Tahiti in March 1791. Of the sixteen men who had remained on the island, two had been murdered. The

others were soon rounded up and the *Pandora* headed
homeward. Its captain, Edwards, makes Bligh seem, by
contrast, a gentle soul. To house his fourteen prisoners he
built a cagelike structure—it was dubbed Pandora's Box
—on the deck and kept them so tightly fettered hand and
foot that they could scarcely move. Then, on August 28th,
the *Pandora* struck a reef in the Torres Strait and began
to sink. Edwards ignored the cries of the prisoners but at
the last moment a boatswain's mate opened the exit scuttle
in the roof of their cell. Only ten men managed to escape
and eventually reach England.

These survivors were soon brought to trial. Of the ten,
the case of midshipman Peter Heywood attracted by far
the most attention: he was very young (he had been only
sixteen at the time of the mutiny), he was well born, and
his young sister Nessy made the most impassioned pleas
on his behalf. But Bligh felt that although he had been
especially kind to Heywood, the lad had deliberately
encouraged Christian. Indeed, when Bligh first returned
to England, and Heywood's widowed mother anxiously
wrote to him for news of her son, his bitterness betrayed
him into a letter of appalling harshness and priggishness.
He wrote:

> Madame,—I received your letter this day, and feel for
> you very much, being perfectly sensible of the extreme
> distress you must suffer from the conduct of your son,
> Peter. His baseness is beyond all description, but I hope
> you will endeavour to prevent the loss of him, heavy as
> the misfortune is, from afflicting you too severely. I
> imagine he is, with the rest of the mutineers, returned
> to Otaheite.

Curiously, Bligh, the leading prosecutor and witness,
was permitted to leave on his second breadfruit expedition
a year before the trial opened. The court, moreover, never
probed the causes of the mutiny, concerning itself only
with the part each man had played in the uprising. Although Fletcher Christian's brother Edward, a brilliant
lawyer, wrote pamphlets as well as letters to the press
defending his brother and attacking Bligh, no proof of the
charges against Bligh came out at the trial itself.

The verdict of the court was: four of the mutineers
innocent and six guilty. Mercy was asked for Heywood

and Morrison, and these two, along with one of the seamen, were pardoned. On October 29, 1792, three of the mutineers (including Ellison, who was about Heywood's age) were hanged.

It is one of the many strange postscripts to the *Bounty* story that Peter Heywood went on to serve in the navy with distinction for forty-two years and was nearing the rank of admiral when he died.

In his second attempt to transplant the breadfruit, Bligh, taking no chances, set out with two vessels, the *Providence* and the *Assistant,* and a detachment of Royal Marines. After an uneventful voyage around the Cape of Good Hope and some exploration of the coast of Tasmania, he reached Tahiti in April 1792 and learned to his satisfaction that Edwards had already been there and gathered up fourteen of the mutineers. This time Bligh took only three months to collect the breadfruit plants—long enough to note, however, a sad deterioration in native dress: dirty shirts and old coats had begun to supplant the cloths they wore with such style. They had also learned how to get drunk.

On the return voyage, Bligh charted the Fiji Islands and is generally credited with having discovered many of them. Once again he threaded the fearful reefs and currents of the Torres Strait; the channel through which he approached the Strait is still called Bligh's Entrance. After that it was relatively easy going to the Cape and across the Atlantic to Jamaica. There he triumphantly landed his breadfruit plants and was promptly voted thanks and a thousand guineas by the Jamaican Assembly.

The expedition arrived in London in September 1793. The crew cheered Bligh as he quit the vessel and he in turn praised his officers highly, but the trial of the mutineers had taken place while he was away and had to some extent turned popular sentiment against him. It seems never to have turned back again.

On his return Bligh found England at war with France, Holland, and other powers. After a time he was given command of the 64-gun *Director* in a squadron, under Admiral Duncan, assigned to keep the Dutch fleet blocked off on its side of the North Sea. The squadron succeeded in doing this until a mutiny, climaxing years of discontent, and inspired perhaps by the Revolution in France, broke out at the Nore in the Thames estuary and spread to Duncan's squadron. The mutiny petered out within a month but the fact that Bligh's ship was one of the first to join the mutineers and the last to abandon them has sometimes been used against him. Although the harshness of officers was one of the grievances, the chief causes of the mutiny were low pay and poor food. It was an ugly episode and Bligh's role in it was hardly a glorious one.

The mutiny ended not a moment too soon: the Dutch fleet was at last moving out into the open. The English squadron intercepted it and the Battle of Camperdown ensued. Bligh reports that after about two hours of pell-mell action, he sought out the flagship of Admiral De Winter and battered her into surrendering; he makes no mention of the ships that had already pounded her or that helped finish her off. But Bligh was awarded the honor of boarding the defeated flagship and taking her in tow.

The outstanding naval action of Bligh's career was, however, still to come. In 1801, learning that the Russians, Swedes, and Danes were supplying the French, the British sent a fleet under Admiral Parker and Vice-Admiral Lord Nelson to attack Copenhagen. In the squadron was the 54-gun *Glatton* under Captain Bligh. At Copenhagen, the *Glatton* fell in just astern of Nelson's *Elephant*, and Bligh thus fought side-by-side with the greatest commander in British naval history. Despite a considerable mauling (Bligh reported 17 killed and 34 wounded on his ship), the English carried the day. Nelson immediately haled Bligh onto his quarterdeck and thanked him for his support. Nothing Bligh's detractors have since said about his courage or his qualities as a commander can diminish the glory of that moment. Later that year he had the additional honor of being elected a Fellow of the Royal Society.

During the next few years Bligh was on inactive service or occupied with surveys for the Admiralty. Once again the periods of half pay must have been very trying for by that time he had six children, all girls, with the oldest of marriageable age. The only noteworthy incident occurred while he was in command of H.M.S. *Warrior*. When one of his lieutenants, John Frazier, complained of a lame

leg and refused to keep his watch, Bligh brought him before a court martial. Frazier was acquitted and promptly
requested a court martial for Bligh, charging that he had
"grossly insulted and mistreated" Frazier and behaved
toward his officers in a "tyrannical, oppressive and un-
officerlike" manner.

At the trial, a few of the ship's men and officers supported Frazier but others came forward in Bligh's defense,
or at least to say, as the boatswain did, that Bligh was
"hot and hasty" but that words "no sooner escaped him
than his passion ended." Speaking in his own defense,
Bligh thus summed up his code:

> I candidly and without reserve avow that I am not a
> tame and indifferent observer of the manner in which
> officers placed under my orders conducted themselves
> in the performance of their several duties. A signal or
> any communication from a commanding officer have
> ever been to me an indication for exertion and alacrity
> to carry into effect the purport thereof; and, peradven-
> ture, I may occasionally have appeared to some of those
> officers as unnecessarily anxious for its execution . . .
> Gentlemen . . . who know and have experienced the
> arduous task of responsibility, and that of the magnitude
> of one of His Majesty's 74-gun ships . . . will, I am
> persuaded, acquit me of any apparent impetuosity . . .
> attributing the warmth of my temper . . . to my zeal for
> that service in which I have been employed . . . for up-
> wards of 35 years . . .

The testimony seems to have borne out the charge that
Bligh used abusive language (which was nearly normal
by the shipboard standards of the time) but not that he
was tyrannical. The admirals and captains who sat as
judges declared that "the charges were in part proved,
and did therefore adjudge Captain Bligh to be repri-
manded and to be admonished to be in the future more
correct in his language." Bligh, who probably felt that he
had became a target for every malcontent, seems to have
considered the decision tantamount to exoneration.

At this point, the last notable, and perhaps the most
important, episode in William Bligh's extraordinary career
began. It took place in what was then truly *ultima thule*—
New South Wales, in southeastern Australia.

In 1805 New South Wales had been settled for only seventeen years. Founded as a penal colony on the edge of an unknown continent, it was still a primitive community. Its population of eight thousand consisted of convicts, former convicts, free settlers and a military garrison. Two governors had come and gone without solving the problems that plagued the colony; the third was weary and had decided to resign. Once again Sir Joseph Banks, long a most influential figure in the colony's affairs, recommended Bligh unreservedly, and Bligh was assured that his naval rank would go on. As Banks pointed out, the job needed a man capable of ruling with an iron hand. Bligh accepted. What he apparently failed to realize was that it also needed a modicum of tact.

After a voyage in which, characteristically, Bligh quarreled bitterly with the cantankerous captain of the convoy escort as to who was in command of the convoy, they arrived in Sydney early in August 1806.

Bligh found that the settlement was wallowing in drunkenness and debauchery and that the chief promoter of this was the New South Wales Corps. Composed mostly of former convicts, adventurers and other unsavory characters, the corps had from the beginning used its control of the liquor supply, and its right to trade privately, to profiteer in every direction. Rum was, in fact, *the* currency of the colony; the government paid wages in it, and men sold their crops, their wives, and their souls for a few gallons of it.

It is therefore hardly surprising that vice flourished: everyone defrauded the government, prostitutes rode to the parade ground with the officers, concubines greatly outnumbered married women, and most of the children were illegitimate. To one evil, land-grabbing, Bligh was unfortunately a party: the retiring governor granted him over a thousand acres and Bligh soon reciprocated—an exchange that even apologists for Bligh deplore.

As soon as Bligh made it clear that he meant to end the traffic in rum, the struggle between him and the corps began. His powers were immense but since the corps was the only enforcement agency, he was doomed from the start.

The leader of the opposition, John Macarthur, had resigned as a captain in the corps and become one of the richest and most powerful men in the settlement. The chief figure in the introduction and development of the Australian wool industry, he is often described as a great national benefactor and, because of his opposition to Bligh, an overthrower of despots. But he has also been reliably characterized as a profiteer, land-grabber, and inveterate schemer. A man of boundless enterprise, rapacious, domineering and pitiless, he was convinced that those who stood in his way were not only his enemies but those of the state as well. He harassed all the early governors of Australia and was probably responsible for the downfall or withdrawal of three of them, including Bligh.

Although outwardly Bligh's first months in office were quiet, Macarthur later claimed that at his first interview with Bligh concerning sheep and a fine wool industry, Bligh had become furious and shouted: "Are you to have such flocks and herds of cattle as no man ever heard of before? No, sir!" and "I have heard of your concerns, sir, you have got 5,000 acres of land in the finest situation in the country; but, by God! you shan't keep it," and, when Macarthur said he had received the land from the Privy Council and by order of the Secretary of State, "Damn the Privy Council and damn the Secretary of State too!" Bligh later categorically denied all this but his critics have accepted the story, and others have treated it as true but perhaps exaggerated. But Herbert Vere Evatt, distinguished Australian jurist, concluded after close analysis that it was for the most part fabricated.

During his first year Bligh worked hard, particularly on measures to aid hard-pressed settlers in getting vital supplies. But two clashes with Macarthur gave warning that his foe was merely waiting for a chance to strike. In one, Macarthur tried to collect a promissory note for a number of bushels of wheat from Andrew Thompson, Bligh's bailiff. But wheat had meanwhile risen four times in value and Thompson offered to pay only according to the original value. When the matter was brought before Bligh, he decided in Thompson's favor. In the second incident, Macarthur refused to give up part of a still that had been sent to him from England. It was seized, and

Macarthur promptly prosecuted. The court decided in his favor.

Late in 1807 a third incident brought the conflict to a head. A notorious convict had stowed away on the *Parramatta,* a vessel owned partly by Macarthur, and had been allowed to get ashore at Tahiti. When the *Parramatta* returned to Sydney, the authorities declared the ship's bond forfeited. But the owners refused to pay. The Port Officer then occupied the vessel, whereupon Macarthur abandoned both the ship and the crew. The Judge Advocate, Atkins, issued a warrant for Macarthur's arrest and when Macarthur defied it, had him brought in by armed police.

At this point Macarthur demanded that Atkins settle a fourteen-year-old debt, plus interest. Atkins (whom Bligh himself described as corrupt and a drunkard) refused, and when the *Parramatta* trial opened, Macarthur challenged his right to sit as a judge. The other six judges, officers of the New South Wales Corps, unheld his challenge.

The following day, January 26, 1808, Bligh in desperation had Macarthur jailed and then summoned the six officer-judges to answer to charges of treason. They in turn called on Major Johnston, commander of the corps, for help. A weak, easygoing man, he ordered Macarthur released, and then, at the urging of Macarthur and a few excited officers, began what is known as the "Rum Rebellion." Leading the troops from their barracks to Government House, he sent in several soldiers to arrest the Governor. But they could not find him, and when they finally tracked him down, they claimed—in what was to become one of the most sensational stories in Australian history—that they had found him hiding under a bed in an upstairs room. Later Bligh declared with scorn and indignation that he had rushed upstairs chiefly to hide important papers.

For more than a year, while Macarthur and the Major waited for word from England, Bligh was kept under house arrest, a difficult situation for any deposed officer but one that was unbearably galling to Bligh. The "rebels" meanwhile took the position that they had intervened to save the settlement from anarchy and Bligh from violence at the hands of an enraged citizenry. But the fact is that a few days after Bligh's arrest, 830 settlers sent him a statement thanking him for his just and beneficial government. Bligh himself never admitted his defeat and when a commander of the corps at last gave him permission to leave for England if he would do so quietly, he promised, and then, once on board ship, branded the regime a mutiny and hovered nearby.

The Home Government finally sent out a new governor, declared that all acts of the rebels were illegal, and that Bligh was to be received in the colony with honor. But they also added that he was to return home. So Bligh left Australia, after three and a half years, and arrived in England in October 1810.

The Crown soon brought Major (then Lieutenant Colonel) Johnston to trial, found him guilty of mutiny and sentenced him to be cashiered. Macarthur was barred from returning to the colony; and it was not until February 1817, after an absence of eight years, that he was permitted to go back—and resume his climb to wealth and influence. After the trial, Bligh was made a Rear-Admiral, but historically far more important is the fact that despite his personal defeat, Bligh's experiences, and recommendations contributed to the recall of the New South Wales Corps, to improvements in the colony's law courts, and other reforms.

In 1813, his wife having died and he himself almost sixty years old, Bligh retired to a fine old house in the country. To the end, which came in 1817, he numbered several eminent men among his close friends.

William Bligh is usually remembered as a cruel sea captain who brought a mutiny on himself and then made an astonishing voyage across the South Pacific in an open boat. Generally forgotten are the four years' service on Cook's great last expedition, the successful transporting of breadfruit to the West Indies, the exploration of Tasmania and the Fiji Archipelago, the ships commanded at Dogger Bank and Camperdown and the commendation from Nelson at Copenhagen, the governorship of New South Wales and the resulting reforms, and the Vice-Admiral's flag.

When all these are recalled, the image that emerges is hardly that of a hero but certainly of far more than a cross-grained, foul-mouthed martinet. Although he had many talents, he lacked imagination, humor, and the vital quality that enables great autocrats to win devotion as well as respect. He was incapable of making allowances, and he permitted the minor virtues of the disciplinarian to assume a major role. But, having conceded that his defects kept him from greatness, let us at least deliver him once and for all from the legend that he was a villain and a brute.

—MILTON RUGOFF

Recommended Further Reading

Evatt, Herbert Vere. *Rum Rebellion: A Study of the Overthrow of Governor Bligh by John Macarthur and the New South Wales Corps.* London: Angus & Robertson, Ltd., 1938.

Mackaness, George. *The Life of Vice-Admiral William Bligh.* 2 vols. London: Angus & Robertson, Ltd., 1931; New York: Farrar & Rinehart, Inc., 1936.

Montgomerie, H. S. *William Bligh of the Bounty in Fact and in Fable.* London: Williams & Norgate, Ltd., 1937.

Rawson, Geoffrey. *Bligh of the Bounty.* London: Phillip Allan & Company, Ltd., 1934; New York: G. R. Gorman, 1937.

Rutter, Owen. *Turbulent Journey: A Life of William Bligh, Vice-Admiral of the Blue.* London: Ivor Nicholson & Watson, Ltd., 1936.

A Note on Bligh's Narrative

As soon as Bligh returned from the South Seas in 1790, he published *A Narrative of the Mutiny on Board H.M.S. Bounty*. This small book covered only the mutiny itself and the voyage in the open boat. Apparently because of the interest it aroused, Bligh then prepared, with the help of an editor, a much longer account, describing the entire voyage from the time of his departure from London to his return. Originally published in 1792, this version is here reprinted in full.

Bligh's detractors have charged that his narrative is marked by omissions and distortions, but others have found it a remarkably dispassionate and reasonable record. Bligh was a master of his calling, and he writes about it with dignity and assurance.